STEPHEN RICHARDSON

The Harvest

Book one

SOWN
PUBLISHING

For Lucy, whose imagination and wonder inspired me to write in the first place.

Contents

Prologue

White.

That's all there is at first. The walls are flat and smooth like they were made in one piece. The floor feels cold through the chair, and the air moves across my skin in little shivers. A bright light hangs above me on a long, bending arm. It buzzes softly.

A screen on the wall shows someone lying in a chair like mine, their head held still while silver tools touch their skin. I think it's… me. A sharp sting hits my temple as I search my mind, grasping at broken thoughts.

Nothing is colored. Nothing has softness. Everything waits, very still. It's quiet.

A voice breaks through the silence. Soft and practiced, but not human enough to be comforting.

"349, please keep your eyes open."

I wince at the sound of the figure's mechanical voice. 349. They keep calling me that. I don't think that's my name… but when I reach for the real one, it slips away like water. I blink again, harder this time.

My wrists sting as I tug on the thin straps chaining me to my seat.

A slow, rhythmic beeping begins behind me. A screen, maybe. A machine. Something that knows more about me than I do. A sudden smell reaches my nose, I don't know how to explain it but it made something shift in my head—like a door creaking open. A flash of color appears behind my eyes: a stuffed rabbit. Warm arms around me. Laughter. A voice whispering, *"Hold on tight."*

The image fades instantly, swallowed by blinding white.

"349, focus on the ceiling."

The voice sounds patient, but there's no emotion behind it—like someone trying to imitate calm. I turn my head toward the sound even though I don't mean to. My muscles move just a fraction late, like someone else is choosing for me.

"Memory interference detected," the voice murmurs—not to me, but to someone else.

I try to lift my hands, but they don't move. My chest tightens. Another voice, deeper this time, says:

"Begin correction."

A hiss. A mask lowers toward my face.

No.

No, I don't want this. I try to say something, fight something, remember something—but the words jam in my throat. A sharp pressure pulses above my ear, followed by a cold rush through my head. The ceiling flickers.

Blood spills over my eyes, and I can smell it as soon as I see it, and then I taste it. For a heartbeat, the room dissolves. I feel warmth on my face. A feeling I can't describe washes over me—not fear. Something good. Something I shouldn't remember.

The memory hits like a wave, too real to doubt.

Then it's gone.

The white room snaps back into place, harsher than before.

"349, remain calm. The correction will resolve the intrusion."

I want to scream that it wasn't an intrusion. That it was real. That I *know* it was real. But I can't remember why. The mask descends. The cold spreads. My vision fractures.

The last thing I hear before everything fades is:

"Prepare for reset. We will try again."

A sting blooms behind my eyes.

Then everything goes dark.

I

Owen Hale

1

Before Five O'Clock

The drive to work was short, but it was the only peace I got all day. I hated saying goodbye to my kids in the morning, but from the second I woke up, Thomas, my oldest, would talk and talk and talk—about dinosaurs, random facts, and questions that spiraled into more questions. It was exhausting trying to keep up, but knowing the only real social interaction he had was with his parents forced me to stay present and listen.

Today was his birthday. He had turned eleven. We had plans for that night; we were going to the dinosaur museum that had just opened, and he couldn't stop talking about it. I tried to fake enthusiasm that morning, nodding and responding when I remembered to, but it's hard to show your kids you love them when you don't care what they're talking about. The thought made my body tense, and I tightened my grip on the steering wheel, annoyed with myself for even thinking it.

My daughter Grace was special. She was four years old and far too smart for her age, excelling at nearly everything she tried. Granted, most of it was still just kid stuff—puzzles, drawing, sounding out words—but she picked things up quickly and seemed to understand more than she should have. She moved through the world with a quiet focus that felt different, even if I couldn't explain why.

Elisabeth was my rock. If it weren't for her, I couldn't be the father I was, or at least the father I tried to be. The thought immediately soured. What kind of dad was I, really, when I had already blown off my conversation with Thomas on his birthday? The guilt sat heavy in my chest, sharp enough to distract me from the road in front of me.

The workday passed in a blur. My mindset shifted as the hours dragged on, and I kept replaying my conversation with Thomas in my head, mentally rewriting it, imagining myself listening better, responding better. I was determined to try again that night. I knew better, and I knew I could do better.

Near the end of the day, I got a text from Elisabeth saying she was going to meet me in the parking lot, and my heart fluttered in a way that surprised me. Just the thought of seeing them, determined to do better, made me feel lighter, like I could finally step out of my own head and into my life.

The last ten minutes of the day went on for hours. Or at least that's what it felt like. I kept pretending to work, glancing at the clock only to find that not even a full minute had passed. The air in the office felt thick, like everyone was waiting for permission to leave but no one wanted to be the first to stop pretending.

That's when I heard the commotion at the pill station. Someone talking loudly, almost to himself. I thought it was Nathan. He was newer, only about a month in, and he already stood out from the others. There was something different about him, something more relatable. Most of the attendants recited the same robotic phrase every morning, word for word, but Nathan would ask how I was doing. He'd make small talk. It felt strange, almost comforting, like he hadn't learned yet that you weren't supposed to do that.

"This isn't RIGHT!" he yelled suddenly.

About half the room turned to look. The rest kept their eyes glued to their screens, typing or clicking through nothing, pretending not to notice so they wouldn't have to deal with anything else this close to five.

I decided that was enough work for the day and logged out a few minutes early. I told myself I was heading to the pill station for my afternoon dose, but the truth was I wanted to see what was going on with Nathan.

When I reached the station, he was curled up in the corner, knees drawn to his chest, rocking back and forth as he tugged at his hair. His voice was low and broken, repeating the same phrases over and over. "It's not okay what they did to me…" "What did they do to my baby…"

My hands started to sweat. For a moment, I considered backing away, skipping the pill altogether and pretending I hadn't seen anything. I didn't have time for something like this today. I didn't want to be pulled into whatever was happening to him.

"Are you… okay?" I asked.

His eyes snapped up to meet mine, moving fast, like something startled out of hiding. His hair flicked wildly with the motion, strands sticking to his damp forehead. Up close, he didn't look sick so much as hunted—eyes wide, jaw clenched, every muscle locked tight as if he were bracing for a blow.

"Are you with *them*?" he demanded, his voice sharp and unsteady, cracking at the edges. "Tell me. Tell me if you're with them."

"I—sorry, I don't know what you're talking about," I said, holding my hands out slightly, palms open. "I just... do you have my pill for today?"

His face collapsed. The anger drained out of him, replaced by something raw and unbearable. His mouth trembled as he shook his head, tears spilling freely now. "Don't take it," he said, the words barely holding together. "Please. Don't take the pill."

My chest tightened. "I... I have to," I said. "It's required."

He laughed then, a broken, choking sound that didn't belong in his throat. "It isn't real," he said, as if the walls were closing in. "None of it is real."

Then he stood up quickly, and everything shattered at once.

His arms flailed wildly, knocking into the shelves beside him. Bottles exploded across the floor, plastic clattering and skidding, pills bouncing everywhere like spilled teeth. Creams and lotions burst open, white smears streaking the walls and counters. The clean, ordered station unraveled in seconds.

"NONE OF IT'S REAL!" he screamed, his voice tearing itself apart. "THEY KILLED HER. THEY KILLED MY BABY."

The words hit like a physical blow.

Before anyone could react, a security guard rushed in from behind, arms wrapping around Nathan's chest, trying to drag him down. There was a brief, violent struggle. Boots scraping, breath grunting, and then everything went wrong.

Nathan's hand shot to the guard's hip.

I saw the gun before my mind could register what it meant.

There was a deafening crack, impossibly loud in the enclosed space. The guard jerked violently, and red sprayed across the white interior of the pill station, painting the walls, the counter, the floor. Someone screamed. Then someone else. Then everyone.

I ran.

I bolted for the stairs, my feet slipping on pills underfoot, heart slamming so hard I thought it might tear free of my chest, but before I could reach them, a metal wall slammed down from the ceiling with a bone-rattling crash, sealing the exit shut.

More guards poured in, weapons raised, spreading out in a slow, tightening circle around Nathan. He turned toward them, gun held stiff, his hands shaking so badly the barrel wobbled in wide arcs. He pulled the trigger again and again, the shots wild, sparks and ricochets snapping off metal and tile. One guard cried out as a bullet caught him in the hip, sending him crashing to the floor.

Then Nathan froze.

His finger stopped mid-pull. His breathing slowed, just slightly. His face—his *expression*—changed. The panic drained away, replaced by something blank, almost peaceful.

I didn't understand what I was seeing until I heard the sound.

A single, thunderous explosion.

What had been Nathan's face erupted outward in a violent red spray, fragments splattering across the room like thrown paint. The force of it knocked his body backward, and he collapsed in a limp heap among the pills and blood.

I could barely hear the screams over the ringing in my ears.

People ran for the walls, where the stairs used to be, pounding on them with open palms and clenched fists, screaming for doors that didn't exist. Most of them were already speckled with blood—fine droplets on their faces, their clothes, their hair, as if the violence had settled on them like dust. Someone stumbled, then disappeared beneath the surge of bodies. I heard a sharp, wet sound, followed by a scream that cut off too quickly. No one stopped. There was nowhere to stop.

I stood frozen in the middle of it all, unable to move, unable to think. My mind refused to catch up to what my eyes were seeing. Shock held me in place, heavy and numbing, as if my body no longer belonged to me.

Then the doors opened. Doors I had never noticed before. They slid apart soundlessly, revealing a white beyond them so blank it hurt to look at. People stepped out wearing white uniforms. Some were older, their movements efficient, but others were young. Teenagers. Maybe even younger than that. Their faces were empty, eyes unfocused, like their body was following instructions they didn't need to understand.

They carried mops and buckets.

They started cleaning immediately.

Blood was wiped away in smooth, practiced strokes. Pills were swept aside without a glance. Two of them bent down and lifted the body of the man who had been crushed, dragging him toward the open doorway. His arm flopped uselessly against the floor, leaving a thick red smear behind him, the color violent against the sterile white. None of them reacted. No urgency. No emotion. Just routine.

A woman nearby lost whatever was holding her together. She screamed, sobbing uncontrollably, striking at the guards with weak, desperate blows. She was hysterical—but who wouldn't be? I wanted to shout at her to stop. *Hadn't she seen what happened to the last person who resisted?*

She never got the chance to learn.

Someone came up behind her and plunged a needle into her neck. Her scream cut off mid-syllable, and her body went slack, collapsing like the strings had been cut.

Slowly, methodically, the guards moved through the room.

Some people fought. They screamed, kicked, clawed, and begged. It didn't matter. Each struggle ended the same way—with a sharp prick, a sudden stillness, and a body hitting the floor. Once someone went down, they were dragged away into the white hall, vanishing behind the doors like they had never existed at all.

As it continued, something shifted.

People stopped fighting.

They watched what happened to those who tried to escape. They watched what happened to those who resisted. Understanding spread quietly through the room, unspoken but absolute. There was no winning. No bargaining. No point.

One by one, people simply gave in.

They stood still. They lowered their heads. They waited.

When the guards finally reached me, I tried to speak. I tried to explain, to reason, to plead. The words felt useless even as they left my mouth. I never saw the needle coming. I only felt the brief, sharp pressure at the base of my neck.

The room began to blur. The edges of everything softened and smeared together. The screaming faded into a distant hum.

And then there was nothing.

[STATUS: DELETED FROM C-2 MEMORY DRIVE]

* * *

I hopped down each step almost gracefully, lightheaded and nearly giddy, because I knew my family would be waiting for me in the parking lot. The stress of the day was finally over, and I was going to be with them, really with them, to celebrate Thomas. I could already picture them. Grace clinging to Elisabeth's hand, Thomas talking excitedly about the museum, unable to sit still. The thought carried me forward.

As I entered the lobby, something felt off.

It was darker than it should have been at five, like the building had already shut itself down for the night. My steps slowed as unease crept in, and I pulled out my phone to check the time, half-expecting it to confirm I was imagining things. It didn't. It was just after eight. I saw the missed calls—thirteen from Elisabeth—and the unanswered messages beneath them. *Hey, we're here. Where are you?* I didn't wait to read the rest.

I ran to the parking lot, my breath coming fast, scanning the rows before I even reached the door. The family car wasn't there. The lot was nearly empty, quiet in a way that made my ears ring. Curtis stood alone near the edge of the pavement, his posture rigid, his face drawn tight. He didn't look away when he saw me, and something in his expression told me he already knew this moment would change everything.

"Owen… Your family…" he said, then hesitated. "There's been an accident."

The words didn't settle. They hovered, meaningless.

"They're… gone."

I shook my head, already backing away, already reaching for my keys. I didn't listen to anything else he said. I drove faster than I ever had, faster than I should have, the road blurring beneath me as I repeated their names under my breath like it might anchor them in place. When I reached our apartment, I tore the door open and stepped inside, my heart hammering as I scanned each room.

No one was there.

The birthday cake sat untouched on the table, candles still in their box. Presents were wrapped and stacked neatly, ready to be opened. Streamers hung from the ceiling, bright and expectant, swaying slightly in the still air. Everything had been prepared. Everything was waiting.

The knock at the door came quietly.

When I opened it, two officers stood in the hallway. Their voices were calm, and distant, like they were reading from something they'd memorized long ago. There had been an accident. They were sorry. There was nothing that could have been done. My family had died.

I don't remember what I said to them, if I said anything at all. I only remember standing there afterward, staring past the doorway at the room behind me, at the decorations and the gifts frozen in place.

The presents and the decorations, never to be enjoyed by my sweet, loving boy. The boy whose birthday it was. The boy I had ignored that morning.

2

The Decision

Five years later
[UNIT C-2 CONSCIOUSNESS AND VIDEO LOG. DATE: MAR 28, 2425]

I remembered the morning I decided to die with a clarity that bordered on peace.

A Friday.

The world outside my window felt unnaturally still. No car horns, no neighbors arguing, no footsteps in the hallway. Just the faint hum of the refrigerator in the other room and the low murmur of the building settling, like a tired old man lowering himself into a chair.

I lay on my back and stared at the hairline crack in the ceiling above my bed. I'd watched that same crack spread over the years, branching out slowly across the concrete, splitting like a dry riverbed. I'd always thought I'd outlast it. Watch it widen, maybe one day give way.

That morning, I knew I wouldn't.

The realization didn't arrive with any dramatic flare. No

gasp, no spike of fear. It was just a quiet understanding that settled in my chest, heavy but certain: I was done. Not in a screaming, pleading way. Just a simple, final sentence in my mind.

I turned my head toward the cheap digital clock on the nightstand. The red numbers glowed in the dim room: 6:07 a.m. The alarm wouldn't go off for another twenty or so minutes. I usually let it ring twice before slapping it off and rolling over, bargaining with myself for *just ten more minutes* of sleep I never really got.

But even before the alarm, I knew I wasn't going back to sleep.

"If I go to work," I whispered into the stale air, "no one will check in on me over the weekend."

My voice sounded thin and dry, like it belonged to someone older. A voice that had been worn down by too many long conversations with doctors and too many short ones with people who said, "I'm so sorry for your loss," and then had the luxury of walking away.

"And if I do it afterward," I added, "they'll have the whole weekend to find my body."

There was a strange, bitter practicality in that thought. The last responsible thing I'd ever do. Time my death so that it inconvenienced people as little as possible. I imagined the landlord's irritation if I skipped rent, the hassle of neighbors smelling something through the walls on a Tuesday. It was stupid, but those were the things my brain clung to when everything else felt untouchable.

Practical. Considerate, even. What a joke.

I swung my legs over the edge of the bed and sat up. The room spun just a little. My joints ached more these days. My back protested. I rubbed my eyes and felt the rough prickle of unshaven stubble on my cheeks.

For a few seconds, I just sat there, elbows on my knees, hands clasped, staring at the floor. The faint morning light pushed through the blinds in thin, crooked lines, catching dust in the air that never seemed to settle. The room smelled like old fabric, with a faint hint of must. Untouched. Somewhere behind me, the mattress let out a tired groan as it adjusted to the shift of my weight. I didn't have to look around to know what was there: clothes in small, defeated piles, the nightstand cluttered with old water glasses, the dresser still holding things that didn't belong to this version of my life, the tv covered in papers. Everything sat exactly where it had for years, gathering layers of dust. The carpet was worn down in the exact spots I always put my feet. Same depressions. Same routine.

My life hasn't always been unbearable. It hasn't always been this… empty.

There have been good years. I used to come home to noise. kids shouting, toys crashing, my wife laughing as she tried to keep everyone from hurting themselves. I used to stand in the doorway and feel like I belonged in the picture. Like I was part of something living.

Then the accident happened, and everything rotted from the inside out.

Nights turned into battlegrounds. I'd wake up choking on air that tasted like fire, certain I could hear my kids calling my name from somewhere I couldn't reach. Their faces hovered inches from mine as I slept. Burned, blackened, distorted— and even when I shook myself awake, I could still feel the heat on my skin. I'd lie there in the dark with my heart pounding, trying not to cry because crying didn't help. Crying didn't bring anyone back.

Days were worse. In the daylight, I saw them everywhere. In reflections. In crowds. In the shape of a stranger's shoulders from behind. Once, I almost grabbed a little girl's hand on the street, convinced she was Grace. Her mother turned around, ready to scream, and I saw it wasn't her. She was older, and her eyes looked different.

I apologized and walked away.

I can't remember why I wasn't there when they died… *Why wasn't I there…* It made my head hurt everytime I thought about it.

Only one fragment survived the blackout. Red. A smear of it, bright and wet, sliding across a surface I can't identify. No shape. No detail. Just blood, suspended in a place my mind refuses to explain.

After that, everything I remember is the aftermath. I didn't see the twisted metal or the burned-out shell of the car. I didn't see their bodies. I didn't stand beside flashing lights and emergency tape or answer questions from officers whose pity was worse than the truth.

In my mind, I replayed that last evening over and over again, like if I tried hard enough, I could slip back into the moment and reroute everything that followed.

What haunts me isn't what happened. It's what I imagine right before it did.

I see the truck long before they would have. Huge. Fast. Moving with momentum you feel before you register it. I imagine the moment Elisabeth sensed something off. The flicker of fear tightening her grip on the wheel. I imagine Thomas going quiet, the way kids do when they understand danger. I imagine Grace blinking awake, confused at the change in motion, the shift in her mother's breathing.

And then everything stops. Frozen in my mind like a tableau right before the fall.

My brain refuses to show me the impact. It only gives me the before. The unbearable before. The half-second of knowing, of realizing, of being unable to stop what's coming.

Sometimes when I walk past the gas station on the corner, a sharp smell catches in my throat. Burning rubber, hot metal, something chemical, and it yanks me back to that imagined moment so hard I have to stop walking. Other times, in that thin place between sleeping and waking, I swear I hear them calling for me. Voices distorted by memory, echoing through some part of me that refuses to heal.

They shouldn't sound real. But they do. And once the echo starts, it follows me through every hour of the day, threading itself through the quietest moments like a warning I can never unhear.

People told me the guilt would fade eventually. That it wasn't my fault. That I couldn't have known. That they were in a better place. That at least they hadn't suffered.

Those people had never seen the things I'd seen in my head.

Therapists called it "trauma replay." They wanted me to talk about it. To "unpack" it. One of them wrote a prescription and told me the pills would "soften the edges" of the memories. "They'll help you sleep," he said. "They'll help your brain process things more gently."

Everyone took them. Or almost everyone. Little orange bottles rattled in purses and medicine cabinets in half the apartments on my floor. Some people called them "forgetful pills." Some called them "numbers." Medication had become its own language of survival.

I took mine.

They dulled some things.

They never dulled enough.

They took the sharpness off my nightmares, maybe, made them less vivid. But they never took away the core truth of them. They never took away the fact that my family was gone—and that I hadn't been there.

After they died, eating barely crossed my mind. I'd stand in front of the fridge and stare at its contents, trying to remember what being hungry was supposed to feel like. Sleeping wasn't any better. Closing my eyes only brought fire with it. And living… living felt like something I was only pretending to do.

The only thing that mattered on that Friday morning in late March was the quiet conclusion I had finally reached: I couldn't keep living as the only one left. I sat at the edge of the bed, the cracked ceiling above me and the cold floor beneath my feet, and let the decision settle into place—not as a plea for someone to notice, but as something final and intentional. When the day was done, I would come home and end my life.

I pictured what that would mean. The stillness. The silence. No more blaring alarms, no more hollow apartment echoing at me, no more phantom flashes of children that weren't really there.

The thought should have jolted me, should have filled me with fear or guilt or something sharp enough to cut through the numbness. Instead, it loosened something in me. It felt like relief.

The kitchen was dim, which was how I liked it. A few thin bars of daylight slipped through the blinds. Enough to outline the room without revealing the details. The paint on the walls had peeled in long, curling strips, exposing gray cement like old skin.

Four chairs still circled the table, but I hadn't sat there in years; it was buried under dust, unopened mail, and dishes I'd long stopped bothering to move. Kids' drawings hung on the fridge, their warped, yellowing paper fading into ghostly colors. The rest of the mess was mine. Mold creeping along bowl edges, plates stacked in the sink, cups left wherever I dropped them. Not the mess of a family. Just the slow collapse of someone who no longer cared enough to clean what was left behind.

I opened the fridge expecting nothing, and nothing was exactly what I found. A mold-slick burrito clung to the back shelf. The lettuce had liquefied into a swamp in its bag. And the milk—still heavy enough to trick me into a moment of hope—slid thickly inside the jug, moving slowly, like something dead shifting in a jar.

I poured it anyway.

The milk hit the cereal in gelatinous chunks, splattering the counter. The smell hit a moment later. Sour, almost chemical. Years ago, I would have gagged. Would've tossed the bowl out and scrubbed the counter before the kids woke up. Elisabeth would've kissed my cheek and teased me for being dramatic.

Now I just stared at it. Ate one bite without tasting a thing. Left the bowl where it sat, a little island of rot in the stale kitchen light.

I wasn't saving the place for anyone anymore.

I shut the apartment door behind me, locking it out of habit. The hallway met me with its usual stench. Damp plaster. Mold. Old carpet fibers breaking down into dust. The smell clung to my clothes and followed me into elevators and meetings until coworkers asked if my building was having "plumbing issues."

I passed the elevator, stuck open as always. Yellow caution tape drooped across the doors. The metal interior was dark, the floor covered in grime. Six years ago, Grace had asked, "Daddy, why is the elevator sleeping?" I could still hear her tiny voice. The way she held my hand like the world was safe as long as I didn't let go.

I followed the familiar path to the vending machine—an ancient, buzzing relic that only accepted coins. I dug into my pocket.

F11. My ritual.

It never gave me F11.

Some days it gave pretzels. Some days it gave a bag of stale barbecue chips. The kids always laughed when I did this, so always did even if i wasn't hungry. It was the best part of my day. Today it spat out a cookie wrapped in plastic so wrinkled it looked mummified.

I didn't eat it. Just carried it.

The stairwell door was cold under my palm. I pushed it open and paused. Sometimes, if I closed my eyes, I could still hear Thomas and Grace begging to drop a penny down the stairwell—their favorite game before it hit Mr. Johnson in the head and before they learned not everyone found them adorable.

Mr. Johnson never smiled after that. He hadn't smiled much before, either. Sometimes I wondered if he'd been grieving someone too, seeing the world in gray the way I did now. I often caught him watching things most people overlooked— a flickering light, a neighbor hesitating mid-sentence, me standing too long with my keys in my hand. Once, I glanced up and found him staring directly at me, as if waiting for me to notice, and then he simply turned and walked away.

Maybe I imagined meaning where there wasn't any. Maybe he wasn't observant—just lonely, the way people get when the world forgets them. Watching others might have been his way of participating in a life he didn't feel part of anymore.

Downstairs, the mailboxes buzzed under the fluorescent light, most of them overflowing. A sour draft seeped in from the exit door, carrying garbage and damp concrete. It curled around my ankles, but I barely noticed anymore; it was just part of the air, the same as the humming lights and sticky tile.

The floor here always looked permanently dirty, like no amount of mopping could cut through the grime, and the front door's cracked pane let in just enough daylight to make the stains on the ground look darker. The whole building had that tight, over-used feeling—like the hallways were narrow, the walls too close.

My box held mostly spam—overstuffed envelopes, glossy coupon sheets, and those smug "exclusive offers" grocery stores kept mailing like there must be someone left in the world who still cuts out paper coupons. I flipped through them with the dull, automatic rhythm of someone bracing for bills they already know they can't pay. Car insurance pitch. Credit card application. Another "0% APR for the first 12 months" lie pretending to be helpful.

I was halfway through tossing everything into the trash when something thin and weightless slid loose from the stack. It didn't fall like paper. It drifted—slow, almost cautious— turning once in the air before settling at my feet. A single folded sheet of plain white paper. No envelope. No smudges. No creases except the one down the center, sharp enough to look machine-made.

I bent down and picked it up. The paper felt smooth, like it hadn't passed through real hands. I unfolded it. Four words, printed in small, eerily perfect type—no ink spread, no texture, no trace of a printer or pen. Just precision. **WATCH FOR THE SIGNS.**

Black ink. Handwritten. Slanted. Imperfect.

A prank, I told myself. Kids messing around. Teenagers with nothing better to do. I crushed the note in my fist, tossed it into the trash, and walked away. I tried not to think about it again—tried being the important word.

The thought followed me out the front door, into the afternoon air.

The bridge felt older than it looked—grimy concrete patched in mismatched squares, railings dull and metallic enough to make your hands smell like iron. I kept mine in my pockets. The river below carried its usual metallic stink, like wet rust and old machinery waking under the surface, but today the smell was sharper, heavier in the back of my nose.

Across the water, the city's glass-and-steel buildings caught the light in clean, bright lines that didn't match the world behind me. The old main street stretched along the riverbank in faded brick and peeling signs, narrow windows clouded by age. Trees squeezed into the tight gaps between buildings, their branches shifting in the breeze. Birds called from somewhere inside the slivers of green, but their voices sounded distant, out of place.

Missing-person flyers lined the railings—dozens of faces I'd memorized without trying. A boy in a red hoodie. A woman with a chipped tooth. A toddler with uneven pigtails. The papers were warped by weather, layered on top of each other like the bridge couldn't bring itself to let any of them go.

I walked slowly, each step heavier than the last. The morning haze broke cleanly over the river, turning it into a dark split running through the town. As I moved toward the taller buildings, the bridge drifted into shadow and the air thickened pressing in around me. I kept my hands buried in my pockets, shoulders hunched, not from cold but from that familiar hollowness settling beneath my ribs.

Halfway across the bridge, something made me stop.

A man stood on the opposite walkway, staring over the railing. He wasn't moving. Not a twitch. Not even a shift of weight. Just… frozen. His coat flapped sharply in the wind, but his body didn't react.

I stared at him for a few seconds.

Still nothing.

It was particularly odd because he looked like a normal man. He was dressed well, and didn't seem to be high or anything like that. I looked him directly in the eyes, and his mouth opened slightly. Drool slowly dripped down his chin, and pooled on his shirt.

I took a step forward, and suddenly felt a low rumble pass under the bridge. Too low to be a boat, and too rhythmic to be pipes. The railing on the bridge vibrated faintly under my hand.

I took another step forward and the rumbling stopped. At that moment the wind died down, the rustle of flyers stopped. Even the river seemed to mute under the sudden stillness.

Suddenly I heard a car horn blare, and I whipped my head around to see where it was coming from. All at once, everything returned to normal.

The man blinked and wiped the saliva from his chin, and

turned and walked the other direction, like a paused scene resuming in a film.

He acted like nothing had happened. He just walked away, hands in his pockets.

I reached the other side and turned toward the office district. Buildings loomed overhead, tall and grave-like. Most were dull beige or chipped white, their windows reflecting nothing but fog. One, though, caught my eye—the city-owned building marked CONDEMNED — MAINTENANCE PENDING.

It had looked lifeless for years, but today a single light flickered in a third-floor window—just once, just long enough to make my stomach drop. I blinked, and the window was dark again. I told myself it had to be a trick of the sun, a bit of glare, maybe a passing car throwing light where it didn't belong.

3

Compliance Review

The file flickered as it opened, lines of old code crawling across the display. Someone had hidden it deep. Buried under layers of false directories, mislabeled logs, dead links. But 349 had learned how to find things they never meant for anyone to see.

A timestamp sat at the top dated over 4 years ago:

[LOG ENTRY-UNIT C-2. DATE: OCT 17th, 2420]

The incident with Supervisor N-64 required immediate action. He remembered pieces of his former life. He tried to speak them aloud. He tried to reach C-2 directly. By the time your team arrived, his mind had already broken through too many layers. Resetting him again would not have held.

He was removed.

Every unit who witnessed the moment has had their memory cleaned. The inconsistencies have been sealed. No one will recall what N-64 said, or what he did.

Cleanup will take approximately three hours. During that time, the building must remain calm and undisturbed.

Regarding C-2: his emotional development had stalled. Without a significant loss event, he would not reach the levels we require. The timing was appropriate. His family has been taken out of his current path. Their absence will deepen his emotional range and make him more responsive during later stages.

* * *

I stepped through the automatic doors of CityLink Communications, the blast of cold lobby air greeting me the same way it had for the last ten years. The place always smelled like musty carpet, burned coffee, and hand sanitizer. The staircase rose to my right, its once-white marble now a tired gray, railings worn smooth from years of use. A few dusty artificial plants hung from the balcony above, doing little to brighten the space.

I knew every fading spot in the carpet, every buzzing light panel, every scuff on the elevator doors. Ten years in one building will do that. A decade ago, climbing the ladder here felt like the biggest accomplishment of my life—something I chased with the kind of desperation only a young father with bills and no time can understand.

About a year after the accident, I was promoted from Renewal Specialist to Behavioral Account Analyst, the highest-paying job you could get without a CityLink Management Certification. Becoming a BAA was supposed to be the peak. Five years in that role and I could move into management, get certified, maybe even run a team. I used to care about all of that. I used to picture the bigger office, the real windows, the better hours. I imagined Elisabeth and the kids visiting, their faces lighting up.

After the accident, the promotion meant nothing. I had more money than I needed and nowhere to spend it. No house to upgrade. No school clothes to buy. No birthday trips to save for. No future worth building when mine had already been buried.

Still, I came here every morning. I stood in this lobby, scanned my badge, and went through the motions because they were the only things left that still moved on their own.

Janice didn't look up when she gestured for me to scan my badge. She never did. I pressed it to the scanner, and the machine beeped sharply through the quiet lobby.

WELCOME Owen, the old green font blinked across the scratched display.

The scanner looked older than the building—yellowed plastic, chipped corners, dust thick enough to write my name in. I sometimes wondered if the whole place would collapse before that little screen ever died.

Right on cue, Curtis stepped out from behind the frosted glass like the beep had summoned him. "You made it right on time," he said in the same crisp, emotionless tone he used every day. "Good. Compliance is easier when we stick to routine."

Curtis always said something like that.

He knew my schedule down to the exact minute. Sometimes I caught him checking his watch right as I walked through the door, nodding as if I had fulfilled some requirement only he understood. I used to think he meant well. These days it felt more like being monitored. Observed.

I forced a smile I didn't feel and said,

"Good to see you, Curtis. How is—"

He cut me off before I finished the question.

He always did.

"Productivity is stable," he said, clasping his hands behind his back. "Your department met 92% of its weekly projection. A slight downturn, but acceptable."

I nodded, even though none of that was an answer to the question I had started. Curtis rarely acknowledged small talk. He answered with data instead of emotions, as if numbers were the only language he trusted.

"That's good," I said weakly.

Curtis gave a single, precise nod.

"Consistency is key. The system works best when the people inside it do."

He meant it as encouragement, probably. Or whatever passed for encouragement in Curtis's mind. He was the kind of man who would pat a crying child on the head with all the tenderness of someone testing a melon for ripeness.

His gaze flicked down to the scanner.

"Your clock-in is registered. Head upstairs. The Compliance Desk is expecting you."

Of course it was.

We all went there first thing every morning.

No one questioned it.

"Right," I said. "Thanks."

Curtis stepped aside in that mechanical way of his, like a sliding door in human form, and gestured toward the elevators.

"Have a smooth day, Owen," he said.

The phrase was standard. Scripted. As if even he didn't believe what he was saying.

I gave a half-smile that never reached my eyes and headed for the stairs. My shoes clicked across the lobby floor, each step echoing louder than it should in a building this empty. I passed Janice at the desk; she didn't look up, just kept tapping the same three keys in that same looping rhythm.

The staircase rose to my right, wide marble steps framed by tired wooden rails. It must've once looked impressive, but now it just felt worn out, too polished for a building that had long given up on modernity. My footsteps echoed off the high ceiling, bouncing around the space until it sounded like someone was following me. As I climbed, the smell shifted from musty carpet to old paper. Files, printed forms, things stored too long in forgotten rooms.

The third floor opened into its usual layout. To the left: restrooms and a cramped break room. Straight ahead: the Compliance Desk under a row of flickering lights. To the right: a grid of cubicles stretching toward a hallway of offices, every door closed, every space identical except for the nameplates screwed into the walls. Curtis's office sat at the beginning of the hall, always slightly ajar. Farther down, narrow windows filtered in washed-out sunlight that didn't make anything feel brighter.

I squared my shoulders and moved toward the Compliance Desk. The routine always hit the same way. The weight in my stomach, the numbness spreading through my chest, the quiet question in the back of my mind wondering if today would be the day I didn't take the pills.

But even as the thought surfaced, I pushed it down.

I joined the short line at the Compliance Desk. The faint scent of rubbing alcohol hung in the air, cold and sterile, settling over the room. Behind the glass barrier sat the bright white counter where everyone received their daily pill. A single white tablet slid across a tray with all the warmth of a processed inventory item.

While I waited, my eyes drifted to the walls. Posters for "wellness" and "youth maintenance" plastered every surface, advertising creams and supplements CityLink conveniently sold on-site. It was almost funny. Forced emotional regulation on one end, cheerful moisturizers on the other.

Beside the counter, the same sign I'd seen for a decade glared back at me:

DAILY DOSE REQUIRED

For Emotional Wellness and Stability

The attendant stood behind the glass, a fixture as much as the desk itself. He'd been here about a year, long enough to lose any edges he once had. He had Janice's stillness but none of her attempts at friendliness. His gray uniform blended into the walls, and his expression never changed. Up close, he always smelled faintly of mint with a sour undertone I could never un-associate from him.

One employee after another stepped forward, and the attendant delivered the same line each time, voice perfectly even, like the words had been installed in him:

"Please take your assigned dose. Hold it under the tongue until dissolved."

Most people ahead of me took their pill without hesitation and headed straight to their desks, moving in smooth, practiced lines. A few lingered to talk about traffic or weekend plans, but they were quickly nudged back to their stations.

When my turn came, I stepped forward, picked up the small pill, and held it under the flickering lights. It looked exactly like the one I took at home. Same size, same shape, same smooth surface.

As I raised it to my mouth, a memory hit hard—Elisabeth

brushing my hand in the kitchen, Grace trying to tell a joke she couldn't finish, Thomas proudly showing me a project he'd worked on for hours. My chest tightened. Taking this pill felt like erasing them all over again. The medication always softened my memories, blurred the edges, made everything easier to bear but harder to keep.

I placed the pill under my tongue, let it dissolve, and swallowed.

"Thank you. Have a great day," the attendant said, voice bright and hollow.

As I walked toward my desk, the familiar burn sparked behind my eyes. I hardly reacted anymore. The sensation spread through my head like cold water moving under my skin. My grief softened at the edges, the anger dulled with it, and the memories blurred—still there, but smudged.

I kept walking, trying to remember what had just been bothering me. Something important. Something sharp. But the thought slipped out of reach before I could grasp it.

I sat at my desk, staring at the monitor while the office blended into a dull hum. Whispers, clicking keys, the heater's constant hiss. Everything routine. Everything predictable. I touched my temple. The world felt soft around the edges, the pill smoothing my thoughts more than it should.

"Owen, are you ready for our meeting?"

Curtis's voice jolted me upright. My heart jumped as I spun in my chair, I had completely forgotten about our meeting. He stood behind me, eyebrows slightly raised, as if my startled reaction confirmed something he'd already suspected.

I nodded quickly, logged out, and tried not to look shaken.

Curtis was… complicated. Everyone swore he was the nicest man in the building, the one who cared the most. I wanted to believe that.

He'd do something undeniably kind—something that should've cemented that belief—and somehow it only made me feel worse.

Like the Christmas I tanked my numbers. I was drowning, bills piling up, no money for gifts, pretending everything was fine. I mentioned it once in passing, not thinking anything of it. That afternoon, every present I'd listed was sitting on my desk. All from Curtis, not the company. He never brought it up, never asked for thanks. It should've made me like him more. Instead, it made him harder to understand.

He opened his office door and motioned for me to enter. As I passed him, a faint, metallic fishy scent hit my nose. I stepped inside quickly and sat in the corner chair.

Curtis closed the door with that careful gentleness he used for everything, then took the seat across from me, folding his hands in his lap.

"So," he began, his voice warm, "how have you been sleeping lately?"

I blinked at the question. "Uh… fine, I guess."

He nodded. "Any moments of waking confusion? Difficulty distinguishing dreams from consciousness?"

"Not really," I said.

"And routine tasks? Any trouble completing them or remembering steps?"

"No. I'm good."

"Your sense of connection to our community values?"

"As good as ever."

He shifted slightly as though advancing to the next line in a script. "Tell me about your grief levels."

"As good as they can be," I muttered.

Curtis didn't react, just continued, "Any intrusive memories today?"

I frowned. "What does that even mean?"

He paused for a beat and his expression tightened, like someone trying to recreate concern from memory rather than actually feeling it.

"Listen, Owen," he said, leaning forward slightly, elbows on his desk. "I'm just concerned. Honestly, I think of you like a friend, and I've been worried."

I stayed silent.

He let the quiet hang there for effect.

"I feel like after the accident… you struggled. Understandably. Then you improved. But lately…" His eyes narrowed a fraction. "Something seems off. Your work is excellent—no issues there. But emotionally… I don't know. I just sense a shift."

My jaw clenched. I'd done nothing to give him that impression. I'd kept my head down. Kept my numbers steady. Kept my personal life sealed tight.

And then, the realization.

Ending everything. That was the thing I forgot.

My heart lurched. Of course. That was why the morning felt strange, and why everything blurred. The plan. The quiet conclusion I'd reached this morning.

I almost laughed at the absurdity of this timing—sitting here being scrutinized by Curtis like a broken appliance ready for warranty replacement. But I swallowed it down.

If today was supposed to be my last day, maybe I didn't need to drag it out inside this over-sanitized office.

"Owen, I'm worried about you," he repeated.

I forced a smile, thin and brittle. "I'm okay. Really. I don't think I've had this much clarity in a long time."

Curtis studied my face for a long, uncomfortable moment before finally nodding. "As long as you're certain." The gesture didn't match his expression; he didn't look convinced. Not even close.

I kept my face neutral because anything else invited more questions. Eventually, I cleared my throat and said, "Actually… I was hoping to leave a little early today."

That got his attention. His eyes dropped to the tablet on his desk, and he tapped it once, then again, slower, like he was checking my request against some invisible protocol. When he looked back up, there was concern in his face, but concern the way actors rehearse it. "Is there a reason?" he asked.

"I'm just tired," I said. "Long week."

"Tired how?" His voice was soft, but the question wasn't.

"Just tired," I repeated quickly. "Need to clear my head."

Curtis tapped the tablet again, and a soft chime sounded, the same sound the doors made when compliance checks were approved. He folded his hands on the desk. "Yes you may go home early."

"Thanks," I said, pushing out the word.

Curtis rose with me, hand resting lightly on the back of his chair as if he needed to steady himself. "And Owen…" Curtis waited until I met his eyes. "Don't disappear on us."

My stomach dropped, heavy and sudden.

I gave a stiff nod, unable to speak. Curtis held my gaze long enough to make my skin crawl, before finally stepping back. But even after I left his office, I felt his eyes on me. The sensation followed me down the hallway, only easing when I turned the corner and broke his line of sight.

4

The Easier Way

As I crossed the parking lot, I kept glancing back at the building, half expecting to find Curtis standing in his office window, tracking my steps. But he never appeared. Nothing moved. Nothing shifted.

Today I caught myself studying everything with even sharper focus than usual. As I crossed back over the bridge, a couple passed me stepping in perfect sync, laughing at something quiet between them. Their joy didn't sting. It actually made something inside me settle for a moment. On the other side of the bridge, a man ahead of me was arguing into his phone, voice sharp and frustrated, but the instant he met my eyes, he softened, gave me a polite nod, and lowered his tone. People were funny like that, snapping from storm to sunshine the moment they realized someone else existed.

As I neared the grocery store, I slowed out of habit. It sat in one of the old red-brick buildings on Main Street, the bricks were uneven in color, some darker from age or weather, some chipped along the edges. Tall windows stretched across the front, their frames painted black years ago but now fading to a tired charcoal. Inside, I could see the familiar clutter of produce bins and fluorescent lights humming against the ceiling, the same setup it had always had. It was wedged between a pawn shop and a boutique that never had customers, all of them stitched together like a long, aging row of teeth. I usually stopped here for groceries on my way home, but I wouldn't be needing anything after tonight. Still, my stomach growled loudly enough to make me wince, and I was suddenly aware that I hadn't eaten since yesterday. I ignored it and looked through the window instead.

Inside, a man stood alone in the cleaning aisle, holding two nearly identical bottles of soap and staring between them like he was defusing a bomb. After a moment of indecision, he pulled out his phone to call his spouse for clarification. Smart move. No one wants to be sent back to the store.

A few feet down, a mother was trying to wrangle her three kids, all of them delightfully feral, grabbing at things, running small circles around her legs. She looked exhausted but determined. I remembered those days. The pressure. The noise. The strangers who stared too long, pretending not to judge while very much judging.

I had always wanted to tell parents like her they were doing fine, that it was okay to look overwhelmed, that kids were supposed to be loud and messy and alive.

My eyes shifted from the bustling scene inside to my own reflection in the glass. The man staring back at me looked worn down by something heavier than a long day. My hair, once dark, had threads of gray creeping through it. My beard had grown uneven, longer than I ever used to let it get. I looked thinner too.

When my eyes drifted back toward the glass, my breath stopped. Mr. Johnson stood inside the store, perfectly centered in the window where my reflection had been a second earlier. He didn't blink. Didn't move. He just stared straight at me, his face pressed close to the glass, as if he'd been waiting for the exact moment my eyes would return. The fluorescent lights behind him flickered, throwing quick, sickly flashes across his features, making the deep lines in his face twitch like something crawling beneath his skin. For a split second it felt like I was staring into an open grave. His eyes—sunken, glassy, and impossibly focused, locked onto mine making the hair on my arms rise.

My stomach lurched and I stumbled backward so fast my foot slipped off the curb. I nearly fell into the road as a car screeched past, horn blaring long and furious. The driver leaned out the window shouting something I couldn't hear, but the tone said enough. "Sorry!" I shouted reflexively, waving an apology he absolutely didn't care about. He responded with a gesture that left no room for misunderstanding.

I forced a shaky smile and turned back to the window, ready to give Mr. Johnson a sheepish wave, maybe some kind of "oops, didn't mean to react like that" gesture. But he was gone. Just… gone. A chill crawled across my shoulders. I hoped I hadn't offended him. But honestly, he had to know he looked like he'd wandered straight out of a horror film.

He was balding, but refused to accept it—letting the long, greasy strands he had left cling to the sides of his scalp like seaweed on a rock. His skin always looked damp, and his teeth, what little I'd seen, were the color of old paper. You could practically smell him before you saw him. Sometimes, walking through the hallway of our building, I'd catch the lingering scent he left behind: stale sweat and mildew, like an old coat left too long in the rain. Unsettling didn't begin to cover it.

Looking at my reflection beside the now-empty window, I could see a version of myself that ended up just like him. A man no one wanted to look at. A man people stepped around in silence. A man who watched others closely because he had no one left to watch him back.

The window's reflection still trembled in my vision as I stepped back onto the sidewalk. My heart hadn't fully settled, and I found myself walking slower than usual, each step hesitant, like my body wasn't sure it wanted to keep moving forward. It was strange. After everything I'd been feeling all day, part of me wondered if maybe I didn't actually want to die. Not yet. Not if the world could still jolt me like that. Not if something as simple as being startled could slam me back into myself so hard.

But the thought didn't hold. It fluttered for a moment and then dissolved as quickly as it formed.

By the time I turned onto my street, the silence had settled again, wrapping around me like a heavy coat. My steps slowed even more. The streetlights hummed. The wind clicked a loose sign against a lamppost. Everything felt distant, muffled, as though the world was drifting a few inches away from where it was supposed to be.

And somewhere in that quiet, a different thought arrived. A simple, treacherous whisper that slid into my mind as easily as breathing.

You don't have to feel like this tomorrow.

I didn't react. Didn't stop walking. Didn't even blink. I just let the thought exist. I let it sit beside me like an unwelcome companion I no longer had the strength to force away. I wasn't planning anything. I wasn't making decisions. I was just letting the possibility unfold in the empty space inside me where hope used to sit.

It was quiet.

And that quiet was the real danger.

Across from my apartment was the playground, the same one I used to take the kids to after work. Even now, in the fading light, it looked almost cheerful. Bright primary colors standing out against the darkening tree line behind it. The paint on the yellow rails was chipped in places, the red posts faded from too many summers, and the blue slide had a long scuff down one side, but none of that mattered. It was familiar. A little island of color pressed up against the wall of trees that always seemed to loom close.

The benches along the walkway were empty, their metal frames cold and dark under the overcast sky. I used to sit there for hours, timing Thomas's runs from the slide to the ladder, pushing Grace gently on the swing until her eyes drooped and her little fists loosened around the chains. From across the street, I could almost hear their laughter, bright and echoing and alive, slipping between the trees like something the forest hadn't managed to swallow.

The few times I'd come back alone, parents had glanced at me the way parents do—quick, tight looks, hands pulling their kids just a little closer. I didn't blame them. A grown man lingering near a playground always reads wrong. So I stayed on the other side of the road, where I could watch without anyone staring. Honestly, that was probably worse, but at least I didn't have to feel their eyes on me.

I was turning toward my building when something shifted

in the bushes behind the play structure. A soft rustling. I paused. Probably a squirrel. Or a raccoon. Or some small, harmless thing.

A rabbit hopped out. Soft, brown, cheerful-looking, sniffing the air like it was searching for treasure. Its nose twitched rapidly as it looked around, and for a strange moment, it felt like its gaze fixed on me. And then, suddenly, it bounded toward me.

It ran in a straight line, ears flopping, its tiny feet skittering across the playground mulch. It appeared almost excited, almost joyful, the way Grace used to run toward me when I came home from work—arms open, hair bouncing, smile wide enough to break me in half. Something about its earnest little dash stirred something warm behind my ribs.

A small boy reached out to grab it, laughing, but the rabbit darted past him. It shot across the road, barely avoiding a speeding car that blared its horn but didn't slow down. Then it reached me. It sat right at my feet, looking up with that same impossible focus, head tilted just slightly as if waiting for me to understand something.

For a moment, it was… nice. Strange, but nice. A tiny gift from a world that didn't offer me many anymore.

Then something shifted in the concrete beside my shoe.

A crack I'd never noticed before was just wide enough for something black to ooze up from the darkness. A snake. Thin, obsidian-scaled, with two white stripes running down its back, slithered into the light. It moved in an unnatural, fluid ripple, its tongue flicking out like it was tasting something rotten in the air.

I froze. Every instinct I had screamed at me to move, but my body locked up before I could decide what to do. The rabbit didn't freeze with me. It backed up once, a tiny startled hop, nose twitching rapidly, then the snake struck.

It was small, barely a foot and a half long, no thicker than my finger. Its two white stripes glinting as it shot forward with impossible speed. It latched onto the soft part of the rabbit's neck and held on with a kind of frantic, desperate violence that made my stomach twist.

The rabbit thrashed, kicking wildly, its hind feet drumming against the ground in panicked bursts. The snake whipped back and forth with the movement, anchored by its tiny jaws. I felt myself take a step back without meaning to, fear spiking sharp and immediate.

As the rabbit fought, something about its movements shifted. Its eyes bulged, reddened, veins spiderwebbing across the whites. Thin trails of blood leaked from places that shouldn't bleed. My heart hammered so hard I could feel it in my teeth. I wanted to move. I wanted to look away. But fear had its hands around my spine, holding me in place.

The rabbit's body tensed, its small frame going rigid as though something inside it had suddenly seized. Its fur puffed outward in a strange, unnatural swell like air was being forced beneath its skin. Then, just as quickly, the tension broke. The rabbit collapsed onto the ground in a limp heap, its body folding in on itself as though all strength had drained away at once. A faint warmth rose from its fur, and the stillness that followed was so complete it made my stomach twist. The rabbit didn't twitch. Didn't breathe. It was simply… gone.

The snake released its grip, its tiny mouth streaked red. It hesitated for a single heartbeat, long enough for its head to angle toward me, and then it slid back into the crack in the concrete with quick, darting movements.

The whole thing lasted seconds. But every second felt too long, too vivid to dismiss.

My breath came out in short, shaky bursts. The air felt warm on my face even though the evening chill still settled around my shoulders. My hands were trembling. My legs felt hollow. Fear pulsed through me in a way I hadn't felt in years. Real fear.

I backed away, one step at a time, not trusting the crack in the concrete, the bushes, or the shadows creeping across the playground. I didn't want to look back. I didn't want to see if anything else was moving. All I wanted was to get inside my building, somewhere familiar, somewhere with walls.

The glass door to the building didn't reflect me until I was almost touching it. And when I stepped inside, the hallway looked emptier than it ever had. I expected to hear a TV from someone's apartment, a conversation behind a door, footsteps on the stairwell. Something. Anything. But the place was still.

I half expected someone to step out, to nod, to at least acknowledge I existed. No one did.

I forced my key into the lock and pushed open my apartment door. The air inside was stale, unmoving. My own life lay scattered where I'd left it. Shoes by the door, jacket slumped over a chair, mail on the counter, but somehow it all felt foreign, as if I'd walked into a stranger's home wearing a stranger's skin.

Nothing met me at the door. No warmth, no sense of home. Only silence, only walls, and the knowledge that whatever I was slipping into wasn't going to let me pretend I was okay anymore.

As I stepped deeper into the apartment, my shoulder brushed the edge of the bookshelf, and a framed photo of

Grace and Thomas tipped forward, sliding off the shelf before I could even react. It hit the floor face-down with a sharp crack of breaking glass. I didn't move toward it. I didn't even flinch. I just stared at the fractured edge of the frame, the way a thin line of glittering shards spread across the floor like a frozen spill. It was strange how quiet the fall sounded. Or maybe everything else in me was just too loud.

My phone buzzed in my pocket, a small vibration against my thigh that startled me only because of how alive it felt compared to everything else. I pulled it out without thinking. A bank reminder. Something about an automatic payment. Nothing that mattered. I locked the screen and let the phone slip from my hand onto the couch, the way you drop something and know you won't be picking it up again anytime soon.

Out the window, a soft tapping caught my attention. A crow had landed on the power line just outside. Alone, perfectly balanced, perfectly still. It didn't blink. Didn't shift. Just stared into my window like it had been waiting for me to look. The wind rocked the line slightly, but the bird didn't move, its dark eyes fixed on me with unsettling patience.

My gaze drifted to the pill bottle on the kitchen counter. I picked it up without ceremony, the plastic warm from the room, familiar in a way nothing else felt anymore. I didn't open it. I didn't turn it over. I just held it. And I didn't put it back.

5

A Crack in the Ceiling

The pill bottle pulsed under the sweat of my hand. I could hear the faint rattle of the pills inside when my fingers tightened, the small dry sound swallowed instantly by the heavy quiet of the apartment. Everything around me seemed to hold still, waiting.

I took a step toward the bedroom, and the floorboards groaned beneath me, just enough to sound like the house whispering its own disapproval. The crow tilted its head, barely an inch, but the movement sliced through me like a blade. Something about it felt like it was reacting to my decision before I'd fully made it.

I walked slowly, each step tugging me deeper into a thick, suffocating calm. That was the part that scared me most. How quiet it all felt. How gentle. No panic. No trembling hands. Just a smooth, sinking acceptance.

In the bedroom, the shadows were longer than they should've been. They clung to the corners like damp cloth, unmoving, observing. I sat on the edge of the bed, the mattress dipping beneath my weight with a sigh that felt almost human. The crow disappeared from view, but I could still feel its presence, still feel the weight of its stare through the wall behind me.

I looked down at the bottle in my hand. The label was creased from where my thumb had rubbed it raw over the past few months.

My chest tightened. My pulse steadied instead of spiking.

I set the bottle on my lap. My fingers curled around the cap, twisting it until a soft click broke the stillness.

The apartment exhaled around me.

And I let myself go quiet.

I lifted the bottle, hesitating for a breath that felt thin, and then dumped them into my mouth. My thoughts smeared at the edges, slipping out of order. The bottle felt heavier now, as if the weight inside it had doubled in the span of seconds.

After a few minutes, the world softened in layers. The corners of the room rounded out. The shadows blurred. My own breath sounded distant, muffled, as though I was hearing it through thick fabric. Even the weight of my body felt uncertain. Anchored one moment, floating the next.

I eased myself onto the bed, sinking into the mattress with a slow exhale. The ceiling tilted a few degrees, then drifted slowly in a circular motion, like a carousel turning at the end of the night after all the children had gone home. My limbs tingled, warmth crawling up my fingers and down my ribs in a slow, creeping wave that made everything feel unreal.

Time loosened. Moments doubled back on themselves. My hand releasing the bottle. My head settling into the pillow. My eyes blinking. Everything felt shuffled, out of sequence, my thoughts being been torn apart and reassembled in the wrong order.

A faint ringing filled my ears, hollow and repetitive. Beneath it came a soft, steady thud. My heartbeat, but distant, as if it belonged to someone lying in a different room. My vision dimmed at the edges, not darkening so much as fading, like the brightness had been turned down on the world.

Then I heard a sound above me.

A quiet, dry crack.

The tiniest shift of concrete.

I stared at the ceiling. At first, nothing seemed unusual. Just the same hairline split that had been there for years. But as the room tilted and breathed around me, the crack seemed to stretch, widening almost imperceptibly. I blinked, and the crack widened again. The concrete pulsed. Something moved behind it.

A thin, black shape pushed through.

Then another.

And another.

My breath hitched as the first snake slithered free, thin as twine, black as ink, with two pale white stripes glowing faintly along its back. It wriggled across the ceiling, its tiny body moving in unnatural ripples. Then the crack yawned wider, splitting open like wet paper.

They poured out.

Dozens at first, then hundreds. Slick, writhing things spilling through the widening gap. Their bodies cascaded across the ceiling in waves, each one marked by those same white lines, two ghostly streaks that shimmered as they writhed over one another. They moved silently, impossibly, their thin tongues flicking out in rhythmic unison.

The ceiling sagged under the weight of them. The concrete

bowed, bulging downward like it was going to burst open and rain snakes onto the bed. Their bodies twisted and knotted and slid across one another in a living sheet of black and white. A few dangled down, stretching like dripping oil toward my face.

I tried to sit up. My body didn't move.

I tried to scream. My throat tightened around a sound that never formed.

The snakes dropped a few inches closer, swaying like they were tasting the air above me. The room dimmed further, shadows pooling around the edges of my vision. The ringing in my ears grew louder. My heartbeat slowed to a distant, underwater thump.

The swarm above me writhed faster, a pulsing black cloud ready to drop.

I felt the first snake slide against my ankle, light as a thread, barely there. Then another, thicker, pressing under the blanket. Then dozens. They slipped beneath my pant legs, cold and wet, their scaled bodies dragging against my skin in frantic motions. The sensation shot up my legs like electric current. My breath stopped as more of them pushed through the fabric of my sleeves, wriggling along my arms, coiling across my ribs, sliding beneath my shirt in a cold, suffocating wave.

They were everywhere. At my throat, my wrists, skittering across my chest in a frantic, suffocating wave. Each time one touched me, a sting shot through my skin, sharp, needle-quick bursts that flared like sparks and faded into numbness almost instantly. Bright flashes of pain that felt like my own nerves misfiring all at once.

The smell hit next. A wet, moldy stench that filled the room, pressing close to my face, crawling into my lungs. A familiar smell.

My chest cinched tight. The shapes writhed higher, circling my ribs like coils, squeezing until my breath came shallow and thin. The room blurred around me, colors draining into a thick black haze that swallowed the walls and ceiling. My limbs stiffened, distant and heavy, like they no longer belonged to me. Pinpricks of light blinked across my vision. My thoughts broke apart, scrambled and slow.

I tried to speak—anything, even a gasp—but the air thickened the moment I opened my mouth. The shadows above me rippled. Something cold brushed my lips, feather-light and quick. At first I thought it was the numbness spreading upward, but then came another touch, and another, like thin lines of pressure tracing across my tongue, testing the shape of my breath.

My throat flexed on instinct. My breath stalled, stuck halfway in my chest. The darkness pressed closer, filling the space where air should have been. A taste rose in the back of my mouth. Earthy, damp, like the smell of a flooded basement. It coated my tongue, thick and suffocating. I tried to swallow, but something pushed gently back.

My body jerked weakly, a useless attempt to sit up as the room swayed. The cold prickled inside my head.. The shadows tightened their grip, and the weight across my chest grew heavier, spreading outward in slow, creeping waves that made every breath feel borrowed.

The room spun. My vision smeared. My lungs refused to work, clenching against the phantom invasion. All I could think was *I'm choking on the dark itself.* My consciousness fluttered like a dying lightbulb. The snakes, the pressure, the suffocating weight, it all blurred together into a single crushing force that pressed me down, deeper, deeper still.

A numb calm washed over me. The terror dissolved, replaced by a hollow acceptance. I let my mouth fall open, let the darkness fill it, let everything go slack. This was it. This was the end. I would finally be with my family again.

Then a hot breath brushed my ear, and a voice rasped, ancient, impossibly close cut through the hallucination like a blade: "Not yet… you don't get to rest. Not until the harvesting." My eyes snapped open. The snakes vanished. The darkness thinned.

And Mr. Johnson's withered face hovered inches above mine, his cloudy eyes locked onto mine with an awareness that felt older than the room, older than the night itself.

* * *

Today was Thomas's birthday. He was turning eleven. At least, that's what the candles said, and the banner on the wall, and what she kept telling herself. But the number didn't feel solid. It wobbled at the edges, like it wanted to become something else whenever she looked away. Dreams did that sometimes.

Time felt warped too. Meeting Owen felt both recent and impossibly far away. Moments overlapped in her mind—or is it my mind—scenes from different years sliding together until she couldn't tell which came first. She tried to picture her big family, but their faces slipped out of focus the moment she reached for them. What stayed clear was simple: she had always wanted children, and she loved them more than anything.

She and Owen had married young. She remembered that

part. Maybe twenty-one. Maybe twenty-two. The exact number wouldn't settle, but the feeling of it did—the warmth of his hand, the look on his face, the quiet certainty she had chosen the right person.

Owen worked hard for them. When he came home, the apartment always seemed brighter. Thomas and Grace would run to him, and he'd lift them both with an ease that made their cramped space feel bigger. He could turn their living room into a whole world—forests, oceans, castles—just by pretending hard enough. The kids loved it. So did she.

Lately she'd noticed the heaviness in him. His smile catching for a second, his eyes dropping before he answered her, but it didn't change how she felt. If anything, it made her love him even more, holding tightly to the pieces of their life that still felt steady in a dream that kept slipping around the edges.

Today was supposed to be special. Owen had planned the whole evening for Thomas. Dinosaur museum first, then the movies, then cake and ice cream back home. Thomas had called him three times that afternoon, making absolutely certain his dad would be home by 5:30. His excitement was so bright it felt like a lightbulb humming inside the room.

But at 4:30, Elisabeth's phone buzzed. Owen's name appeared on the screen, though the letters seemed to waver, shifting subtly as if they weren't entirely settled into place. She opened the message.

Honey! Curtis scheduled a meeting for me tonight that I didn't know about, but it's with a promising client. Might get me the promotion! I'll still try to be home by 5:30, but I could be a little late.

In the dream, she read the text twice, then a third time, the words bending and straightening with each pass. The lines didn't hold still; they rippled like they were being rewritten in front of her. And as I watched the scene unfold through her eyes, something inside me tugged hard, cutting through the dream's fog.

That isn't right. I didn't send that message. I didn't stay late.

She texted him: *No problem! What if we picked you up at work?*

No response.

Elisabeth kept checking the time, though every glance seemed to show a different number. 5:12. 5:18. 5:15. Finally the clock steadied at 5:15. Still nothing from Owen.

"Mom, can you see if Dad is on his way yet?" Thomas asked, bouncing with the kind of excitement that made the room glow brighter.

"Just checked where he is on Maps," she said, though the little dot flickered strangely on the screen. "Looks like he hasn't left the office yet, sweetie."

She checked again. 5:33. The numbers stretched slightly, like they were printed on rubber. She dialed his number. It went straight to voicemail. She called again. Same thing.

The map showed his location frozen at the office. Frozen like the world was holding still.

"Okay, kids," she said, clapping her hands with forced cheerfulness. "We're gonna go get Dad!"

She typed another message: *The kids are getting restless, so we're just gonna grab you! Love you!*

The dream made her press send twice, though she didn't remember tapping anything.

They picked him up from work often. It kept the evenings smoother, and gave them more time together as a family. That part felt true, even if everything else wavered at the edges.

At the car, Grace immediately began her usual battle with the car seat, insisting every stuffed animal needed to be buckled in too. Elisabeth tried gentle logic, then patience, then bribery. None of it worked until suddenly, finally, the buckle snapped closed. Elisabeth exhaled like she'd just finished a marathon.

Thomas filled the car with his voice as soon as they pulled out. Dinosaurs, fossils, theories he was inventing on the spot. In the dream his words ran a little too quickly, like someone nudged the speed up without telling him.

Grace's crying started halfway through his explanation of a triceratops horn.

"Use your words, sweetheart. I can't help if I can't understand you."

Her tone stayed gentle, but the dream warped the moment. The sound in the car grew dense, Thomas's excitement, Grace's sobs, the steady thrum of the road. It pressed around her like the space was shrinking and stretching at the same time.

"Thomas," she said, forcing sweetness into her voice the way she always tried to, "I love what you're telling me, I really do. But would it be okay if we sang to Grace so she could get a quick nap in?"

"I guess…" Thomas sighed, dramatically, as only children can. In the dream, his voice sounded older for a moment, then young again. The way sounds blur underwater.

Elisabeth began to sing.

Twinkle twinkle little star, how I wonder what you are. Up above the world so high, like a diamond in the sky…

She sang the lullaby again and again, the melody stretching slow and warm. The car dimmed at the edges as she watched

Grace's eyelids flutter, then finally close. A soft smile touched Elisabeth's face. For a moment, joy filled her completely. She loved these kids more than anything.

But somewhere behind the scene, I watched the dream unfold differently than I remembered.. Something was off. But I did know that the sweetness here was always the last calm breath before—

"MOM!!!"

Thomas's scream tore through the car like a blade. The vehicle lurched, the world tilting violently. I tried to close my eyes, but it wasn't my eyes watching. The roar of a semi truck flooded the dream, a deafening wall of sound that swallowed everything else. Elisabeth's hands jerked the steering wheel left, then right, her foot slamming the brake so hard her leg jolted. Grace woke in a shriek of terror, her cry splitting the air in a way that made the dream flicker like a glitching film reel.

And then, stillness.

The semi rushed past them, missing the car by inches. A graze, a scrape, a breath too close, but they were fine. Completely fine.

My subconscious recoiled. *This wasn't how it happened.* This wasn't how it ever happened. Something was wrong. Something was rewriting itself.

The car sat trembling in the lane, a thin scratch marking its side. Elisabeth's heart hammered as she unbuckled her seatbelt and stepped out. The air smelled different. Sharper almost.

The car looked the same as always: the old beater they'd bought for a thousand dollars from her coworker. A new scratch meant nothing. But the fact that they were all still alive meant everything. And nothing. And too much. I couldn't keep the facts straight. My mind kept insisting they weren't supposed to be here.

She looked up and saw the truck driver sprinting toward them, his face pale, terrified, melted around the edges like the dream was struggling to hold him together.

"Ma'am—are you all okay? I'm so, so sorry!"

"Yes," she said, voice thin and shaking. "We're okay. But what if I hadn't gotten out of the way? You could have killed my family."

The words came out stern but quiet, warping slightly as if spoken underwater.

"What can I do to make it up to you? I'll grab my insurance—just one second."

"No, that won't be necessary. We're in a hurry."

She climbed back into the car and pulled the door shut. The slam sounded wrong. Too soft and delayed by half a second. She gripped the wheel, breathing hard as the rage surged inside her, hot and sharp. He could have killed them. Should have. Or—*hadn't he? Wasn't he supposed to?*

She took three slow breaths.

Somewhere far away inside the dream, I whispered, confused and trembling:

This isn't right. This isn't how it happened.

* * *

Sound came back to me in thin, broken threads. A low murmur. A sharp hiss. Something metallic clattering onto the floor. None of it connected. None of it felt anchored to the room. I floated somewhere between the ceiling and the bed, my awareness stretched thin like a string being pulled too tight.

Mr. Johnson's voice bled in from a great distance, muffled and warped, "…stay…with…me…"

The syllables bent and twisted, folding in on themselves until they barely sounded human.

I tried to lift my head, but gravity felt off. Sideways, heavy, syrup-thick. The room swayed in slow circles, colors leaking at the edges of everything like wet paint running down a canvas. I blinked, and Mr. Johnson's face flickered into view above me. Blinked again, and he was yards away, shouting into what looked like a phone but stretched and bent like rubber. Blink. He was right beside me again, his hand on my shoulder, his lips moving too fast for the sound to keep up.

"…breathing…stay…stay…"

The words reached me out of order, cracked like shattered glass. I couldn't tell if I was hearing him or remembering him.

Somewhere else far beyond the apartment walls, a high, rising wail began to thread through the air. Sirens. Close, then far, then close again, like they were jumping locations every few seconds. Red and blue light spilled through the window, swelling and shrinking in slow, dreamlike waves.

I felt hands on me. Didn't know whose. Didn't know how many. Gloves brushed my cheek; a strap tightened across my chest. A voice near my ear shouted something firm and sharp, but it fractured in my mind into three overlapping echoes. My vision shuddered as the ceiling tilted past me, then disappeared completely as I was lifted, weightless, and carried through a corridor that stretched far longer than it ever had before.

Strangers' faces swam above me, distorted, elongated, like

reflections in warped glass. Their mouths moved, but the only thing I heard was the lingering, gravelly whisper from before, curling around the edges of my fading consciousness:

Not yet... not yet...

The night air hit my face in a cold roar as they carried me outside

Lights. Voices. Motion.

But it all felt far away.

Like I was being pulled through two worlds at once and neither one wanted to hold me steady.

* * *

Elisabeth pulled into the parking lot of Owen's workplace and shifted the car into park. The engine ticked softly, cooling in uneven clicks. The clock on the dashboard glowed 6:13, though she could've sworn they left the apartment only ten minutes ago. The numbers looked warped, slanting downward as if they were being pulled by gravity.

The car went quiet. Grace wasn't crying anymore. Thomas wasn't talking. Even the sound of traffic felt muted.

Elisabeth stared through the windshield at the building Owen worked in. The lights inside flickered in a strange rhythm—bright, dim, bright, dim—as if unsure how to behave. She squinted, trying to remember why they were here. The thought hovered just out of reach. Something about a meeting? A birthday? A promise? The memory dissolved whenever she tried to grasp it.

"Mom?" Thomas's small voice cut through the stillness. "Are we going to go in and get Dad?"

She blinked. Once. Twice. The world snapped back into

focus with a disorienting jolt.

"What?" she asked, her voice sounding like it belonged to someone sitting three seats away. "Oh—yes. Yes, we're going in to get Dad. Sorry."

As she said *sorry*, she turned to face Thomas fully.

And froze.

His eyes, usually bright, warm, and alive. The light from the parking lot shimmered across them in a way that made her stomach twist. She opened her mouth to ask if he was feeling okay, but her words died in her throat.

Something else was moving behind him.

Slowly, like a shadow deciding whether or not to become real, a thin black shape slid through the open car window. It stretched across the interior like spilled ink coming to life.

The snake eased inside with stillness. Black as oil. Small, with two white lines glowing faintly across its back like someone had painted them there with trembling hands.

Time stuttered.

Elisabeth tried to scream. Tried to snatch Thomas into her arms. Tried to slam the window shut. But her body wouldn't move. Her fingers twitched uselessly against the steering wheel.

The snake lifted its head, tongue flicking in slow pulses. It paused when it sensed her fear, almost tasting it in the air. Then it turned toward her.

Before she could react, before the dream could decide whether she deserved another second, something sharp pricked the side of her neck.

A needle-like sting.

A flash of heat.

Then, nothing.

Her breath collapsed in her chest. The world tilted sideways. The parking lights outside smeared into pale streaks as her vision doubled, then tripled. She tried to gasp, but the air fled her lungs like it had been yanked away by invisible hands.

Thomas screamed—at least she thought he did. The sound came out warped, slow, stretching across the car like a tape being eaten by a machine.

Then she heard it. A small shift of movement, just a soft whisper of friction at first, then another, and another. Her eyes snapped around the car, searching for the source until she finally saw them: snakes. Dozens of them. Maybe hundreds.

They poured through every crack, every seam of the car. Through the air vents, beneath the seats, under the floor mats. They threaded through the fabric, slithering from shadows that hadn't been there moments ago. Each one identical: black bodies, two white stripes, eyes like tiny burning embers.

They poured into the car in heaving waves, climbing the seats and coiling around the headrests. Snakes slid between her ankles, pressed against her spine, even crawled over Thomas's legs as the swarm filled every inch of space.

Wrapped around Grace's stuffed animals, covering the bright colors.

Their bodies scraped, hissed, writhed, filling every inch of space with cold, hungry movement.

Elisabeth tried to move, but the venom had hollowed her limbs. Her breath came in tiny, useless gasps as the swarm closed over her lap, her chest, her face.

Dream logic twisted the scene. The windows began to fog from something pulsing inside the snakes, something that radiated heat and cold at the same time. The interior of the car darkened as scales layered over the glass, blocking out the last of the daylight.

The last thing she saw before everything drowned in black coils was Thomas's small hand reaching toward her, trembling, trying to grab hers.

Then the world disappeared behind the swarm.

My world.

* * *

Cold air crashed against my face as the EMTs wheeled me out of the apartment building, a shocking contrast to the thick, suffocating heat of the dream. It felt sharper than it should've, like the temperature had been turned down just for me, just for this moment. I tried to lift my head, to see where I was, but my neck wouldn't move. My vision dragged across the night sky in blurring streaks as the stretcher jolted over the uneven pavement.

Everything looked stretched thin like the world was being pulled at the edges, elastic and fragile. The buildings tilted slightly, then straightened again. The night hummed with a low vibration I couldn't place, like electricity running through water.

Voices echoed around me, but none of them belonged to the people I could see. They bounced off the inside of my head, too far away and too close at the same time. I tried to focus on one but they slipped through my fingers like smoke. My breath made thin, foggy wisps in the air, and each one seemed to fade slower than the last.

Streetlights passed overhead in long, warped arcs. The light smeared across my eyes every time I blinked, leaving streaks that hung in the air.

Someone asked me a question. I opened my mouth to answer but only managed a soft gasp. The sound didn't feel like it came from me. My chest tightened as the stretcher lifted into the ambulance. The metal doors clanged shut, the noise splitting into two overlapping echoes in my mind. One real, one from somewhere deeper.

I don't remember anything about the ride to the hospital. Whatever happened between the apartment door and the ambulance dissolving into the night vanished before it could settle. All that remained was the feeling. A cold, hollow emptiness that clung to my skin like frost.

Fear was still there. Of course it was. Dread too, heavy and familiar, pressing against my ribs the way it always did after I dreamed of them. But underneath all of that, something new wound through the panic, something thin and sharp

Confusion.

The dream never changed. Not once. It always ended at the same point: the semi-truck, the impact, the sudden impossible silence. But this time… it didn't. This time the truck missed them by inches. For a heartbeat, a tiny impossible breath, it felt like everything might be different. Like maybe they would live.

But then the snakes came.

They poured into the car—hundreds, thousands—an impossible tide of black bodies with white stripes, filling every gap, every crease, every inch of space. I could still feel the weight of them, their cold scales sliding over skin, hear the choked scream that came from Grace, see the way Thomas reached for her. They didn't die the way they always died. They didn't die the way I remembered.

Why would my mind do that? Why twist it into something

even worse? Why change the ending now, after years of the same nightmare playing on loop?

Nothing made sense. Nothing felt real. And the emptiness followed me, clinging to the fading edges of consciousness like something that wasn't finished with me yet.

The questions looped in my head until they unraveled completely, leaving only the hollow ache behind them. The ambulance jolted to a stop, the doors swung open, and cold air swallowed me whole. Hands steadied the stretcher and guided me out. Streetlights smeared into trembling halos above, bending and warping like they were underwater. My name was shouted somewhere nearby, but it sounded distant, like it was meant for someone else. They pushed me toward the hospital entrance.

Then something cut through the fog—a sudden rush of wings overhead, a dark shape slicing through the light. A crow.

It dipped low, passing directly above me, its feathers catching the glow of the lamps in a way that made them glisten like oil. Something small glimmered between its claws just for an instant before falling. It hit the pavement beside the stretcher with a sharp, ringing clink.

A penny.

The sound cracked through the haze like lightning. I didn't analyze it. I didn't question it. I just... felt it.

Grace. Not alive or truly present, but somehow watching. Reaching.

A sign from heaven dropped into my path at the exact moment I was slipping away. A whisper from somewhere beyond, small and impossible and meant only for me.

The stretcher rolled forward. The hospital doors opened.

White light swallowed the edges of my vision.

As consciousness slid out of my grasp, I clung to that one fragile feeling—warmth pressed against the cold:

She sees me. She remembers who I am.

6

Night Doses Enclosed

A week had passed since I was admitted to the hospital, though my body didn't seem aware of it. Everything still felt tilted like I was waking up underwater and the world above me refused to snap into place. My thoughts kept drifting back to that evening, to the crow on the power line outside my bedroom window watching me in a steady, unblinking way.

The more I thought about it, the more certain I became that someone was watching over me. Maybe it was God. Maybe it was Grace, reaching through in the only ways she could. Maybe it was both. Because how else would Mr. Johnson have known to check on me right at that exact moment? He wasn't supposed to walk in. But he did, right when it mattered most.

It didn't feel like a coincidence. It felt like protection. Like guidance. Like a reminder that I wasn't done yet.

But then... what did he say?

Something about... a harvest?

The words drifted through my mind like a misplaced memory. Too sharp to ignore, too strange to make sense of. Had he actually said that? Had I imagined it in the panic?

I rubbed my forehead, trying to clear it. I told myself it didn't matter. I was alive. I was watched over. That was enough.

A nurse stood at my bedside, reading through the discharge instructions as if they were simple, obvious things. Rest. Hydrate. Follow up in ten days. She spoke clearly enough, but the words slid through a layer of cotton in my mind. I kept nodding like I understood, even though I knew I was agreeing to something I wouldn't remember.

She handed me a clipboard. My name was printed neatly at the top. The line for my signature waited below. I gripped the pen, but my hand didn't feel like mine. When I scribbled my name, the letters slanted in strange directions, uneven and sloppy. It looked like someone else had signed it for me.

I stepped outside the sliding doors of the hospital and the air hit me like a slap. Colors felt unnaturally bright, like someone had turned the saturation up on the world without warning. Cars passing on the street sounded crisp in a way that hurt.

I stood there for a minute, swaying slightly, adjusting to the brightness and the sudden sense of being untethered. Every breath felt like it was waking up parts of me that hadn't quite returned yet. "It's fine," I whispered to myself. "I'm just recovering." But even as I said it, the ground seemed to hum under my feet, and the world felt off in ways I didn't have words for yet.

Curtis was waiting for me just outside the sliding doors, standing perfectly still in a pressed suit that looked too crisp for visiting a hospital. His posture was relaxed, almost gentle, as if he had rehearsed looking approachable. When he saw me, his expression didn't change, but he stepped forward like he knew it was the right moment to do so.

"Owen," he said, voice soft, careful. "I can take you home. You shouldn't be walking yet." The words sounded like concern, but his face was a blank surface. No worry in his eyes, no tension around his mouth. Just a flat, almost polite emptiness.

"I'm okay," I said. "I want to walk."

Curtis nodded slowly, the motion measured, like he was checking a box on a list titled *How to React When Someone Declines Help*. "Of course. If that's what you want." His tone dipped into something that *should* have been understanding, but there was no real feeling behind it.

Then he added, "Just… if you need anything… anything at all… you let me know."

The words were comforting in theory, but coming from him, they didn't land right. He said them with the exact rhythm of empathy, but none of its weight. A traced outline of human warmth without the color filled in.

He held my gaze a second too long. Then, as if remembering people are supposed to smile in moments like this, he manufactured one. His lips stretched upward, but nothing else moved—no cheeks, no eyes, no life.

"I'll… keep that in mind," I muttered.

Curtis didn't move as I walked away. He just kept watching me go, like he was waiting for me to turn around and give him a different answer. I felt his eyes follow me all the way down the sidewalk, steady and unblinking. I just kept my head forward, focused on putting one foot in front of the other, glad to finally be outside and on my own.

Halfway down the block, the adrenaline wore off, and the reality of the last week hit me all at once. I was starving.

So I figured I'd stop at the grocery store. Just grab a few things. Something easy to make. Something real. Something normal.

The automatic doors opened, and the lights inside were harsh. Every sound echoed. The carts rattling, a scanner beeping somewhere near the back, footsteps on tile that seemed to follow me even when no one was behind me.

I grabbed a basket from the stack by the entrance and nearly dropped it. My hands still felt weak, like they weren't convinced they worked properly yet. "Just fatigue," I whispered, trying to brush it off. "You're fine. You're just tired."

As I walked through the aisles, muscle memory kicked in, the old routines surfacing without my permission. I used to shop differently. Buying in bulk was easier back then: big bags of potatoes, cheap cereal, gallon jugs of milk, giant jars of peanut butter that lasted weeks. Back then, meals made sense. Throw everything into a pot, stir, hope for leftovers, and if there weren't any, that was fine too. Feeding little mouths was simple.

I moved on autopilot. Oranges. Bread. Jam for PB&Js. Frozen burritos. Milk. The kinds of things that didn't require much effort or thought.

But the memories hit anyway when I wasn't ready—Grace sitting on the counter swinging her legs, Thomas asking if he could help stir, Elizabeth stealing bites before dinner.

Those memories ached.

Even now, years later, they pressed against me like bruises I kept forgetting I had.

At self-checkout, the machine greeted me with a sharp beep

that felt like it went straight through my head. I scanned the first item, barely lifting it off the scanner before the voice snapped, "Please place item in the bagging area."

I blinked at it. "Nobody is that fast," I muttered under my breath. The machine didn't care. It beeped again, louder this time, like it was offended I hadn't obeyed instantly.

An attendant noticed the flashing red light and wandered over with the tired look of someone who'd been fixing the same problem all day. She swiped her badge, tapped a few buttons without even glancing at the screen, and said, "You're good now," before drifting to the next machine in distress.

I tried again, scanning each item more carefully, but the machine still seemed to rush me—beeping before my hands even cleared the scanner, telling me to "please wait for assistance" when nothing was wrong. I took a breath, reminded myself I'd been through worse than an impatient checkout machine, and kept going. One scan at a time. Bread. Oranges. Jam. Frozen burritos. Milk.

When the last item finally registered, the screen asked if I wanted cash back. I hit "no" with more force than necessary. The printer whirred loudly and spit out the receipt in one long curl, warm from the machine.

I folded it in half and slid it into my pocket without looking at it. My mind was already somewhere else—on food, on home, on the vague exhaustion weighing down every part of me. I just wanted to get outside, breathe real air, feel the day on my skin instead of fluorescent lights in my eyes.

It wasn't until I was halfway to the exit, the cool rush of air from the opening doors brushing across my face, that I finally reached into my pocket.

I pulled the receipt out of my pocket and unfolded it without thinking, my mind still half on dinner, half on getting home and lying down. I started to look at the front—just prices, nothing special—but something made me turn it over.

And then I froze.

My feet stopped moving before the rest of me realized why. I just stood there in the middle of the walkway, people moving around me, the automatic doors opening and closing behind me, letting in bursts of cold air that didn't register.

Because the back of the receipt… wasn't blank. A pressure bloomed behind my ribs, sudden and unwelcome, stealing the air from my next breath.

A single word was scratched across the paper in uneven, shaky letters:

Dad

It looked off on the page.. Not something printed, not something neat. It was written in a messy scrawl with the kind of pressure kids use when they're gripping a pencil with their whole fist. The D took up half the line, huge and crooked. The a was tiny beside it, like it was trying to hide. And the last d dipped down like the writer forgot where the baseline was supposed to be.

This wasn't adult handwriting. Not even remotely. Not the handwriting of someone practiced or confident or intentional.

It was the handwriting of a child.

A very young one.

Four, maybe. The exact age Grace was when I lost her. When she still wrote letters too big for the paper and traced the ones she wasn't sure about. When she'd write her name with backward Gs and oversized loops and look up at me to ask, "Is that right, Daddy?"

My knees went weak, and the entire grocery store seemed to tilt slightly to the left. I reached out blindly and grabbed the nearest cart just to keep from stumbling, knuckles going white around the metal handle. The fluorescent lights blurred at the edges of my vision. For a moment I honestly thought I might pass out.

And for a heartbeat—just one—I felt like I was standing on the edge of something impossible, something my mind wasn't ready to accept, something too close to hope and too close to heartbreak to be safe.

Before I could even blink, the ink on the receipt shifted, then the letters themselves began to bleed. The sharp edges softened, the lines sagging into each other like wet paint.

The word warped, the curves of the letters bending in slow motion, smearing across the paper. I blinked hard, once, twice, but it didn't stop. The ink thinned, fading into pale gray, then into nothing at all, dissolving back into the fibers of the receipt until it was perfectly blank—like it had never been touched.

I stared down at the empty paper, my heart still pounding from what I'd seen—or what I thought I'd seen. I walked back toward the self-checkout attendant, holding the receipt out.

"Did you… print this?" My voice cracked in the middle.

She glanced at it, confused. "Yeah. Just a normal receipt. Want another one?"

She was already reaching to hit reprint, her face open, casual, completely unaware that my entire world had tilted sideways. I didn't know what I was expecting her to say. Something. Anything that made sense of what just happened.

But she looked at me like I was just another tired customer.

I forced a smile, shaking my head. "No. It's fine. Have a good night."

"Yeah, you too," she said, already turning away.

I folded the receipt and shoved it into my pocket, my hand trembling walking out of the store like nothing had happened, even though my pulse was still racing and my legs felt like they might give out beneath me.

Outside, I pressed my back against the brick wall of the store, trying to steady myself. The cold evening air hit my face, but it didn't help. I was sweating, trembling so hard I had to brace one hand against my knee just to stay upright. My heart wouldn't slow down. It felt like it was trying to crawl up my throat.

I was tired. I was overstimulated. I was imagining things. That was all. Anything else I refused to consider.

But some part of me knew deep down that something had cracked. Something small but real. A fracture I couldn't see the edges of yet.

I arrived home and walked down the empty halls of my apartment building, the fluorescent lights buzzing faintly overhead. When I reached Mr. Johnson's door, I stopped. My hand hovered in the air for a long moment.

I didn't even know what I wanted from him. Clarity, maybe? Or reassurance? Or just to hear his voice say something normal, something that proved I hadn't imagined that strange sentence in the middle of everything. *Harvest.* Had he really said that? Or had my brain been scrambling nonsense together while it shut down?

I swallowed hard and finally lifted my hand to knock. Before my knuckles touched the wood, a voice came from behind me.

"He's gone," the neighbor across the hall said. Her words hit me like a jolt, sharp and sudden.

I turned. "Gone?" The word came out weaker than I meant. "Like… gone gone?"

She shook her head quickly. "No, not dead. Relax." She pushed her door open a little wider, leaning against the frame. "He said he was in some kind of trouble. Headed to a place called… I don't know. The nether? Something like that."

"The nether?" I repeated, trying to make sense of it.

She shrugged. "Who knows. He's a pretty confused guy. Could be nothing. Could be something he saw on a TV show. He packs up and leaves every few months anyway. He'll be back later I'm sure."

Her tone was casual, almost dismissive. Mr. Johnson wasn't confused. Not in the way she was implying. Not to me.

I nodded slowly, though I didn't feel any calmer. "Right. Thanks."

"Sure thing," she said, already stepping back inside her apartment. "Have a good night."

The hallway went quiet again as her door clicked shut, leaving me staring at Mr. Johnson's empty doorway.

When I reached my door, I noticed a small cardboard box sitting neatly on the welcome mat. My name was printed across the label in clean black text, the same as always. Same size. Same weight.

It was my night doses.

Work handled the morning and after-shift pills, handing them out like clockwork to everyone who needed them. But the nighttime set was always delivered straight to my apartment, timed perfectly so the new box arrived the day the last one ran out. I never ordered them. I never asked. They just showed up.

I picked up the package and held it in my hands. It felt

strangely heavy for something so small.

I brought it inside and set it on the counter. The silence in the apartment settled around the box like it was waiting to see what I'd do.

I knew the routine by heart: tear it open, pop one out, swallow, wait for the night to smooth out until I didn't feel anything sharp or complicated or painful. It was what I'd been told to do. What everyone told me would help.

But standing there in my doorway, the box unopened, something inside me pushed back. Hard.

If I was still here—if I was still breathing after everything— then maybe it wasn't because of the pills. Maybe it was because I was meant to hold on, meant to feel something, meant to stay connected to the parts of my life that still mattered.

And the truth was, those pills took more than they ever gave. They dulled the memories I wanted to keep. Softened the edges until Thomas's laugh felt distant, until Grace's little voice sounded like a memory of a memory. Even Elizabeth's face blurred at the corners on the nights I took them.

If staying alive meant I had to feel everything, even the worst parts, then maybe that was okay. Maybe feeling the pain meant I still had something left to lose. Something left to love.

I slid the box farther down the counter, away from me.

"No," I whispered. "Not tonight."

7

Snakes

That night the dream was different. Not in a good way. The moment it began, I felt it—an uneasiness under my skin, like my mind was bracing itself for something it already knew was coming.

I was standing in a white room. Not just a room—an expanse. Bigger than any store I'd ever been in, bigger than any building should be. The floor stretched out in every direction, polished and cold, fading into the horizon like a blank sheet of paper. I turned slowly, waiting to see a wall, a door, anything that marked an ending.

There wasn't one.

I picked a direction and started walking. My steps echoed loudly, the sound bouncing off nothing and coming back to me delayed, distorted. I walked faster. Then faster still, until my walk turned into a jog, and my jog into a full sprint. But the room didn't change. No matter how far I ran, no matter how hard I pushed my legs, everything stayed the same—white floor, white ceiling, nothing in between but space.

Finally, I stopped. My breath came in hard, uneven pulls. Sweat slid down my back. And that's when I noticed it.

The faint smell of mildew.

It crept in slowly at first, just enough to make me wrinkle my nose, then strengthened as I focused on it. A damp, musty scent, like old concrete in a flooded basement or the inside of a forgotten room. I didn't know why it stood out, but it did. It felt familiar somehow, like something from a memory I couldn't fully access.

I turned toward it instinctively, shifting a few degrees to the left, and started walking again. The scent grew stronger with every step, guiding me like a trail only I could sense. The fluorescent lights above me flickered—just once at first, then again, longer this time.

I walked deeper into the void.

With every flicker, the room dimmed. Slowly, but definitely. The bright white ceiling began to gray. The shadows lengthened, thin lines stretching across the floor even though nothing cast them. The further I went, the more the light faded, until the whiteness around me felt less like a room and more like fog being eaten away at the edges.

Something in me wanted to turn around, to go back to where it was brighter, safer, more familiar. But the mildew smell kept pulling me forward. Each breath filled my lungs with its damp heaviness, urging me to keep going.

And so I did, step by step, into the growing dark ahead.

Eventually, the light around me thinned into almost nothing. Just a single, faint glow in the distance, like someone holding a dying flashlight miles away. Everything else was swallowed by a thick, soupy darkness that felt alive—like it was breathing with me, waiting for me to slip. My steps slowed, but the pressure in my chest only tightened. I wasn't wandering. I knew that now. I was *searching* for someone. Someone who mattered. Someone who shouldn't be alone here.

But before I could focus on that feeling, something slid against my leg.

Cold. Smooth. Alive.

I froze.

A rush of terror erupted beneath my skin, primal and immediate, like an old nightmare snapping its jaws shut around me. I knew that feeling. Snakes. My nerves remembered every detail—the icy glide of their scales, the way they moved with intent, the way they appeared in places where nothing should be.

My hand twitched, useless in the dark. I didn't dare look down.

The snake didn't curl around me. It didn't strike. It didn't even hesitate. It just slid past, its small body whispering across the floor like a line of cold ink being drawn into the dark.

Something was different.

A sinking dread clawed up my throat. It wasn't interested in *me*.

Which meant whoever I was searching for—whoever pulled me into this endless room—*wasn't safe*.

Air scraped in and out of my lungs while my pulse thundered beneath my skin.

The snake picked up speed, gliding straight toward that faint, dying glow ahead.

I didn't think—I just sprinted into the darkness. My feet slamming against the floor, my breaths coming out ragged and broken. The faint glow ahead pulsed once, like a dying heartbeat, and suddenly the shadows around me exploded with movement.

Snakes—hundreds of them—poured in from every direction. From the floor. From the ceiling. From the corners where the dark was thickest. Small bodies whipping, curling, surging toward the same point I was running to. Toward *them*.

I pushed harder. My legs burned but I didn't stop. I couldn't. Someone was out there, and the way the snakes moved—fast, desperate, purposeful—made my blood turn to ice.

There were too many to dodge.

Cold bodies slid over my shoes, my ankles, my shins. Scales scraped against my skin. I kept running, stomping through them, feeling tiny bones crunch under my feet, hearing soft, wet pops as I crushed them mid-stride. They writhed and coiled around my ankles, slipping under my soles, sliding between my fingers when I swung my arms for balance—living ropes that tangled and twisted and tried to pull me down.

Still I ran. Through dozens. Hundreds. No—thousands.

The darkness had swallowed everything now. No ceiling. No floor. No horizon. Just movement and the suffocating sound of scales scraping against each other like whispers in a language I shouldn't understand.

I didn't care. I ran faster. Harder. My lungs screamed, my knees buckled, but I ran.

And then something grabbed me.

A hand—ice-cold, long-fingered—shot out of the dark and yanked my ankle with impossible strength. I pitched forward, my body flipping through the air before slamming into the ground with a sickening crack.

Pain exploded through my skull. My vision shattered into white stars.

Then, silence.

The snakes were gone. Instantly. Completely. Like they'd never existed.

I lay there in the dark, gasping, my head ringing, blood trickling warm down the side of my face.

A light snapped on above me.

Blinding. White. Violent.

I lifted my head, eyes stinging, and froze.

In front of me, under the harsh white lights, sat a woman in a metal chair. Her head was shaved, and her skin looked pale in the brightness, like the light was draining the color from her. She slumped forward in a strange, stiff way, as if she had been sitting there for a very long time.

Her mouth hung open a little, but it didn't look like breathing. Her eyes were half-open too, staring upward at nothing, unfocused and cloudy in a way that made my stomach flip. She didn't blink. She didn't move. She didn't react to me at all.

A faint glimmer of moisture traced down her chin, catching the light as it fell. The room was so quiet that I could hear it drip onto the metal below.

Something was off…

Like someone had pressed "pause" on her body and forgotten to unfreeze it. Like she had been emptied out from the inside, leaving just the outside sitting there, waiting.

And she *was* waiting—perfectly still, perfectly silent.

For me to find.

A dark streak trailed down her forehead, catching the light as it moved in a slow, unbroken line. For a moment I couldn't tell what it was or where it started. Then, with my heart thudding in my chest, I forced myself to look upward. Two long metal needles were attached to the sides of her head, tucked into her skin in a way that made my heart sink. They weren't placed carefully or gently—just stuck there, tilted toward each other, connected to a thick black cable that dangled from the ceiling.

I didn't want to touch it. I didn't even want to stand this close. But something inside me—panic or instinct or something I didn't have a name for—made my hand reach out anyway. My fingers closed around the cool metal, and I pulled. Slowly. Carefully.

The sound that followed was small but awful, a soft pop mixed with a sticky tug, like pulling tape off skin. The woman's body jerked once, a sharp twitch that made me stumble back, my heartbeat pounding in my ears. For a second I thought she might wake up.

She didn't.

She slumped forward in the chair, her head falling to the side, her mouth just barely open like she was about to say something but never got the chance. She didn't move again. Not even a little.

I stared at her—this empty, ruined shell of a person—and felt sweat bead down my spine. I looked down at the cord in my hand, intending to throw it away, to fling it across the room, to get it off me—

But it moved.

The thick line twisted sharply, wriggling against my palm like a trapped animal. The cord writhed up my wrist, contracting, reshaping. In seconds, the long black cable wasn't a cable at all.

It was a snake.

The same color. The same pattern—jet black with two

white stripes running the length of its body. But this one was enormous, thick as my forearm, muscles coiling and bulging beneath its slick scales. Its tongue flicked out, tasting the air inches from my skin.

I stumbled backward just as it lifted its head, pupils narrowing into razor-thin slits. It drew back, jaw stretching just enough to show the curved, ivory fangs inside.

Then it struck—

And that was when I woke up.

I lay there in my bed, heart pounding so hard it felt like it might bruise my ribs from the inside. Sweat soaked my shirt. My hands wouldn't stop trembling. The dream still clung to me—every sound, every smear of blood, every breath of that massive snake—like pieces of it were still hidden in the dark corners of the room.

For the first time, I understood something I'd refused to admit. I always thought the pills were just to take the edge off the nightmares, to soften them, to keep them from tearing me apart at night. I thought they were supposed to make the dreams less vivid, less consuming, less real. And I had complained so many times that they never worked.

But after this—after what I saw, after what I felt—I realized the truth.

They had worked.

They had been working the entire time.

The pills hadn't failed me. They'd been holding the nightmares back, muffling them, dulling them, blurring the sharpest edges. I had no idea how deep the dreams went without them, how bright the horrors could become when nothing stood in their way.

Now I did.

Because for the first time, I wasn't sure if the pills had saved me from the nightmares…

or saving me from remembering something I wasn't meant to see.

8

Watch for the Signs

Monday morning came quick, the way it always did. My alarm went off earlier than usual, and for a few seconds I couldn't remember why I had set it that early. The sound felt harsher than normal, cutting through the last fog of sleep. Everything around me looked the same as always, nothing out of place, yet an uneasiness clung to me the moment I opened my eyes. Maybe it was just the weight of everything I'd tried to escape waiting for me again. I'd told myself I'd accepted it, that dealing with it was just part of moving forward, but it still sat strangely in my chest.

The building would keep deteriorating. The crack in the ceiling above my bed would keep inching wider, no matter how much I pretended not to notice. Thinking about it sent a shiver down my spine. I couldn't stop myself from remembering the hallucination—the snakes sliding silently through that growing split, their bodies disappearing into shadows that hadn't been there. The memory tightened something in my stomach, and I forced myself upright before the image could solidify. Movement helped. Distraction helped.

Then I remembered why I'd woken up early. The doctor's appointment. My follow-up. Another obligation I didn't want but couldn't avoid

As I sat on the edge of the bed trying to shake off the morning, the real reason for my uneasiness settled in. I'd been off the pills since Friday night. Three full days. This was the first day I'd have to be around people again. Everyone at work watched each other's moods so closely that even a slight difference would stand out. And I still had to get through the pill station at the beginning and end of the day without raising suspicion.

The doctor would notice things too. He'd ask about the prescription refill, ask how consistently I'd been taking it since the overdose, ask questions designed to see whether I was still a risk to myself. He'd be evaluating everything I said, everything I didn't say, every expression I made. I would have to be careful.

* * *

When I stepped into the clinic, the receptionist glanced up from her phone and forced a smile that didn't match the amusement she'd been showing a second earlier. "Hi, welcome in. How can I help you?" she asked in that overly-bright customer service voice people use when they'd rather be anywhere else.

"Just following up on a hospital visit from last week," I said.

"Okay…" she said, her voice uncertain, like she'd never

handled something as simple as a patient checking in before. She looked at me as if this was the first time anyone had ever walked into a doctor's office and asked for an appointment.

"I do have an appointment, right? Owen. Owen Hale."

"One moment," she snapped, the shift in tone abrupt. She clicked through her screen with sharp, impatient movements. "Just looking through the schedule… Here you are," she said, smiling again. But the smile stretched too far, wider than it had any right to be. Her eyes locked onto mine, unblinking, until it felt like she wasn't looking at me at all—she was looking through me. The smile faded slowly, draining out of her face until nothing was left but a blank, slack expression. Somehow that was worse.

"Are you okay?" I asked.

She blinked once, twice, and then forced her smile back into place. "Hi, welcome in. How can I help you?"

I stared at her. Had I imagined the last thirty seconds? Had I walked in twice? Had my mind skipped?

"Yes…" I said weakly. "We were just talking about my appointment. For Owen Hale."

"Oh, look at that—you're already on the screen! Go ahead and take a seat and I'll call you back."

I sat down slowly, watching her from the corner of my eye, trying to figure out if she had truly forgotten our entire interaction or if something else had happened. The déjà vu clung to me, thick and stubborn. I felt like I'd lived something almost exactly like this recently—an interaction that reset halfway through, a person who froze and then continued as if nothing had occurred.

But I couldn't place it. Everything from the last few weeks blurred together, sharp moments buried under exhaustion and confusion. Still… I was sure something like this had happened. A man freezing. Or was it a child? I couldn't remember. I only knew it hadn't felt normal then either.

My eyes drifted to the wall-mounted TV behind the receptionist—the digital calendar glowing faintly in the washed-out morning light. I had to squint to make out the text from where I sat, leaning forward a little as if that would help bring the screen into focus. There I was. **Owen Hale.** First on the list. A small relief, at least something today was working the way it was supposed to.

Then the screen flickered—just a quick static distortion, like the picture had been pulled sideways for a fraction of a second. When it settled again, my name was gone. Completely gone. I let out a slow breath, already annoyed at the idea of a system malfunction. They'd think I hadn't shown up. They'd skip me. I'd wait around even longer, get even further behind for work. The irritation was normal enough that for a moment, I didn't think anything of it.

But when I looked back at the screen to find myself again, something else caught my attention. At the very bottom of the list, a name appeared that made my stomach drop so fast I thought I might be sick right there in the chair. **Thomas Hale.** My son's name. Written casually, as if it belonged among the day's appointments. For a second I couldn't move, couldn't blink, couldn't breathe. A piercing ring filled my ears, drowning out the noise of the office, and the edges of my vision began to blur like someone had smeared the world with their thumb.

I forced my eyes to the far right of the screen for the date. It wasn't today's. It wasn't even close. **October 17th. Five years ago.** The night of the accident. The night of his eleventh birthday. His last birthday. His last day. The memory hit with such force that the entire room seemed to tilt around it, like everything else lost its shape while those words burned themselves into my mind. My hands tightened against my knees as if holding myself still would keep the world from slipping further out of place.

The waiting room around me dimmed at the edges, shapes losing clarity, the colors draining until the only thing I could truly register was his name still sitting there on that glowing screen. Every muscle in my body felt locked, as though if I moved even an inch, the image might change—or worse, stay exactly the same. It felt impossible, too cruel to be a glitch, too specific to be meaningless.

"Owen? Owen Hale?"

The voice cut through the haze, snapping me back hard enough that it felt like my head jerked. I turned toward the nurse standing in the doorway, her expression neutral, unaware that she'd pulled me out of a spiral I hadn't even realized I'd fallen all the way into. I looked back at the screen, desperate and terrified to confirm what I had seen.

But the list showed only today's date—**April 7th**—and my name was right at the top where it had been before. No trace of Thomas. No trace of the wrong date. No trace of anything that could explain what I'd just seen. I swallowed hard, forcing myself to my feet, trying to steady the trembling in my hands before following the nurse down the hall, each step feeling like it belonged to someone else.

It was about fifteen minutes before the doctor finally came in, and I didn't mind the wait. The longer I sat there, the more I convinced myself I'd imagined the whole thing on the screen. Stress could do that. Withdrawal could do that. And that was the problem I kept circling back to—should I tell him I was seeing things? The answer kept coming back the same: absolutely not. If I said the wrong thing, if I even hinted that something felt off, they'd know I hadn't been taking the pills. They'd start asking questions I couldn't afford to answer honestly.

These things had only started when I stopped taking the medication. That had to mean it was withdrawal. A temporary imbalance. Something explainable. Something survivable. If I confessed to anything, they would treat it as instability, as danger, as a reason to pull me back into a place I'd only just escaped from. Sometimes, to keep your freedom, lying becomes a form of self-preservation. Sometimes the doctors didn't feel like they were there to help you—they felt like they were there to keep you in line.

A knock came at the door, sharp enough to startle me out of my thoughts. I cleared my throat and managed a quiet "Come in," my voice cracking at the edges, the way it always did when I had to speak before my mind caught up. The door opened and the doctor walked in. A new doctor that I had never met before, but something in his face tugged at my memory, familiar in a way I couldn't pin down.

"I heard it's been a rough week for you, Owen. I truly apologize," he said, each word slow and deliberate, the same careful pacing Curtis used whenever he wanted to sound empathetic. It was the kind of speech pattern that told me he understood the script of emotion but not the feeling itself. After he apologized for my suicide attempt, he paused in a way that didn't feel natural, as if the sentence had run out and he didn't know how to transition to the next one.

Then he looked at me. His eyes were blank, drained of life,

the same hollow, distant expression the nurse had given me, the same vacant stare I'd seen too often in medical rooms. It was an expression that made people feel seen but not understood, watched but not cared for. Curtis had looked at me like that too.

Wait. That's where I'd seen him. Or... was it? The familiarity pressed against my mind like a half-remembered dream. I knew this man from somewhere, but the moment I tried to trace the connection, the thought slipped away, just out of reach.

The bridge. That's where I knew him from. A week and a half ago, early morning, cold air, halfway across the span. He'd been there—standing on the opposite walkway—watching me like he was part of the scenery. That same stillness. That same blank expression.

I remembered the way he hadn't reacted. The way the world had stuttered around us. The vibration under the bridge. The silence that fell like a curtain. The drool he didn't wipe until everything snapped back into motion. All of it returned to me in one punch of clarity. I didn't need every detail to surface to feel the weight of it again; the feeling alone was enough. The certainty.

These glitches hadn't started when I stopped taking the pills. They'd begun before. I didn't know when, exactly, or how many I'd forgotten. But they weren't new, and they weren't tied to withdrawal. They'd been happening long enough that pieces of them had slipped out of reach, buried under something I didn't understand.

I'd been dreading this appointment, planning my answers, trying to make sure it wasn't obvious I'd gone off the pills. But now my ears were ringing again, drowning out the doctor's voice. When had all of this really begun? Was there ever a clean beginning, or had it always been there—quiet, creeping, waiting for me to finally notice?

"Owen?" the doctor said, his voice cutting through the fog in my head with an odd precision. Everything snapped back into place—the room, the chair beneath me, the fluorescent hum overhead. I blinked hard, remembering where I was.

"Yes. Sorry," I said quickly.

"I just wanted to confirm that the pills are… going okay. After the overdose." He said "overdose" like it wasn't a word he fully understood, like he was repeating it from a file and waiting to see if I'd correct him.

"Um, yeah. As good as it can be going," I said, forcing a small laugh that felt brittle. "Trying to stay consistent. Which I have been, of course. And I feel… clearer. So that's good."

He nodded with an oddly measured rhythm, each dip of his chin the same depth as the last, like someone matching a pattern rather than reacting. "Do you feel like you are a danger to yourself?" The question came out with no shift in tone, no softening, no hesitation—just a clean, direct prompt.

"No, no, not at all," I answered too fast. "Or—I mean, I understand why you're asking, but… no. I feel better than I have in years. Honestly. Going through everything, realizing the weight of it, it kind of snapped me out of whatever I was stuck in. I don't foresee any more problems. I'll stay consistent with the pills and follow up." I tried to pack as much reassurance into one explanation as I could, hoping it would cover any other questions he might have queued up. I needed time to think, not more scrutiny.

"Well I'm very pleased to hear that," he said, the words spaced out perfectly, almost evenly metered, as if he were reading them from a script designed to sound comforting. His face didn't quite match the tone—his expression shifted a second too late, the smile appearing after the emotional cue rather than with it. "Please notify me immediately if you experience any recurrence of suicidal ideation. I am here for you."

There was no warmth behind it. Just a line delivered because it was the correct line to deliver. A response generated to fit the moment, regardless of whether he felt anything at all.

* * *

The third-floor hallway opened into the Compliance area with its usual stale chill, the same humming lights, the same laminated posters about "Corporate Wellness Through Daily Consistency." Nothing about the space ever changed, which was exactly why stepping into it made my chest tighten. I knew the ritual by heart. Every employee did. Name, dose, dissolve, swallow, move on.

But today, because I was late, the pill station sat behind a lowered metal shutter—sealed shut like a bank vault. No line. No chatter. No attendants. Everyone else had already come through, taken their dose, and scattered to their desks. For a second—a small, dangerous second—I stood alone with the shutter and the quiet and the thought that maybe, just maybe, I could slip past without anyone noticing. If the booth was closed, no one could hand me anything. No witness, no pill, no questions. I could keep walking.

I shifted my weight forward. One step.

"Morning, Owen!"

Curtis's voice materialized behind me. I froze. He gave me

his usual composed smile. "Let me get the attendant to bring your morning pill."

"Thanks," I said, trying to keep my tone neutral, steady.

Curtis turned and walked back down the hall, leaving me at the shutter with my heart pounding hard enough to make my fingertips feel warm. I could have still walked away, but the window of possibility had vanished the moment he said my name. The seconds stretched out, thick and uncomfortable, before the shutter rattled and jerked upward into the ceiling.

The attendant stepped into place instantly, as though he'd been standing motionless behind the metal the whole time. His expression was fixed—no greeting, no shift, just that blank, practiced readiness. "Name," he said, flat and precise.

"Owen," I replied.

He typed with that same measured rhythm I'd heard a hundred times—keys pressed with identical pressure, identical timing. A click sounded, and a single white pill dispensed into the small tray. It looked the same as all the ones before it. Same size. Same smooth surface. Same nothingness.

The attendant watched me like he was checking boxes in his mind. With the station empty, I felt completely exposed, as if the entire floor had turned its attention on me even though no one else was around to see it.

I reached for the pill, acting carefully, purposefully. It felt warm from the machine—warmer than I expected. I lifted it toward my mouth with the same routine motion I'd used for years. The fake grimace, the tiny throat movement, the swallow of nothing. A perfect imitation of compliance.

The attendant's eyes lingered on me for a single, hovering moment before he gave a small, mechanical nod.

I nodded back and walked quickly toward my cubicle, trying

to match my pace to something normal, something unremark-able. My fingers closed around the pill in my pocket—the same pill that should have been dissolving under my tongue. The tiny shape pressed into my palm, an unnerving reminder of what I'd just done.

I kept moving. No one called out. No alarms went off. No correction was issued. But with every step down the hallway, the pressure in my chest grew tighter, like at any moment someone might appear behind me again, saying my name the way Curtis always did—calm, controlled, knowing.

But no one did.

I walked to my desk with the pill in my pocket instead of dissolving in my bloodstream.

I stared blankly at my computer screen, my mind drifting while the familiar default background glowed back at me. Everyone at CityLink had the same one—a wide field of wheat, gold and heavy under a pale sky. In the center stood a lone man holding a scythe, his back turned, face hidden. I'd seen the image a thousand times but never really looked at it. Today, for some reason, I did.

My eyes traced the horizon. There was a small church tucked behind the wheat, its steeple barely visible beyond the stalks. A few scattered buildings. And far beyond them, almost lost in a faded haze, a distant city skyline. It had always been there, part of the wallpaper.

The screen flickered.

Just a flash—barely a blink—but enough to catch my eye.

Around me, the office noise began to thin. The soft clatter of keyboards, the murmur of small conversations, the faint hum of printers—all of it began to fade like someone was slowly turning down the volume of the entire floor. My ears strained against the silence, waiting for something familiar to latch onto.

Instead, I heard whistling.

Faint at first. Cheerful. Almost playful. But the sound carried a strange hollowness, like it was drifting through a long, empty tunnel from someplace impossibly far away. The notes echoed in a way that didn't belong in an office filled with people.

I turned in my chair, scanning the cubicles but nobody was whistling.

Lights overhead began to dim, slowly, gradually. The fluorescent glow softened into a dull, sickly gray that made every corner of the room feel further away. I turned back to my computer screen because I didn't know where else to look.

The man in the wheat field was no longer standing still.

His shoulders shifted first, a slow, unnatural roll—like his joints had to remember how to move. Then his arm lifted, the scythe glinting with a sheen I had never seen on any screensaver. He brought the blade across the wheat with a fluid, sweeping motion.

And the whistling grew louder.

I watched, frozen in my chair, as he continued harvesting row after row of wheat. The stalks fell too realistically, bending and snapping like real plants instead of pixels. The sound of the scythe slicing through them was faint but unmistakable.

Then, slowly—painfully slowly—he turned.

His head rotated first, followed by his shoulders, until he was facing the screen. Facing me. His eyes were dark, and they locked onto mine as if he had been waiting for this moment.

His expression twitched at the corners, a flicker of something that might have been recognition. Or amusement.

Then he smiled.

And all the while he kept cutting. The blade rose and fell with eerie precision, each swing timed perfectly with the tune he was whistling. But the whistle began to shift, bending and tightening until it wasn't just a tune—it was a song.

A song meant for me.

A song he sang as he worked.

"The harvest is near... oh, the harvest is near," he sang.

As he sang the first line, his smile stretched upward, pulling too high on one side as though something beneath the skin was tugging the muscles the wrong way. His scythe kept moving, cutting through the wheat in perfect, rhythmic arcs, but his eyes never left mine—not even for a blink.

"You can feel it in your bones when the sky turns clear."

The sky behind him brightened unnaturally, shifting from muted gray to a harsh, overexposed white. The wheat stalks glowed at the edges, outlines burning like film caught in a projector. The man's pupils shrank painfully small, almost disappearing as his face tightened with anticipation.

"Those who wander off never reappear—"

The wheat behind him rippled violently, bending in synchronized waves as if something massive was pushing beneath the field. The ripples grew closer, racing toward him—and toward me through the screen—yet he didn't flinch. His smile only grew.

"And the ones that come back... ain't the same, my dear."

His voice softened, almost tender, and that was somehow worse. As he said "dear," his mouth twitched once, twice—and then his lower jaw sagged unnaturally, stretching open wider than any human jaw should be able to.

He kept his eyes locked on mine.

He kept cutting.

But his face began to change.

His eyes bulged outward, swelling like balloons under pressure as the skin around them darkened. His cheeks sagged. His lips peeled back. His entire expression melted into something slack and disturbingly eager.

He never stopped singing.

"Moonrise hums on the metal and stone," he continued, voice vibrating unnaturally as his features began to slide downward. His skin drooped like wax heated from beneath, dripping in slow, sticky strings onto the wheat field at his feet.

"Fields don't grow like they used to, you know."

A laugh rattled out of him between lines—wet, bubbling, delighted. The sun behind him dimmed suddenly, shrinking to a dull red glow as his face sloughed off in thick sheets. Beneath the falling skin was another face—raw, incomplete, forming itself as though molded from the inside out.

"Heard the low call hummin' under the gear..."

The wheat stalks behind him turned black, curling inward, collapsing. His new face pushed forward through the dissolving remains of the old one—same bone structure, same hollow eyes, but different. Distorted. Familiar. His teeth stretched long and thin, chattering in rhythmic excitement.

"Best keep quiet now... the harvest is near."

With the final line, the sun on the background suddenly blinked out—total darkness swallowing the field. In that black vacuum, what looked like an outer layer of his body, collapsed inward with a sickening, gelatinous sound, bones snapping and sinking into a puddle of blood and tissue.

And like a snake slipping free of an old skin, another figure rose from the dim shape left behind.

It was the same face, but altered—neither the farmer's nor a stranger's. Curtis's features surfaced from the darkness, sharp and too defined against the black. His smile stayed fixed, but his eyes shifted in a way that made it seem like he was looking past me... or straight through me.

"You've felt it, haven't you?" he whispered. "The shift... the pull..."

He leaned closer to the screen, voice dropping.

"It's already started."

His smile widened just enough to show he wasn't talking about the field anymore.

"Watch for the signs."

9

F11

Everything snapped back to normal so fast it made my head throb. The lights brightened and the office noise surged in—keyboard clicks, chair wheels, casual chatter—like someone had unmuted the world. A message blinked across my monitor: **SYSTEM REBOOTING — IT ISSUES DETECTED**. Chairs creaked around me as people leaned toward their screens, confused murmurs rippling across the room. Every monitor I could see showed the same message.

"Did you… see that?" I asked the coworker nearest me—Tom, a heavyset guy whose shirt always looked rumpled no matter how often he washed it. He brushed orange chip dust off his front and nodded.

"Yeah, popped up right in the middle of everything," he said. "Shut down all my tabs. Annoying."

He wasn't talking about anything I had seen.

"Right," I said carefully. "But before it rebooted—did anything weird happen on the screensaver?"

He frowned. "Screensaver? No. Why?"

My fingers twitched, and I tucked my hands under the desk before he noticed the tremor. *Watch for the signs.* I'd heard that before. Somewhere. Maybe recently, maybe years ago—my memory wouldn't land on it.

Across the office, people were settling into the downtime the reboot had created—chatting about sports, weekend plans, daycare pickups, spouses, commutes. Completely normal. No one was unsettled. No one had seen a face melt on a screen or heard a song crawling out of a speaker. To them, it was just an IT glitch.

I stood, but my legs felt strange—heavy and hollow at the same time. The floor seemed farther away than it should've been. My movements lagged a fraction behind my thoughts, like something inside me was misfiring. People walked past toward the break room or the restrooms, their movements perfectly ordinary, perfectly human.

I didn't feel human.

I moved toward the restrooms but stopped at the drinking fountain instead. Cold water hit my face, sharp enough to sting. That wasn't a hallucination, I told myself. That was real. I was the only one who saw it. The only one meant to.

"Owen?"

Curtis's voice cut through my thoughts like a blade. He stepped out of the restroom, drying his hands with slow, precise motions. His eyes locked onto mine immediately as if he'd been waiting for me to turn around.

"Did you get the memo about the meeting?" he asked. "It's short notice. We need you in the conference room right away."

Curtis didn't wait for an answer. He stepped aside in a smooth, deliberate motion, gesturing for me to walk ahead of him. I listened, even though every instinct told me to turn around and run in the opposite direction. The hallway to the conference room looked longer than usual—stretched somehow—and for a second I felt dizzy, like the floor was tilting under my feet. I blinked hard, and the hallway snapped back to its normal length. A coworker passed by carrying a stack of files, humming under his breath, completely unaware anything had shifted. "Rough morning?" he asked.

When I reached the conference room door, my hand hovered over the handle—and Curtis was suddenly beside me again, arriving at the exact same moment. He gave me a polite, neutral smile that didn't reach his eyes. "After you," he said.

Inside, the lights were dimmed for the projector, leaving the room washed in a low amber glow. The conference room was big enough to fit ten people around the polished wooden table, but somehow it still felt cramped—like the air didn't know how to settle with only the two of us inside it. The projector hummed loudly with a mechanical whir that sounded like it was straining to stay alive. Its fan rattled as it cast a grainy light onto the screen at the far wall, where the client window flickered while the connection finalized.

I took the seat farthest from the screen, the one I always used when I wanted to keep some distance between myself and whoever might be on the other end of the call. The chair creaked under me—comfortable, but old enough that the springs protested every shift of weight. Curtis didn't sit beside me. He sat directly behind me instead, close enough that I could hear the faint, steady rhythm of his breathing and the soft click of his pen tapping against his clipboard. It made the whole room feel smaller, like the walls had leaned inward a few inches the moment the door closed.

A dying plant slumped in the corner, its leaves crisp at the edges as though it had given up weeks ago. Next to it stood the water cooler stocked with tiny paper cones that never held more than a swallow of water. The cooler hum blended with the projector until both sounds melted into a single, low vibration crawling along the floor. On the wall behind the projector hung a whiteboard covered in half-erased scribbles from someone's forgotten meeting—arrows, circles, a list of initials no one cared about anymore.

The call began to ring through the speakers. A soft echo, a digital chime. Curtis leaned forward slightly, not enough to touch me, but enough that I felt the space around me tighten. I tried to breathe normally.

The connection clicked, and the client's face began to form on-screen.

The client appeared on-screen: a man in his early sixties with neatly trimmed nearly-white hair, a tidy gray shadow along his jaw, and a crisp white shirt that made him look more put-together than anyone I'd talked to in years. He wasn't polished in a corporate way—more like a grandfather who still ironed his shirts out of habit. He smiled warmly as he picked up a pair of glasses from his desk and slid them on. "Hi, Owen. Thanks for taking the time. I know this was short notice."

His office behind him looked bright and organized, sunlight pouring through big windows onto clean surfaces and tall buildings outside. I didn't really take in the details—my focus kept drifting, my attention pulled backward by the presence at my shoulder.

"Sorry it had to be last-minute," Garrett continued, adjusting his glasses. "I've got to run and oversee some maintenance out near the west edge tonight. When the alerts start going off, they want someone on-site." He spoke casually, like this was standard. "Could be seismic readings. Could be something else. Hard to tell until we're out there."

I blinked. "The west edge?"

"Yeah—near the boundary wall." Garrett said it like it was obvious. "Always something cropping up out there."

Curtis leaned in so close behind me I felt his breath warm against my neck. "They have a construction boundary wall," he whispered, slow and deliberate. "That's what he means." His voice didn't match a whisper; it matched a correction. I nodded quickly, pretending it clarified anything at all.

Garrett didn't notice the tension behind me. He shuffled a few pages, smiling again. "Anyway, thanks for moving the meeting up. Just need to review the renewal terms and make sure everything's squared away."

I tried to focus on the document pulled up on the screen, but Curtis's chair creaked behind me as he shifted forward, closer, the scratch-scratch-scratch of his pen hitting the notepad in an unnervingly steady rhythm. He wasn't writing notes about the meeting—I had the sharp, intrusive sense he was writing about me.

Every time I spoke to Garrett, Curtis breathed out softly through his nose, like he was evaluating something. Measuring something. Waiting for something.

Garrett continued explaining a billing change in his warm, patient tone, but my pulse drowned out half of it. I nodded at the right moments. Or the moments that felt right. I wasn't even sure.

Honestly, I barely heard a word he said.

Not because of Garrett.

But because of the constant sense of someone leaning just an inch too close, breathing just a fraction too softly, watching every micro-expression I made as though the meeting weren't about the client at all.

But about me.

At this point, I should've been able to slip into my usual script—welcome the client, review their plan, offer upgrades, secure the renewal. But my throat felt tight. The words hovered somewhere behind my tongue, refusing to come out cleanly. My heart wouldn't slow down. Garrett kept talking, explaining a recent service issue, and I could barely track the meaning of his sentences. I kept seeing the man in the wheat field. The skin melting. The face beneath it. Curtis's face.

Curtis sat behind me the whole time. Not close enough to touch. Just close enough to watch, I could feel his warm breath on my neck. "Everything alright?" Garrett asked. "You look like your connection froze for a second." I forced a quick smile. "Sorry. Rough morning. Please go on." But even I didn't believe myself.

Curtis's reflection hovered faintly in the conference room screen—arms clasped, posture rigid, eyes fixed on me with an unblinking attentiveness that felt like a spotlight. I heard his voice in my mind: *Don't disappear on us.*

The meeting lasted ten minutes, though it felt like an hour. Garrett thanked me, said he appreciated my help, and the call ended with the screen fading into its idle glow. The moment it disconnected, I exhaled like I'd been underwater.

Curtis stepped closer, far closer than anyone should stand during a normal conversation. His breath touched my cheek first—warm, and humid. Then the rest of him followed, an inch at a time, until I could see every detail of his face: the tight, unmoving skin around his jaw, the way his lips rested in a strange almost-smile that looked practiced rather than felt, the faint shine of saliva catching on his teeth when he spoke. He didn't blink. Not once. His eyes stayed fixed on mine with a chilling steadiness, pupils flat, unchanging, as if they were printed onto him instead of alive.

"You seemed… distracted." He enunciated the last word with deliberate care, tongue pressing hard against the roof of his mouth, like he wanted to make absolutely certain I heard the shape of it. The sound of the "t" clicked crisply, a sound that didn't belong to a tired supervisor but to someone rehearsing a script.

"I'm fine," I said, but my voice sounded thin even to me.

Curtis didn't react—not in any normal way. His expression didn't shift. Didn't soften. Didn't frown. It simply stayed… set. A mask deciding what expression it *should* mimic but not quite arriving there. His eyes scanned my face in tiny, mechanical sweeps, studying every twitch and swallow with a precision that made my skin crawl. His lips parted again, and this time I saw his tongue briefly flick forward to wet the corner of his mouth, slow and deliberate, like a predator tasting the air.

"Any trouble focusing?" he asked, pausing unnaturally between each word. "Any emotional… irregularities today?" His breath smelled faintly sterile, like antiseptic diluted with something sweet and rotten beneath it. The tone he used was gentle—almost soothing—but the phrasing wasn't. It was diagnostic. Examining. Cutting.

"No," I said, because telling the truth felt like handing him a knife.

Curtis tilted his head a fraction to the left. Not enough to be human—just enough to make me feel uneasy, like he was listening to a sound only he could hear. The angle exposed the inside of his mouth slightly, and I could see a thin thread of saliva stretch between his teeth before snapping. His lips twitched at the corners, shaping into a smile that had no warmth behind it, only intention.

"Your affect seems slightly different," he murmured. "Let's make sure the rest of the day is… consistent." He clicked the last word sharply, and for a moment the echo of it seemed to bounce in my skull.

Behind him, the fluorescent light flickered. For an instant the afterimage of that melting face from the wheat field slammed into my mind—the bulging eyes, the slackening jaw, the skin draping downward in long, dripping sheets. I could almost see it behind him, superimposed over his features, like his flesh might slide off at any moment to reveal whatever was underneath. I felt a phantom sting behind my eyes, the same sting I had felt when the farmer's face peeled back and Curtis's own eyes stared out from inside the sludge.

Watch for the signs, the echo of that voice whispered through my memory—not his voice, not exactly, but close enough that the hairs on my arms rose. Something in Curtis's stare seemed to wait for that recognition, to assess it, to record it.

He stepped back finally, hands still clasped neatly behind his back. His shoulders moved in a smooth, measured way— too smooth, not a single muscle twitching out of sync. "If you notice anything unfamiliar," he said softly, "you'll let me know." The way he shaped the words made it sound less like a request and more like an order disguised as courtesy.

Without waiting for an answer, he turned and walked away with the same steady rhythm, spine straight, footsteps even.

Not hurried. Not relaxed. Just perfectly calibrated. I watched him go, and for a moment the fluorescent light flickered again—just enough to cast a long, distorted shadow across the floor that didn't seem to match his movements.

My pulse hammered. My throat tightened. Because now, more than ever, the words rattled in my skull like a warning I'd heard before but couldn't place. *Watch for the signs.* And Curtis—standing too close, enunciating words like commands, studying my face as if it contained data—looked like someone who already knew I finally had.

Back at my cubicle, something felt immediately off. The moment I stepped into the small square of carpet that made up my workspace, uneasiness tightened around my ribs like a belt being cinched. Nothing dramatic jumped out at me. Nothing obviously wrong. But it was the *small* things—the kind that only someone who lived their life on repeat would notice.

My stapler was sitting on the left side of the desk. I had never once put it there. Ten years of habit had trained my hand to reach for it on the right, just beneath the corner of my monitor. Seeing it on the wrong side wasn't a big deal to anyone else. But to me, it was like walking into my apartment and finding a chair turned an inch to the left. Minuscule. Insignificant. But unsettling in a way that crept down the spine.

A coworker waved at me from across the aisle. "Hey man, I dropped off that form you needed earlier," he said casually, oblivious to the dread slowly rising in my chest.

"I… didn't get anything," I replied.

He squinted, confused for a long second before shaking his head. "Huh. Weird. Maybe I left it at my desk." Then he turned away, already forgetting the interaction, already moving on.

Nothing impossible. Nothing supernatural. Just wrong. Wrong in the microscopic, invisible way that made my teeth ache. It felt like stepping into a room where the air pressure was slightly off—barely, but enough to notice.

I stood there staring at the left side of my desk longer than anyone should stare at office supplies. My heartbeat felt loud, my skin felt tight. It was all so subtle. So ordinary. But something underneath the surface was tilting, like the world's foundations had shifted and only I felt the slope.

Then, like a whisper rising from the back of my skull, one thought drifted up:

Watch for the signs.

The words brushed through my mind with a familiarity that made me blink hard. I'd heard them before. Not on my screen. Not in the farmer's voice. Somewhere else. A drifting piece of paper. A quiet moment. A message I had seen… or read… or imagined. I couldn't grasp it—it slipped away every time I tried, dissolving into static at the edges of memory.

But the feeling it left behind was unmistakable.

A warning.

A reminder.

A thread pulling me backward toward something I had forgotten.

My fingers hovered above my keyboard but never touched it. The office noise around me—typing, laughing, the whir of printers, the ding of microwaves—felt distant, like it was happening behind a thin wall. People moved normally. Spoke normally. Laughed normally. But it all had the hollow quality of a staged scene, actors hitting marks on a script I suddenly didn't believe in anymore.

I swallowed, throat tight. The stapler on the left stared back at me like an accusation.

Whatever this was—whatever was happening inside my head or outside of it—it wasn't random.

And it wasn't new.

As I sat down, a sheet of paper drifted off someone's desk and floated toward the floor. Not falling the way paper normally does, not dropping in a simple arc—this moved slowly, unnaturally slow, turning weightlessly in the air like time had thinned around it. The moment I saw it fall that way, something loosened in my mind, like a latch unhooking.

My mailbox. The stack of junk ads. The coupons. And the one folded sheet that had slipped from the pile in the exact same, impossible way. WATCH FOR THE SIGNS. The memory didn't just return—it surged, sharp and intact, clearer than it had ever been. And I understood why. It wasn't fading anymore. It wasn't smothered. Because for the first time in years, I was off the pills. My head wasn't fogged over or muffled. The things that were supposed to stay buried weren't staying buried anymore.

Someone had placed that note in my mailbox. Someone had wanted me to see it. Now the meaning cracked through all at once—and it hit even harder because those same words had come out of the collapsing, melting face on my screen. WATCH FOR THE SIGNS. Spoken through that smile. Pulled through tearing skin. Echoing in the song. And as vivid as Curtis was in my thoughts, as sharply as his voice curled around every memory, one thing settled in my mind with unnerving certainty: he hadn't written that note. Whoever had warned me—whoever had slipped that message into my mailbox—was someone else entirely.

As if the computer sensed the exact moment something shifted inside me, a pop-up snapped onto my screen: FILES NEEDING TO BE UPDATED. It didn't slide in or fade the way alerts usually did—it appeared instantly, like a shutter blinking open.

The office noise behind me dulled, as if someone had closed a door between me and the rest of the world. Curiosity pressed against my ribs.

I clicked the alert.

A list of system files unfolded across the screen—lines of code, internal logs, timestamps. All ordinary. All forgettable. Except for one in the center. F11. It sat there with the same blank font as the others, but something in me recoiled, recognizing it before I consciously understood why.

F11—the vending machine button that never dispensed the right snack. The one Thomas used to insist I press because the wrong candy made Grace giggle until she hiccuped.

The sound of their laughter hit me so suddenly it almost knocked the air from my lungs.

My finger clicked before I even decided to.

A black window burst open—no loading bar, no lag—just a void swallowing the screen. One sentence appeared in white text:

DO YOU SEE IT YET?

The words flickered once, like a pulse, and vanished. I didn't move.

I didn't breathe. Because for the first time in years—I finally felt awake.

10

The Harvest is Near

The dream was different tonight. Clearer. As if coming off the pills hadn't just lifted the fear and the fog and the numbness they wrapped around everything—it had given the good things back too. Joy felt sharp again. Real. Present in a way I hadn't felt in years. In the dream, I stood in front of our apartment building. It looked exactly the way it does in real life: a tired gray sentinel on the corner, a blocky, weather-stained structure with too many windows and not enough life behind them. The concrete held that same dull shade between ash and old paper. The sharp edges, the harsh shadows across the cracked sidewalk, the peeling paint, the crooked signs—every detail was unchanged. The world hadn't softened just because my feelings had.

Across the street, the park looked the same too. No dream-filters, no brightened colors, no nostalgia glow—just the exact park I see every morning. The same reds and yellows. The same sun hitting the metal slides at the same angle. The same trees forming their quiet green wall. Ordinary. Familiar. But for the first time in a long time, looking at it didn't hurt.

The building behind me felt like a memory that never quite settles. The park felt like one that never fades.

Over here, everything was gray and stiff and tired. Over there… it wasn't.

I've thought it a hundred times, but in the dream it felt truer: how can two places sit on the same block and feel like different worlds? And why do I always end up on this side of the street?

When I looked at the park, my children still existed—just as they were, exactly where time left them. But when I turned back toward the apartment… the other truth waited. The one I wake up to.

I turned back to look at the park one last time, but instead of being across the street, I was suddenly standing inside it— right on the winding path that curved between the swings and the bright metal slide. There was no moment of crossing, no sense of movement. One breath I was on the sidewalk; the next, I was surrounded by the familiar sights and sounds of the park.

The air felt warmer here. Softer. Like late afternoon in early summer, the kind of day when time slows down just enough for kids to stretch it out with laughter. A young girl rode past me on a small bike, the wheels clicking rhythmically as she pedaled. She looked eight or nine—caught right in the middle of childhood, where bravery and uncertainty are always overlapping. Her two braided pigtails bounced against her shoulders as she hit each uneven patch in the path. Every few seconds, she turned her head to look back at me with this bright, proud smile, like she wanted someone—anyone—to see how far she'd gotten on her own.

There was something so normal about her. So easy. She

was just a kid having a good day. The kind of day I used to take for granted.

Then her front wheel caught on a shallow crack. Her bike jerked sideways. She gasped, wobbled, and toppled forward all at once, her small body tumbling over the handlebars. She hit the ground on her hands and knees, the breath knocked out of her. A thin, trembling cry escaped her lips.

"Dad, come help me!"

The word pierced straight through me. Instinct pulled me backward, scanning the park for her father—some guy on a bench, someone standing under the trees, someone I could wave over. A child calls; a parent rushes in. That's the order of things. That's how it should work.

But no one moved.

A couple sat frozen on a blanket, mid-conversation. A jogger stayed in perfect stride, suspended mid-step. A mother pushing a stroller didn't even turn her head. The whole park seemed to hold its breath.

I turned back to the girl.

The bike was gone, as if it had never existed. And she wasn't kneeling anymore. She was standing tall, balanced, still as a statue but somehow more alive than anything else in the dream.

Her clothes had changed too. Instead of jeans and a T-shirt, she wore crisp white slacks and a white tunic, the fabric pressed and structured. The outfit looked like a uniform—not for a child, but for someone with rank. Someone with purpose. Someone with a burden.

The two bouncy pigtails were also gone. Now her hair was slicked back into a tight ponytail that revealed her whole face. And it was her face that made the air around me shift.

She still looked eight or nine. The roundness of her cheeks. The youth of her features. But her expression... her expression wasn't young at all. There was something behind her eyes—a weight, a knowing, an ache—that didn't belong to childhood.

She stared at me with that steady, unwavering concern, like she was trying to warn me gently even though the warning was heavy enough to crush her.

I took a step toward her— I knew that face.

The girl blinked slowly, as if gathering courage. When she spoke, her voice was layered—still the voice of a child, but threaded with something older, something shaped by everything she should never have had to carry.

"Dad..."

The word felt both familiar and brand new, like hearing a memory spoken out loud.

She looked me straight in the eyes—brave, steady, hurting, but determined—and said,

"The Harvest is near."

Her words were almost drowned out by a distant static, faint at first, then slowly growing louder, like something was trying to push through the edges of the dream.

* * *

Static rang in my ears as the echo of Grace's words moved through my body like a shock. She had been older in the dream, a different version of herself, shaped by something I couldn't name, but it was still her. I sat straight up in bed, lungs tight, trying to pull air into them. At first, I thought the static was just leftover noise from the dream, something my brain hadn't shut off yet. But it didn't fade. If anything, it grew louder, weaving itself into the stillness of my room with an unnatural hum that made the hairs on my arms lift.

I looked around, confusion tugging at me until my eyes landed on the television. That didn't make sense. It hadn't been turned on in years. I didn't even have it plugged in. The power cord still dangled against the wall with a thick layer of dust clinging to it. The static rose again, this time pulsing like a warning or a signal. My heart stumbled in my chest as I sat perfectly still, listening. "Is this still the dream?" I whispered, though some part of me already knew the answer.

A muffled sound pushed through the static, like someone trying to speak from underneath a mattress. The screen flickered with a soft, unsettling glow. A vague silhouette began to form—just the suggestion of a person outlined in white noise. The shape moved as if speaking, but the words wouldn't come through. My stomach twisted as the outline sharpened for a split second before the entire screen snapped violently into full color.

A cheerful news anchor appeared, mid-sentence, smiling as though nothing strange had happened. "…and temperatures should warm up nicely next week—finally feeling like spring again," he said in his bright, practiced tone. I stared at him, barely breathing, because something wasn't right. The room still felt thick with static, as if the broadcast was layered over something else trying to break through. And then I heard it: a faint hum behind the anchor's voice. A soft, childlike humming that didn't belong to the broadcast at all.

The sound crawled under my skin. I knew the tune instantly. It was the same melody Curtis had shown me on my computer, the same haunting rhythm that had etched itself into my mind.

I didn't need lyrics to recognize it. My thoughts supplied them automatically, like they'd been carved into my memory. *Those who wander off never reappear—*

The hum grew clearer, cutting through the anchor's voice. He kept talking about warm fronts and sunshine, oblivious to the intrusion. "…and that warm air should come just in time for spring break. It's been a long winter for all of us…"

The girl's hum threaded itself between his words. *And the ones that come back… ain't the same, my dear.*

The anchor showed no sign he could hear her. "…we did notice some strange cloud formations lingering past the wall far in the distance…"

Then the humming stopped all at once. The silence that followed was sharp enough to feel. The anchor paused mid-sentence, blinked once—as if something inside him had shut down and restarted—and slowly lifted his gaze away from the camera.

He wasn't looking at the lens.

He was looking at me.

In a voice that was still bright and polite, still perfectly shaped for morning television but hollow beneath the surface, the news anchor began to speak—but before the words were fully out of his mouth, I heard them sung beneath his voice. The girl's voice. Small, trembling, terrified. They layered over each other in perfect unison, her soft, wavering melody weaving through his cheerful cadence like two versions of the same sentence colliding. Together—his broadcast tone and her frightened, breathy song—they delivered the same message: "Best to run now… the Harvest is near."

The words slammed into me, louder than they should have been, ringing through my skull as if amplified by the static itself. The anchor didn't blink. Didn't shift. He just kept staring, smiling, as if waiting for me to understand something I wasn't ready to understand. Then, in the same cheerful tone he'd used to talk about the weather, he added, "Be sure to look up at the sky this fine morning. It's a beautiful day."

The static roared in my ears again, louder than before, swelling like a warning tearing through the last thin layer between dreams and reality.

The two voices—hers trembling and melodic, his bright and polished—overlapped so perfectly that the sentence felt like it existed twice in the same moment, one version sung in fear and the other announced like breaking news. *Best to **run** now... the Harvest is near.* The words clung to the air even after they finished, vibrating inside my head as the screen flickered violently. The news anchor's smile froze. His eyes twitched toward something off-camera, and for the briefest instant, real panic flashed across his face—sharp, unmistakable, human. Before I could process it, the screen snapped to black with a crack that sounded like the cord had been ripped out of the wall.

Static exploded in my ears, louder than before—thick, full, alive. The floor vibrated beneath my feet as though something massive stirred under the house. I wasn't dreaming anymore. Or if I was, the dream had pulled itself into the real world. The walls groaned. The air hummed with a low frequency that made my teeth ache. Instinct took over. I ran.

I threw open the front door and stumbled outside into the cold morning air. The street looked the same as it always did—the sagging apartment building, the quiet road, the park across the way still and empty—but something beneath it all felt off. Tilted. A deep rumble rolled through the sky, not overhead but everywhere at once, like the atmosphere itself was straining. I stepped farther into the street, my heart pounding in my ears, and looked up.

The rumble built until it felt like it was sinking into my bones. Then came the sound—sharp, electric, violent—like lightning ripping through metal at close range. It wasn't a crack of thunder. It was an act. Something breaking. Something opening. My head jerked upward.

A jagged, uneven rupture ripped across the horizon, white at the center, frayed at the edges, shaped like a wound carved by something with claws instead of precision. I thought it was lightning at first, but it didn't look natural. The tear pulsed with flickering light around the edges, but the center was impossibly white. The edges of the tear twitched, like the sky wasn't just broken but struggling to hold itself together. The wound widened for a breath I swear I felt on my skin. And then, with a sudden, violent motion, the tear snapped shut— pulled tight from both sides as though the sky had elastic memory and was forced back into place..

Silence fell instantly.

The world around me sat in perfect stillness, unchanged, pretending nothing had happened. Something had settled inside me—cold, heavy, impossible to ignore. Grace had tried to warn me. The voices had tried to warn me. And now I'd seen it. The sky had torn open like a curtain pulled back just long enough to show that something else existed behind it. Something bright. Something watching.

For a long moment, I stayed in the middle of the street, staring at the sky like it might tear open again. My pulse thudded in my ears, echoing the last remnants of static, but beneath all that, something else pushed forward—an urgency so sudden and overwhelming it felt like instinct. A pull toward action, as if standing still was the most dangerous thing I could do. I didn't know where I needed to go, but I knew I couldn't stay here. Whatever had just happened in the sky wasn't random. The warning—whatever it was—was meant to move me.

I turned and ran back toward the apartment, my legs moving faster than my thoughts. I wasn't running to hide. I wasn't running from something. I was running *toward* something, a direction I didn't have words for yet. The door slammed behind me as I burst inside, heading straight for my backpack. My hands shook uncontrollably, but not out of fear—out of the sense that time had suddenly sped up around me and I needed to catch it before it slipped out of reach. I grabbed clothes without looking at what they were, shoving them into the bag with frantic, uneven movements. Someone out there knew what I had just seen. Someone out there knew what was coming. And if I could find them, maybe I could understand any of this.

Shoes, jacket, backpack. My breathing came fast and shallow as I moved into the kitchen to grab my keys. The morning light poured through the window above the sink, bright and clean, landing directly on the fridge in a solid beam. Normally the light made the room feel warm, almost peaceful. This morning it felt deliberate, like it was pointing at something. Guiding me.

I stepped closer, and the beam illuminated the one drawing that had stayed pinned to the fridge for five years. I had looked at it every morning—sometimes too long, sometimes barely at all. I knew every line of it. Every wobble of the crayon. I knew it the way you know a wound.

Which is why my footsteps faltered as soon as I saw it wasn't the same.

I blinked, hard, then leaned closer as if my eyes had simply misremembered. But there was no mistaking it. The lines were shaky in that familiar, childlike way, the style unmistakable. But the picture itself—this wasn't the one I'd kept on my fridge for half a decade. The original drawing had been simple: a house, two stick figures, a sun in the corner. But now the sun was gone.

In its place hovered something else. My first thought was a rainbow, but the shape wasn't soft or curved. It wasn't whimsical. It was structured. A domed shape arching over the house, drawn with a trembling hand that seemed uncertain of how to capture it. It looked like an outline of something enclosing the sky. Something overhead. Something watching.

My heart thudded harder. I lifted the paper from the fridge, the magnet clattering to the floor. The edges felt crisp. New. The colors bright, as if they'd been drawn hours ago, not five years in the past. My throat tightened as I stared at it, trying to make sense of why it felt both familiar and foreign at the same time. I didn't recognize the scene—but I recognized the hand that drew it. A child's hand. One I hadn't seen in years.

Then I saw the words.

Three uneven, shaky words written beneath the house: "We're still here."

The air left my lungs all at once. The urgency in my chest sharpened into something clearer, heavier, truer. I didn't fully understand what the message meant—not yet—but I knew with absolute certainty who it was meant for. And who had written it.

It wasn't a dream, or a memory, or some kind of mistake—it

was a message. She was reaching out. Grace was still here.

I clutched the drawing tighter, the paper bending under my fingers. For the first time in years, something warm surged through me so fast it almost knocked me off balance. Hope. Sharp, electric, flooding every hollow place inside me that grief had carved out. I didn't know how she had reached me or how this drawing had changed or what force had pushed it through the cracks of my life, but the moment I felt that spark ignite, everything in me shifted. She wasn't gone. She wasn't lost. And she wasn't done trying to get to me.

The memory of the dream pressed in at the edges—not in images, just in feeling. The voice, the plea, the certainty threaded through it. "Dad, come help me." Those words hit different now. They weren't symbolic. They weren't part of some surreal dream-script. They were real pain reaching for me—the kind a child feels when there's no one else who can hear them. The kind that's meant to pull a parent to their feet. And when a child calls; a parent should rush in. That truth wrapped around my ribs and tightened until I had to steady myself on the counter just to breathe.

My eyes drifted back down to the drawing—the structure over the house, the uneven strokes, the words she'd added— and that rising hope twisted into something far more dangerous. Because hope didn't just mean she was alive. It meant she was out there somewhere hurting. It meant she was calling out because she needed me. And it meant that whatever was happening around her was getting worse. The change in the song echoed faintly in my mind, shifting from a whispered warning to a desperate command: "best to run now, the Harvest is near." She wasn't telling me to stay quiet anymore. She wasn't telling me to brace myself. She was telling me to move.

I held the drawing to my chest and let the weight of it settle into me—hope and fear braided tightly together. Hope because she was reaching out. Fear because if she was still here… so was the thing she was trying to warn me about.

II

349

11

Designation Assigned

I awakened to white. Color so complete it replaced shape, replaced depth, replaced everything. For a moment I wasn't sure if I had eyes or if this was simply the first thing I had ever seen. The world around me existed without edges. No corners. No shadows. No place where one surface ended and another began. Just white, smooth and endless, like I had opened my eyes inside a blank thought.

I sat up slowly, and for a moment I wasn't sure if I was actually sitting or just imagining the motion. My hands pushed against the surface beneath me, and it felt strange—smooth and cool, but not as hard as it looked. When I pressed down, it pushed back just a little, like it was trying to decide what it was supposed to feel like. I didn't have a name for it, but it wasn't familiar. Nothing was familiar. Even the idea of familiarity felt new.

The light above me was the next thing I noticed. It didn't glow the way I expected light to glow—soft at the edges, fading into shadows. This light didn't fade at all. It was everywhere at once, pressing against my eyes so sharply it made them water.

I didn't know where I was. I didn't know what the place was called. I didn't even know if places were supposed to have names. My mind felt like it was trying to start, like a machine turning over for the first time—slow, unsure, catching on thoughts that didn't have words yet.

When I looked to the side, I saw others waking up too. Dozens of them. Mostly boys, but some were girls like me. They moved differently than I did—like they already knew how. Some sat up quickly, their backs straightening in one smooth motion. Others blinked with long, heavy blinks, as if figuring out how eyelids worked took effort. They were bigger than me. Their arms, their legs, their shoulders—they all stretched past the edges of the beds beneath them. My bed fit me almost perfectly. Theirs didn't fit them at all. But none of them looked bothered by it. Maybe they were used to waking like this. Maybe they had done it before. I couldn't tell.

The room around us stretched farther than I could see at first. I had to look and keep looking before my eyes caught the end of it. The floor, the walls, the ceiling—they were all made of the same smooth, white material. It reminded me of stone but softer, like someone had taken something natural and sanded down every part of it that made sense. The air felt cold on my skin, but not sharp. I breathed in, and the air slid into me without any smell at all, like it had been scrubbed of anything that might tell me where I was.

There was no sound. Not real sound. Just the quiet movements of the others—beds shifting, skin brushing against fabric, deep breaths taken at almost the same time. As if they were all following the same pattern without needing to be told. I tried to match my breath to theirs for a moment, just to see, but it felt strange to me.

I let my feet touch the floor. It was colder than the bed, and the surface didn't soften under me like it had under my hands. It felt firm, solid, but still smooth—like it didn't want to hold the shape of anything that touched it.

At the far end of the room, a door broke the endless white. A single outline. A rectangle cut into a wall that wasn't supposed to have shapes at all. Through the thin opening at the bottom, I could see the start of a hallway—long and empty, glowing the same unnatural white as this place. No windows. No markings. Nothing to explain what was on the other side or why the door existed when everything else felt like it didn't need one.

I didn't know why, but my chest tightened when I looked at that doorway. Not in fear. More like a feeling that the space beyond it mattered—like it held something I was meant to understand, even though I didn't understand anything yet.

I looked around again, at all the others waking in perfect rows, on beds that held them like objects instead of people. I wasn't like them—or maybe they weren't like me. I couldn't tell which. But as I sat there blinking against the bright light, the thought lingered long enough to form my first real question: why was I awake?

A sound shivered through the air. It wasn't coming from speakers; I didn't see any. The noise simply existed, vibrating both in the space and inside my head. "Units awaken. Remain seated." The others complied immediately, placing their hands neatly on their knees. I followed a moment later, my movements slower, less certain.

"Designation will now be assigned. State acknowledgment upon hearing your identifier." One by one, the voices around me responded with crisp precision. "341 acknowledged." "342 acknowledged." "343 acknowledged." The numbers continued climbing. I counted them automatically, the sequence arranging itself in my mind like pieces falling into a pattern I didn't remember learning.

When the voice reached me, something tightened in my chest. "349." My own voice startled me. "Acknowledged," I said, though I didn't fully understand what I was agreeing to.

The naming continued without pause, as if my existence was just one more item in a long list. But I held the number carefully in my mind. 349. 349. I repeated it until it felt like it belonged to me, or perhaps until I belonged to it.

Then the walls changed. Panels appeared where there had been nothing, sliding apart without seams or hinges, as if the white itself had decided to become something else. Figures stepped through. They were taller than the others, movements smoother, faces expressionless in a way that seemed designed rather than natural. They scanned us without emotion, their gazes sharp enough to feel like pressure against my skin.

When one of them looked at me, I felt something cold coil at the base of my spine. Not fear. Not exactly. Something more complex. Like recognition. Like remembering a nightmare you've had too many times to pretend it isn't real.

But I didn't know this place. I didn't know these people.

I didn't know anything at all.

Except one thing:

I was 349. And whatever that meant was about to begin.

Cold, synthetic voices began speaking from everywhere and nowhere at once, slicing through the white with perfect precision. They weren't speaking to us—not truly—they were cataloguing us. Sorting us. Slotting us into functions we were apparently built to serve.

"117: Logic Matrix Cohort."

"208: Neural Modulation Cohort."

"349…"

The moment my designation echoed, something in the room tightened—so subtle I could have imagined it, but I didn't. The others kept their faces neutral, their movements efficient and precise. But I felt a shift, like the system itself had tilted its attention toward me.

"349: Cohort Nine. Illusion Engine."

Just that. No instructions. No direction to follow.

I didn't feel chosen. I felt… flagged. Placed with intention I didn't understand.

The hallway stretched out in front of me, wider than I expected, though I wasn't sure what I had expected. The walls, floor, and ceiling were all made of the same white material as the room I'd woken in—smooth, polished, glowing from within, as if the brightness wasn't coming from lights but from the walls themselves. There were no colors anywhere. No markings. No doors. No shapes. Just endless white, high ceilings, and a narrow shadow cast by the bodies moving with me.

Cohort Nine walked ahead, not in perfect unison, but in something close to it. Their steps landed with the same rhythm, the same timing, the same quiet certainty. I tried to match them—to place my feet the way they placed theirs— but something in me hesitated each time. It was as if they were following instructions they'd been given long before now, instructions I somehow didn't have. My steps were smaller. Slower. A fraction behind. A fraction off.

Still, I kept walking.

The hallway hummed around us, a faint vibration in the walls that I felt more than heard. No voices. No machines. No distant echoes. Only the hum and the footsteps—dozens of them, soft and steady, all belonging to people who moved like they knew exactly where they were supposed to go. The calmness of it all pressed in on me. Like everyone around me understood something I didn't. Like I had missed the explanation, the part where someone told us what this place was, who we were, what we were walking toward.

I glanced at the others beside me. Their faces were relaxed, their eyes forward, their breathing slow and even. No questions in their expressions. No hesitation in their strides. They walked through the white hallway as if they'd traveled it a hundred times. As if the brightness didn't sting their eyes. As if the cold didn't raise goosebumps on their arms.

I tried to let their calm guide me, but it didn't fit right. It slid over me like clothes in the wrong size. They looked like they belonged here. I didn't feel the same. I felt… different. Like there was something I was supposed to know, some memory or instruction or instinct I was meant to have, but my mind stayed blank no matter how hard I reached for it.

The hallway continued forward without turning, without branching, without offering any hint of where it led. It felt endless, but no one around me acted like it was. They just kept moving with that steady rhythm, as if they were following a path drawn inside them. I followed because I didn't know what else to do. Because something in my chest tugged me forward, a pull I couldn't explain.

But with every step, the same thought pressed against the

inside of my skull, quiet but persistent.

I'm not like them.

And they're not like me.

By the time we reached the end of the hallway, my legs were already tired. The walk felt longer than it should have been, like the distance stretched beneath our feet without changing shape. When the doorway finally opened into the next room, I froze for a second. It was the same size and shape as the place we'd woken in. Same high ceiling. Same glowing white surfaces. Same cold, perfect air. For a moment, it almost felt like we'd walked in a giant circle, giving someone enough time behind us to clear away the beds and replace them with something else.

Rows of workstations filled the space now. Cubicles made from the same white material as the walls, each just big enough for one person to sit in and no more. The terminals inside them glowed softly, their curved screens wrapping around each user like a shell. Everything was smooth, seamless, too clean to ever have been touched by real hands. Yet the room hummed with life.

People—bigger than us, were already seated and working. Their fingers moved in rapid clicks and taps, hands gliding over the glowing surfaces with inhuman speed. The sound of it filled the room in a steady rhythm, a chorus of motion that didn't break or slow. Their movements were fast, and identical. I watched the way their arms swept across the curved screens, how the symbols shifted and rearranged as if obeying their touch instantly. It looked impossible..

A figure at the front made a sharp gesture toward an empty row—no words, just a flick of the hand. The others in my cohort moved toward the terminals immediately, sliding into their cubicles as if they had done this a thousand times. Maybe they had. Or maybe something in them knew the motions before they did. I didn't.

I sat because they sat. I copied because copying was the only guide I had. The seat molded around me, adjusting until my back was straight, my feet flat, my hands lifted toward the glowing surface. The curved screen in front of me flickered to life, wrapping my vision in shifting symbols that fell in long columns. I didn't know what any of it meant.

The screen pulsed, and a translucent keyboard appeared beneath the streaming symbols—white squares with no letters, no markings, nothing that told me how to use them. I stared at it, waiting for my mind to explain something, anything. But nothing came. My head felt scraped clean, empty except for my designation: 349. It echoed faintly, a label with no explanation.

Around me, the others were already working. Their hands flew across their screens in silent storms of motion, symbols forming and adjusting under their touch faster than I could follow. Watching them made something inside me constrict. If this room was where people came to work, to build, to create whatever this was… why was I here? I was smaller. Slower. Out of sync. There had to be a mistake.

The symbols on my screen cascaded again, brighter this time, almost expectant. I reached out hesitantly, touching one of the empty squares. The surface warmed instantly beneath my finger, and a string of code snapped into place across the screen as if I had known exactly what to type. I hadn't known. Not really.

And yet…

And yet something inside me stirred—something deep and

instinctive, something that recognized patterns before my mind did. It scared me, but it also pulled me forward. The others worked like machines. Maybe I was supposed to work like that too.

Maybe the mistake wasn't that I had been brought here.

Maybe the mistake was thinking I didn't belong.

No one had taught me anything. I didn't even know what these symbols were—shapes with straight edges, shapes with curves, tiny marks that repeated in patterns I couldn't decode. They looked cold and rigid and meaningless, like pieces of a language that belonged to someone else.

But I lifted my hands anyway.

The instant my fingers touched the glowing keys, something inside me snapped into place. Not a memory. Not knowledge. More like a switch being thrown, or a muscle waking up that I hadn't known existed. It didn't feel like I was typing. It felt like I was watching… like my hands belonged to someone else, and I was just following the movement the way you follow a scene in a movie—detached, certain, weightless.

The symbols on the screen—letters, numbers, lines, all arranged in rows—began to shift as my fingers moved. I didn't know what I was making. I didn't know why the symbols were rearranging themselves or why my hands seemed to know which ones came next. I didn't even have words for what I was doing. But somehow, the chaos began to form patterns. The shapes grouped together. The repeated marks lined up. Things that shouldn't have made sense began to stack into a rhythm that tugged at something deep inside me.

Then the pain hit.

Sharp and dull at the same time, like a heavy pressure inside my head was cracking open from both sides. My hand twitched toward my temple, instinctively trying to touch the ache—but it didn't move. My fingers stayed locked to the screen, gliding across it in a blur I couldn't slow down. The more I tried to pull away, the faster my hands seemed to move, as if stopping wasn't an option my body had been programmed with.

Around me, the others worked with terrifying speed, their fingers dancing in perfect storms of motion. But no one looked at me. No one noticed me. It was as if I was invisible, or as if this moment—*my* moment—existed outside of their world entirely. Their presence faded until I barely registered the sound of their typing. The whole room slipped away piece by piece until it was just me and the glowing surface beneath my hands.

And the strangest part was…

It felt easy. Like my hands had been waiting for this exact task, this exact sequence, this exact moment. The symbols kept forming, faster and faster, and the pain in my head sharpened again—but instead of fear, something else rose up in me. A spark. A pull. A sense that this wasn't wrong at all. It was right.

It felt like destiny.

Like I had been made for this.

And even though I didn't understand a single thing I was typing, excitement flickered in my chest—bright, wild, impossible to ignore.

Because for the first time since waking, I felt like I was moving toward something meant for me.

12

C-1

Time feels weird here and memories were even weirder. All I really remember is that I'm typing on this screen. The lights always stay on, I have never seen a window. Time blurs here. Nights come and go too fast to count. We sleep, we work. Meals arrive at our stations and disappear just as quickly, hands moving in silence before returning to their tasks.

Each time my fingers slide, something new happens on the surface. A line bends. A dot stretches. A group of symbols pulls together like they're magnetized. I don't know what any of it means. But my hands seem to know what they're supposed to do, so I let them. It's easier than thinking. Thinking makes my head hurt.

Someone is standing beside me. I can see their arm moving up and down, writing. Sometimes they shift their weight or breathe out quietly. I want to turn my head and see their face, but my neck won't move the right way. Every time I try, something inside me tells me not to. So I keep my eyes on the screen.

The surface under my hands feels warm in some places and cold in others, like the glowing symbols are breathing.

The lights above me hum softly, but the hum feels constant, like it's part of the air instead of coming from anywhere specific. The whiteness around me makes it hard to tell how big the room is. When I glance forward, it just looks like the wall keeps going even though I know it has to stop somewhere. My fingers keep moving. They don't wait for me to catch up.

I shift slightly in my seat, just enough to feel the chair under me—hard, smooth, and cold. There's no pattern, no texture, nothing that feels familiar. Even the floor looks like it's made from the same material, stretching out without seams. I look down at my feet for a moment, and they look strange on the blank surface. It makes my chest tighten, so I look back at the screen again.

My fingers pull another set of symbols into a line. The line bends in a way that feels off, so I straighten it. I don't know why I think it's wrong, but the feeling pushes at me until I listen. When I make it straight, something clicks lightly beneath my fingertips. A soft, tiny sound. Like the screen is satisfied.

The watcher beside me adjusts their stance. I hear the faint scrape of their shoe. I try again to turn my head just a little, to see if I can catch more than the side of their sleeve, but the same invisible pressure stops me. My neck stiffens. My gaze stays forward. My fingers slide faster, like they're trying to hide the fact that I got distracted.

I blink, and the screen flashes white for a second—so bright and fast I almost think I imagined it. I drag my fingers back over the spot where it happened, just to check if something broke. But the symbols pull themselves together again, like nothing happened at all. I decide I must have done something out of order. I fix the pattern the way my fingers tell me to.

I don't know why I know what "fixing" is supposed to look like. But I do. Or my hands do.

There's a sound to my left. A chair shifting. Someone adjusting their posture. I never hear talking. Nobody talks. Only the quiet sounds of working. A steady rhythm. Pens. Footsteps. My fingers tapping—a soft, twitchy beat against the screen.

A faint pressure builds in my temples. The more I ignore it, the more it fades. So I keep ignoring it. I keep my eyes on the glowing symbols. I keep my hands moving.

But then—after a long time or maybe a short one—something breaks the rhythm. A sharp, choked gasp.

I freeze, but not fully. My hands don't stop; they twitch nervously on the surface, stuttering through movements they no longer understand. I glance at the reflection in my screen, just a flicker of my eyes, enough to see a figure at the end of the row push back from their desk.

Their hands hover above their screen like they were caught mid-thought. Their shoulders jerk once. Then again. Then drop. Their head lowers, slow at first, tilting forward as if gravity suddenly doubled.

And then they fall.

The chair tips backward with a scraping, dragging sound that slices through the room. The body hits the ground landing in a way that makes the air shift. Like everything inside it went quiet at once.

My fingers stop moving. Fully. Completely. The pressure in my head spikes into something sharp.

Two men enter—or maybe they were already here and I didn't notice until now. They move fast but without fear, like this is normal. Like this is routine. One kneels beside the fallen person and lifts an arm. It dangles from his hand, limp and loose, as if the body forgot how to be a body.

"Nether," one of the men says.

The sound hits me like a physical shove. My breath catches halfway up my throat. I know that word. I don't know how, but I do. It pulses with something dark, something cold, something that makes the back of my neck prickle. A color flashes in my mind—red.

I blink and the color vanishes.

The men drag the body away. Its feet trail behind, toes turned inward, sliding over the smooth white floor. No one helps. No one even looks. The watchers keep writing, steady strokes of pen on their tablet, like nothing just happened. Like this is normal.

My stomach twists hard, heat rolling through my chest in a fast, nauseating wave. Just keep moving. Don't pause. Don't let yourself overthink it.

I force myself to breathe, but my breaths feel thin and jagged. I place my fingers back on the screen. They shake as I touch it, trembling against the glowing surface. When I drag one of the symbols, it jumps, jittering like my hand startled it.

I swallow hard and try again. My hands have to move. They have to keep moving.

Because now I know—stopping is dangerous.

Nobody else moves at all. Nobody notices what just happened. It's like the sound of the fall never existed. Like the body wasn't dragged through the room. Screens glow. Fingers glide. Pens scratch. Everything keeps moving except the person who fell… and me.

Someone steps behind me—just one step. A soft shift of weight, barely a whisper against the floor. But it's enough. Enough to make every muscle in my body lock into place. Enough to make my breath stop halfway out of me.

I don't know who it is, but I don't want to find out. I rush to correct the shaking symbol, forcing my trembling fingers into steadiness. I smooth the pattern, pull the shapes back into the lines they were supposed to follow. The symbols slide together more quickly this time as if the screen wants me to hurry. As if it's also afraid.

The person behind me goes still. Not stepping away. Not stepping closer. Just waiting. Watching. Listening to whether or not my hands keep moving.

So I move.

My fingers race across the surface, faster and faster, the glowing marks blurring under my touch. My eyes sting from staring so hard, but I don't dare blink. I don't dare breathe loudly. I don't dare look away—not even for a second.

I don't know what the Nether is.

But I know the person who fell is never coming back.

I feel a hand touch my shoulder, and the shock of it sends a thin, electric shiver straight down my spine. It isn't a hard touch—just the tips of fingers, barely any pressure at all—but it might as well be a clamp locking every muscle in place. My hands freeze on the screen, my breath trapped in my chest, and for a moment the whole world narrows to the cold imprint of her fingers. Slowly—carefully, like sudden movement might be dangerous—I turn my head. A woman stands beside me, close enough that I can see the reflection of the white room softening across her cheek. I have never seen her before. I'm certain of it. But there is something in her expression that tells me she knows me, deeply and completely, in a way I don't understand.

"349," she says. Her voice slices through the room, calm and steady, the perfect opposite of the panic crawling up my neck. "Come with me." She doesn't raise her voice, yet it somehow echoes, bouncing softly across the walls as if the air itself is hollow.

No one reacts. Not a single head lifts. Not a single hand slows. Everyone sits frozen in their synchronized movements—the tapping fingers, the dragging motions, the unblinking stares. It's as if her voice doesn't exist to them, and only I can hear her.

I stand, legs trembling, and follow her out of the room. She walks with long, quick steps that barely make sound on the smooth white floor, and I trail behind her with the same careful distance. Whenever I have to shuffle faster to match her pace, she instantly turns her head and locks eyes with me. I lower my gaze each time, trying not to do anything wrong, though I don't know what wrong even means here.

We walk for minutes—endless minutes—down identical halls with the same blank walls and same cold hum beneath the silence. I can't tell if we're going deeper into something or walking in circles. Nothing looks different. Nothing ever looks different.

Nether. I didn't know what it was, but as I walked behind her, I kept thinking… *what if that's where she was leading me?*

Finally, the woman stops in front of a door on her left. She presses her hand against the surface and it opens without a sound. She steps inside, and I follow.

The room is small. Claustrophobic even. The air feels thick, as if there's less space to breathe, and no room for thoughts to stretch. When the door closes behind us, it seals with a soft click that feels final. The walls seem to push inward, or maybe that's just my chest tightening.

Two benches slide out from within the wall—smooth, silent, like they were waiting just beneath the surface, and the woman gestured for me to sit.

"349, my name is C-1," she said. Her voice was steady, and practiced. "I'm in charge of this division, and I ensure that everything remains correct for the Steward. The Steward works hard every day to ensure everyone, including you and your peers, maintains a steady life." She studied me as she spoke, her eyes unmoving, waiting to see if her words landed the way she expected them to. The white walls around us echoed faintly with her voice, as if the room itself was listening.

I nodded slowly, pretending I understood, even though the words felt big and heavy. Steward. Division. Steady life. None of it made sense, but she seemed like the kind of person who expected agreement, not questions.

"Ever since you arrived a year ago," she continued, "we have been very impressed by your ability to code the illusion engine for the Nursery." She said it calmly, like it was the most ordinary fact in the world, something I should already know and accept.

My ears rang. *A year?* The sound pulsed in my head, drowning out her voice for a moment. I felt my heartbeat climb into my throat. I thought... I thought maybe a few days had passed. Maybe a week at most. Time didn't make sense here, but I never imagined it could disappear like that— swallowed, erased.

She tilted her head, her expression tightening just enough for me to notice. "349," she said quietly, "are you okay?"

I nodded.

She moved on immediately, accepting the nod as permission to continue. "I anticipate that over the years, if you continue performing the way you are now, you'll earn regular promotions. Eventually, you may learn more about the nursery than most of the coders here. Does that sound all right to you?"

I didn't know what any of that truly meant, but the words lit something warm and restless inside me. Excitement. Fear. A strange desire to impress her, to prove something I didn't fully understand. I hated how much I wanted her approval. C-1 scared me—her stillness, her voice, the way her eyes always looked like she already knew my answers—but part of me wanted her to look at me and see value.

"Your first promotion will be effective immediately. You're being assigned to the Continuity Engine."

She watched my face, saw the confusion, and continued anyway. "This division is far more fast-paced than the Illusion Engine. The Illusion Engine changes, but slowly. Sometimes years pass before an update needs to be processed. Most of the work is maintenance—patching minor openings, reinforcing weak segments, ensuring nothing ruptures through."

She tapped her fingers together once, sharply, like she was punctuating the shift. "The Continuity Engine is different. It changes constantly. Every day. Every hour. You'll be monitoring for inconsistencies, correcting any behavior that loops too often, removing glitches before they're noticed. If something feels unnatural, it's your responsibility to smooth it out."

Her eyes narrowed slightly, assessing me in a way that made

my stomach twist. "Your job is to make everything feel real. Seamless. Understand?"

I nodded again, even though my mind was spinning. I didn't understand any of it—not really. But I understood that she expected me to. That she expected perfection.

"I'm putting a lot of trust in you," she said softly, but there was an edge in her voice that felt like a blade. "Don't let me down. I had to pull a lot of strings to get you placed here. I can tell you're… special."

The word "special" hit me the wrong way. It didn't feel good. It felt like being marked. Noticed. Exposed.

As I followed her down the long white hall toward my next assignment, the air felt heavier with every step. The lights buzzed faintly overhead, flickering like they were struggling to keep up.

Something was wrong. Deep down, I could feel it. A pressure behind my ribs. I was different.

And she had just confirmed it.

13

Continuity Engine

My station in the Continuity Engine didn't look important at first glance. Just a display filled with shifting geometric grids, colored sequences, and moving symbols that pulsed in steady, rhythmic patterns. Everything was organized, symmetrical, and quietly hypnotic—as if the entire interface was breathing in a way my mind already recognized.

I sat down, and something in me settled. The steady hum in the room, the faint clicking of keys, the drifting lines across the display—it all felt strangely familiar. Not like remembering something, but more like stepping into a posture my body had held a thousand times before.

My first assignment appeared in clean, simple text: Drift Correction.

A glowing marker moved along a thin curved guideline stretching across the display. It glided smoothly for a moment, then drifted outward, wobbling just off the track as if pushed by an unseen force. Then it tried to right itself, swaying back and forth in small uncertain arcs.

It looked straightforward—like a calibration drill to test how well I could make a pattern behave.

I typed the correction sequence, matching the shape and rhythm. The keys responded softly, each one clicking with a satisfying, precise weight. The sequence felt natural under my fingers.

I pressed enter.

The marker snapped neatly back onto the line. The entire grid around it quivered for the briefest moment, lines vibrating like a plucked string. Then everything steadied. A soft tone chimed. Confirmation.

I watched the next cycle begin. The marker drifted again, this time in a slightly different direction, testing a new threshold. I didn't need to check the reference guide. My hands already knew the adjustments. Before I fully thought through the pattern, I had already typed half of it.

Enter.

Correction.

Chime.

Another cycle. Another drift. Another correction.

After a while, the work fell into a rhythm—steady, predictable, almost peaceful. The drifting marker, the subtle adjustments, the quiet sound of success—it all repeated in a way that felt meditative. The repetition didn't bore me.

Time passed in a way I couldn't measure. The overhead lighting never changed. No one around me spoke. All I had was the grid, the drifting marker, and the sense that with every correction, I was settling deeper into a pattern I wasn't sure I had ever learned, yet somehow understood completely.

If anything, the more I corrected the drifting line, the more it felt like I was aligning something inside myself—something that had been waiting for the rhythm of this place.

Next came Segment Linking.

The shift happened quietly—no announcement, no signal— just a soft rearranging of the display. The drifting marker and curved lines vanished, replaced by a wide grid filled with rectangular color fields. Dozens of them. Maybe hundreds. Each one a different shade or texture, floating in slow, deliberate motion across the interface.

Some of them pulsed in a steady rhythm, others flickered as if struggling to hold their color, and a few drifted lazily, moving on a current I couldn't see.

At first it looked random, but the longer I watched, the more I realized the fields weren't drifting without purpose. They were circling one another in patterns—subtle ones—but patterns I could feel more than understand.

A prompt appeared in the corner of my display: LINK COMPATIBLE SEGMENTS.

I hesitated. I didn't know what "compatible" meant. There were no instructions this time, no reference chart. But when I focused on the drifting rectangles, two of them drew my attention almost immediately—a pale-blue field with a soft glow around its edges, and a darker blue one pulsing in a slow, steady rhythm.

They didn't match exactly. They didn't form any obvious pair. But something in me recognized them—like the way you can hear two notes and know they belong to the same chord long before you understand why.

I selected the pale-blue segment. It brightened with a soft glow, as though acknowledging me. Then I selected the darker blue one. For a moment, nothing happened—just the slow drifting of shapes across the grid. Then the space between them contracted all at once, not sharply, but with a gentle inevitability, as if the grid itself had been waiting for this combination and simply pulled them back into alignment.

I expected a gradient or some kind of transition effect, something to show where one piece ended and the other began. But there was no seam at all. The line between them didn't blend—it disappeared, erased so completely that I couldn't remember where the two had originally been divided. They didn't overlap, didn't fade, didn't mix. They simply became one.

The newly formed segment pulsed once, a clean, confident thrum of light that rippled across its surface before settling into a steady rhythm. It felt less like completing a puzzle and more like correcting something that had been wrong for a long time. Like restoring a shape that had been split apart and was finally whole again. The screen reacted instantly, expanding the grid slightly, opening more empty space—as if preparing for whatever link came next.

More segments drifted forward, catching my attention even before I consciously noticed them. A faint yellow rectangle flickered rapidly, its edges shimmering like static, while a muted gold one glided with slow, patient consistency. They didn't share a shape or brightness or texture, but the moment they moved near each other, something inside me tightened with recognition. I didn't know why they belonged together— only that they did.

My fingers selected the flickering yellow piece first, steadying it under my touch. Then I selected the gold one. The connection happened immediately. The rapid flickering stopped as though calmed, the two pieces sliding together in a single smooth motion. The boundary dissolved cleanly, effortlessly, leaving behind a unified shape with a warmth that hadn't been there before. Another perfect merge.

I watched the grid shift again, patiently, expectantly, as if waiting for me to continue. And for reasons I couldn't explain, linking them felt less like training and more like remembering—like recognizing pieces that had always been meant to fit.

Then came Dip Repair. The transition into this task was smoother than before—almost unnoticeable. The drifting segments dissolved from the screen, replaced by a broad grid filled with hundreds of tiny squares arranged in perfect rows. At first they all held steady color, but after a few seconds, small flickers began popping across the display like distant sparks. A cluster of squares shifted from their normal hues to a dull gray, then to stark white, then flickered back again as if they were struggling to decide what they were supposed to be. I assumed they were just graphical hiccups—data that hadn't fully rendered or was losing integrity. The patterns didn't seem threatening; they just looked... tired, like pieces of a system that needed refreshing.

I selected one of the flickering squares, and a repair sequence appeared in the corner of my screen. It was simple enough—just a series of inputs meant to rebuild whatever the square had lost. I followed the pattern carefully the first time, expecting it to require exact precision. But the moment I finished typing, the square snapped back to full color immediately, the flickering stopping all at once. The grid around it shifted in a subtle wave, almost like the entire system took a breath of relief before settling again. Nothing about it felt difficult. If anything, it felt natural—like brushing dust off something delicate.

I worked through more dips, repairing them one by one. Some needed only a single correction; others pulsed stubbornly until I repeated the sequence several times. The grid stabilized each time, colors smoothing across the display in soft, satisfying waves, and the hum of nearby stations blended into a background rhythm that made everything feel strangely meditative.

Then, without warning, the entire screen flashed white. Not for long—just a single blink, an instant so quick I wasn't entirely sure it had actually happened. The moment the light faded, the grid returned, stable and calm, as if nothing unusual had occurred. No alarms sounded. No one around me paused or looked up. All the other coders continued their work with the same steady focus they always had, their fingers tapping methodically, their eyes untroubled.

I forced myself not to react, matching their stillness. If they weren't concerned, I assumed I shouldn't be either. The system had its quirks. This, I told myself, must simply be one of them. And so I kept going, repairing the next dip, and the next, until the flickers on my screen became just another part of the quiet rhythm of the Continuity Engine.

After the error, my hands moved automatically to the file that had triggered it. I selected the malfunctioning components and dragged them into a folder labeled Cognitive Directive Station.

Then there were the Loop Alignments. The display shifted again, dissolving the repaired dip-squares into fading light before rebuilding itself into a new interface. This time, dozens of small symbol-clusters floated in looping formations across faint, curving tracks. Some clusters moved in wide arcs, others in tight spirals, some in slow unfolding patterns that resembled petals turning toward an invisible center. Each cluster had its own rhythm, its own logic, its own pattern of motion. I watched them for a long moment, letting my eyes adjust to the constant movement, listening to the soft hum that synced with their cycles. It felt like watching a complicated dance I somehow already knew the steps to.

Most of the time the clusters behaved perfectly. Their movements glided from one frame to the next with a natural flow—rotation slipping into contraction, sliding into expansion—repeating in a way that felt intentional rather than mechanical. It didn't take long before I became familiar with the loops, memorizing their timing without meaning to. My mind settled into the work easily, tracking each movement with the same strange instinct I'd felt during Drift Correction. The repetition was soothing, almost meditative.

But every now and then, one of the clusters would falter. A shape would rotate at the exact same angle twice, or slide in a way that matched its previous motion precisely. The errors were tiny, barely noticeable, but something inside me picked them up instantly.

Resetting a loop was simple but delicate. The correction sequence had to match the rhythm of the cluster, and I found myself tapping the keys in time with its motion. When I pressed enter, the faulty cluster paused. Its symbols froze mid-motion, wobbling as if disoriented, then staggered into alignment before resuming their normal flow. The correction always ended with a subtle shift, a tiny pulse through the grid that made the entire display settle.

I repeated the process over and over. Watch. Wait. Detect. Correct. The cycles blurred together, but not in a confusing way—more like slipping into a pattern that my mind recognized deeply, quietly, without explanation. At some point I realized my breathing had synced with the clusters' motion, rising and falling with their unfolding and retracting. Time felt soft, stretched, unimportant. There were no obvious markers of hours passing, only the smooth glide of loops and the quiet click of keys under my fingers.

I looked up from my workstation and noticed a fellow coder a few seats down, the identifier on his desk glowing softly with the label 201. He wasn't behaving like everyone else. While most recruits sat perfectly still, absorbed in their tasks with the same quiet, practiced focus, he kept glancing toward the watchers that circulated through the room. His nervousness wasn't loud, but it was visible in the way his shoulders tightened and the way his eyes flicked toward the floor every time a watcher passed near him. It made me pause, because I wasn't used to seeing anyone else react to the watchers at all. Usually I felt like I was the only one who ever noticed them. But 201 wasn't good at hiding his tension. I watched one of the watchers turn its head sharply in his direction, and 201 immediately dropped his gaze, his fingers freezing over his keys. The watcher lingered a moment longer than usual, then lifted its tablet and wrote something down in a slow, deliberate stroke. I couldn't see what it recorded, but I knew—without a doubt—that the note was about him.

Hours blurred together in a way I couldn't track. There were moments when I was fully aware of every symbol, every correction, every shift in the display. And then there were stretches where my focus seemed to narrow and widen without warning. The patterns moved, I responded, and the work continued, but I couldn't remember the exact moments in between. Sometimes the grid reorganized itself while I was in the middle of typing, the lines reshaping into new configurations that felt both surprising and familiar. Other times I'd blink, and half of the corrections on my screen were already complete. I would scroll up and see sequences I didn't remember finishing—smooth, precise, perfectly executed— like someone else had slipped into my hands for a moment and done the work for me.

It didn't alarm me. It should have, but it didn't. The flow of it felt natural, and easy to fall into. It was like drifting in and out of a dream while still moving, still thinking, still accomplishing something. My body stayed at the station, my fingers on the keys, but my sense of time stretched into something soft and indistinct, guided by the steady rhythm of the tasks.

When I mentioned the strange gaps during orientation, they told us syncing was normal. Everyone went through it. It was part of adapting to the Continuity Engine, part of learning to work with the system rather than against it. They said it helped efficiency. That it meant we were adjusting well.

Syncing with what, I didn't know. But the more it happened, the less I questioned it. It felt like becoming aligned with something larger—something I couldn't see, but could feel in the way my hands moved, steady and sure, even when my mind drifted somewhere else for a moment.

* * *

At rest-cycle, they brought me to a bed beside 297. The beds were arranged in perfect rows, each one identical, each one glowing faintly from the base as if lit from beneath. 297 was already sitting upright on his mattress, spine straight, hands folded neatly in his lap. He looked over at me with a single, measured nod—acknowledgment without warmth, gentle in its own way but with an edge that made it clear he didn't bend rules. He seemed carved from discipline.

"There are rules here," he said, his voice low but firm. "Don't get out of your bed when the lights dim. Don't speak during rotations. Don't touch any unassigned panels." His eyes didn't leave mine as he listed them, as if he needed to be absolutely certain I understood. Nothing in his tone was threatening, but something about him made it impossible to imagine breaking those rules anyway. He didn't raise his voice. He didn't move. He didn't need to.

I heard a sound and turned toward it. 201 was sitting upright on his bed, shoulders squared, his posture rigid but not in the trained, robotic way everyone else held themselves. He was taller than most in the room and broader too, his frame marked by a natural strength that made him stand out even in stillness. But beneath that strength was something unsettled. His knee bounced in a rapid, uneven rhythm, and every few seconds he shifted slightly, as if trying to shake off a feeling he couldn't name. I had noticed him before—always alone, always quiet, but not empty the way the others were. The others felt synchronized with the routine. He felt like he was resisting it without meaning to.

The lights were still bright overhead, so I knew it wasn't time to sleep yet. That meant it was safe to get up, though a thread of uncertainty tugged at me as I slipped off my bed. Even so, something about him drew me in—the way his eyes darted toward the far corner of the room, the way his breath came unevenly as if he were trying to steady himself. I felt connected to him in a strange, undeniable way, as though we shared something buried beneath the surface. He was older, stronger, more imposing than I was, yet standing beside him didn't scare me. Instead, his presence felt familiar.

"Hi," I whispered, keeping my voice soft so it didn't carry through the quiet room. "I'm 349."

He startled slightly, his head lifting just enough for our eyes to meet. There was confusion in his expression—real confusion, not the blank, orderly emptiness I saw in most recruits. His gaze flicked toward the supervisors' hallway before returning to me, as though he was weighing whether speaking could get him in trouble. He didn't seem afraid of the rules, though. He seemed afraid of himself, or of the thoughts pressing against the inside of his mind.

"Hi…" he murmured, his voice low and almost tender, like he was trying to remember how to say the word. His knee kept bouncing.

"Do you know what we're doing here?" I asked. I didn't expect an answer, but I hoped for one.

He shook his head slowly, his brows knitting together as if the motion hurt. "I don't know fully," he said. His voice wavered, but he forced steadiness into it. "But I know it's important. I know that it's… bigger than any of us." His hand tightened around the edge of his mattress, knuckles white. "How many stations have you been to?"

"This is my second," I told him.

He nodded once, like that piece of information settled something in him. But before I could ask what he meant, a sensation prickled at the back of my neck. I turned, and my stomach tightened.

297 was watching me from across the room. His posture

was perfectly straight, his expression unreadable, his eyes locked onto mine with a quiet intensity that made the air feel heavier. It wasn't anger, but it was a warning—clear, controlled, unmistakable. A reminder that even if I didn't know all the rules, I was already close to crossing one.

The lights slowly began to dim, the shift so gradual it felt like the room itself was exhaling. "I better get back to my bed," I whispered, and he nodded without speaking, his knee finally still. I turned away and moved quickly, trying not to draw attention as I crossed the rows of identical beds. When I climbed back into mine, the mattress cool against my palms, I couldn't help looking back toward him. 201 was still watching me, his face softer than before, the nervousness smoothing out for the first time since I'd noticed him. He gave me a small smile—barely there, but real—and for a moment his entire demeanor shifted, like my presence had steadied something fraying inside him.

14

201

Days went by, or at least I think they did. Every day followed the same outline—Drift Correction, Segment Linking, Dip Repair, Loop Alignments— yet none of it ever felt repetitive. The work had a rhythm, a quiet pull I didn't want to step out of. Even when I couldn't tell what day I was on, I never grew tired of the patterns. I only fell deeper into them.

And through all of it, every so often, I would look up and see 201. He was always somewhere in my peripheral awareness, even when I wasn't consciously searching for him. Something about him stood out from the others—not because he was stronger or bigger, but because he seemed awake in a way no one else was. He wasn't synchronized the way the rest of the recruits were. Sometimes his expression shifted mid-task, as though a memory had brushed against him and startled something loose. Other times he paused, blinking at nothing like he was trying to hold onto a thought before it slipped away. Whenever I caught sight of him, a strange familiarity stirred in me. I couldn't tell if we were similar, or if I knew him from someplace I couldn't reach, or if it was simply that he was the only one who felt... human. Whatever the reason, the feeling lingered each time our eyes met—quiet, persistent, and impossible to ignore.

As the cycles continued, the tasks shifted in small, delicate ways. Drift Correction never presented the exact same drift twice. Each time the glowing marker appeared, it hovered at a slightly different angle or distance from the guideline, drifting off-path in new patterns that required tiny variations in the correction sequence. My hands always seemed ready for those changes, typing with confidence. Sometimes I would look down at my fingers and realize they were moving faster than my thoughts, adjusting values I didn't consciously choose. But the corrections were always right, and the soft chime of success felt like proof that instinct was enough.

Segment Linking shifted too, though the changes were even subtler. The color fields drifted in new pairings every cycle— slightly different shades, slightly altered textures, pulses that dimmed or brightened by degrees. The rectangles that belonged together weren't always obvious, but the instant I saw them, something in me recognized the connection. The merges were always seamless, always satisfying, and never quite the same as the cycle before. It felt less like solving a problem and more like finding something misplaced and returning it to where it belonged.

Dip Repair grew more complicated as time blurred. The flickering squares didn't all behave the same way anymore. Some dimmed slowly as if fading out, others flashed erratically like misfiring lights, and others glitched in sharp, sudden bursts that demanded quicker responses. The repair sequences changed in tiny ways too—sometimes requiring different intervals or adjusted values—but I always knew what to type. Sometimes the entire grid flashed white again, only for a fraction of a second, so fast I doubted it had happened at all. No one else reacted. No one even blinked. Their calmness made me wonder if it was part of the system or part of me.

Loop Alignments remained the most mesmerizing. The symbol-clusters drifted along their tracks in elaborate cycles—rotating, folding, contracting, sliding—with a grace that felt almost alive. Over time, their repetitions became more intricate. The errors were subtle: a shape folding too sharply, a rotation repeating with identical timing, a contraction that paused a fraction too long.

Every correction required feeling for the loop's rhythm, slipping into its pattern, nudging it back into motion. My fingers moved with the flow of the cycle, as if syncing not just to the code but to something deeper, something the whole room breathed in and out. The more I aligned the loops, the more natural it felt, as if I'd been realigning patterns like this my whole life.

I glanced up from my display and noticed 201 sitting completely still, his hands hovering above his keys, his eyes locked onto something only he could see. His posture wasn't controlled or obedient the way everyone else's was; it was frozen, tense, as if some hidden part of him had suddenly surfaced and taken hold of him. He whispered something under his breath, too soft to catch, but I knew instantly it wasn't a code or a sequence. The shape of the word didn't fit the sounds we were used to. He whispered it again, louder this time, his voice cracking just slightly. "Mom."

The word struck something deep inside me, stirring a tiny,

unformed memory or longing I couldn't place. It felt familiar, achingly familiar, even though I couldn't remember why. Did we know the same person? Had he remembered something I hadn't yet found? The thought clung to me in a way that felt both comforting and terrifying.

The watchers turned immediately, but they didn't approach him. Instead, they signaled sharply, and two guards entered the room within seconds. They moved with heavy, deliberate steps, the kind that broke the quiet rhythm of the floor. Without hesitation, they grabbed 201 by the arms and pulled him from his chair, which toppled loudly onto its side. He didn't resist. His face remained distant, almost peaceful, as if the word he'd spoken still echoed through him louder than anything happening around him.

Before I could think, before I could stop myself, the words tore out of me louder than I had expected. "Where are you taking him?"

My voice cut through the room like a jagged tear. Several recruits flinched. The guards didn't. They didn't turn, didn't pause, didn't even acknowledge I had spoken. They just kept walking, escorting 201 toward the door with mechanical certainty. Embarrassment and fear crashed over me at once. I swallowed hard, forcing my voice down, pushing the panic out of it until I sounded calmer—smaller. I turned toward a watcher instead, lowering my volume almost to a whisper.

"Are they taking him to the Nether?"

That made the watcher react. He stopped mid-step and turned its head toward me with a sharp, unnerving stiffness, as if the question itself was a breach it hadn't anticipated. For a moment he said nothing, his posture rigid, like he was weighing what he was allowed to tell me—or whether he should say anything at all. When he finally answered, his voice carried a strain I had never heard from a watcher before. "No," he said slowly. "Not for something like this."

He paused again, his gaze still fixed on me. "He will be realigned and returned."

The tone didn't reassure me. But I nodded, pretending it did, even as the door closed behind the guards with a heavy, echoing thud and 201 disappeared from sight.

The guards were gone long before my thoughts settled. I kept working because everyone else kept working, but none of it felt connected to me anymore—my fingers moved, my eyes tracked the shifting grids, but my mind was still back at 201's station, at the word he'd said, at the way he'd been dragged out like something fragile that had finally cracked. By the time the lights dimmed to signal the end of the cycle, I felt hollow, like the day had stretched far longer than it should have. We walked back to the beds in our usual lines, silent and orderly, and for once the quiet felt suffocating instead of calming. When I climbed into my bed, I lay there for a moment staring at the ceiling, trying to shake the lingering unease crawling through my ribs.

I turned my head—and froze. 201 was sitting in his bed across the row. Back. Returned. As if nothing had happened. Except everything about him was wrong. His hair was gone completely, shaved down to bare skin the way it had been when we all first arrived, only now his scalp was wrapped in a wide white bandage that cut across the top of his head. He sat perfectly straight, his hands resting flat on his blanket, his gaze unfocused. He didn't shift or fidget or bounce his knee. He didn't look aware at all.

I slid out of my bed as quietly as I could, moving slowly so the watchers wouldn't notice. I wasn't even sure why I was walking to him—fear, concern, curiosity—they all tangled together until I couldn't separate them. When I reached the edge of his mattress, I whispered, "201?" hoping something in him would flicker like before.

He turned his head toward me, but his eyes didn't show any sign of recognition, no spark of the soft, nervous awareness he'd shown me before. And seeing him like that—shaved, bandaged, hollow—hit me with a force that nearly knocked the breath out of me. I didn't expect it to hurt. I didn't expect it to remind me of anything. But the sight of that bandage triggered something deep inside me, something I didn't know was waiting.

A memory snapped into place.

A woman slumped in a chair. Her hair shaved unevenly. A device—sharp, metallic—pressed against the top of her skull. Her face twisted in pain, her mouth open in a silent cry. It hit so suddenly I stumbled backward, gripping the frame of his bed to steady myself. The memory vanished as quickly as it came, but it left a hollow ache behind, a sense that I had seen something important—something I wasn't supposed to see.

And as I looked at 201's blank expression and the fresh bandage across his head, I couldn't stop trembling, because I knew—whatever they had done to him, whatever "realigned" meant—I knew I didn't want it to happen to me.

* * *

I had something happen in my head that night, something I didn't have words for. It wasn't thinking, not exactly, and it wasn't the blank nothing that usually came when rest-cycle started. It was… a place. Or maybe a picture. Or maybe not a picture at all, because it moved and shifted and didn't follow any rules I understood. It felt like my mind was awake even though my body wasn't. I didn't know what to call it, but it felt strange and soft and frightening all at once.

I saw a world with color. These colors weren't arranged in grids or floating segments or blinking squares. They came in swirls and smudges, mixed together. They didn't stay still. They weren't precise. They were wild. A soft red that glowed around the edges. A yellow that warmed me without light. A green that wasn't a code, wasn't a command, but something growing, moving, alive. The colors weren't shapes. They weren't numbers. They weren't tasks. They just… existed.

There were sounds too, not the hum of circuitry or the quiet taps of keys. These sounds rose and fell, almost like breathing but not quite. I followed them even though I didn't know how. They felt familiar in a way that scared me, like something inside me recognized them before I did.

And then there were pieces—just flashes—of something else. A hand reaching out, fingers brushing something soft. A room that wasn't white. A shape bending over me, warm and solid. A voice saying something I couldn't understand but somehow wanted to hear again. None of it stayed long enough for me to hold onto. The more I tried to look directly at the images, the faster they crumbled, like they were made of smoke. But the feeling stayed. A feeling like I had been somewhere before all of this, somewhere outside the walls and the screens and the routines.

I didn't understand any of it. I didn't even know how to ask myself what it was. When I opened my eyes again, lying in the dim light of the sleeping room, the only thing I could say for certain was that whatever I had seen—it wasn't something that happened during waking hours. It wasn't a memory from here. It was something different. Something my mind made on its own. I didn't know the word for it, but it felt like my thoughts had gone wandering without me.

I heard a crash so loud it shattered the quiet, followed immediately by the tangled sounds of bodies moving, fists hitting fabric, the sharp scrape of metal against the floor. I sat up instinctively, my heart hammering, but I kept my legs tucked under the blanket. I didn't dare leave my bed. The rules pressed against my ribs like a physical weight—lights were dim, and breaking a rule now felt like stepping off a ledge. Even so, I couldn't stay still. I craned my neck, searching for the source of the chaos.

And then I saw it. 201—who had returned earlier with shaved hair, a fresh bandage across his head, and empty eyes— was no longer sitting in that eerie, silent stillness. He was on his feet, wild and shaking, his arms thrashing as a guard struggled to restrain him. The bandage was slipping, half torn, hanging crooked across his scalp. His face twisted with something raw and desperate, nothing like the quiet, confused boy I had talked to before.

"Take me back to my mom!" he shouted, the word "mom" hitting the air like a foreign object—too real for this room. The sound of it sent a chill through me, the same strange familiarity sparking again deep inside my chest. He kept yelling it, louder each time, like he thought volume could tear open a hole back to whatever he'd remembered.

The guard tried to pin his arms, but 201 was bigger and stronger than almost anyone here. He twisted sharply, ripping free, and drove his fist into the guard's face. The guard stumbled back, blood spraying in a quick arc before disappearing into the dim light. Another punch, harder this time, landed against the guard's jaw, and I heard a crack I felt in my own teeth.

The guard recovered quickly, swinging back with sharp, practiced blows that thudded against 201's ribs and shoulder. But 201 didn't slow down. It was like something had snapped awake inside him—something fueled by more than adrenaline. His movements sharpened, focused, driven by a memory that refused to stay buried.

He kicked the guard square in the chest. The impact echoed through the room, and the guard flew backward, hitting the ground with a heavy, breathless grunt.

He didn't get up. He lay on the floor, arms slack, head tilted in a way that made my stomach twist. But 201 wasn't done. Whatever the "realignment" was meant to suppress—fear, pain, anger, all of it—it had torn free with terrifying force.

Before anyone could react, 201 grabbed the guard by the collar and hauled him upright with alarming ease. The guard sagged in his hands, barely conscious, but 201's expression didn't change.

Then 201 slammed the guard's skull against the corner of the bed. The impact made a horrific crack that rang through the room and made my vision blur for a heartbeat, and the sound of the collision was so final it seemed to steal the air out of my lungs. But he didn't stop. He lifted the guard's head again and brought it down harder this time, then again, and again, each strike driven by something feral and desperate. The guard's body jerked once in reflex before going completely limp, but 201 kept going, lost in the violence, unable or unwilling to see that there was no fight left.

Blood burst outward with each impact. It splattered across the white surface in sharp, violent streaks that crawled down its surface like cracks spreading through ice. Against the white beds, the red looked impossibly bright, almost glowing. Droplets scattered across the floor in chaotic patterns, rolling toward the drains in thin, broken lines. Some of it sprayed across 201's hands, staining the skin between his fingers. And some reached the beds closest to him—small, bright freckles landing on the white uniforms of kids lying frozen beneath their blankets. I saw one girl flinch when a spot hit her cheek, but she didn't move. None of them moved.

The room had gone completely silent. No whispers. No breathing. Just the sickening, wet sound of stone meeting bone over and over. I couldn't look away. My heart hammered against my ribs so hard it hurt. He wasn't fighting anymore. He was unraveling, and whatever memory had broken through inside him had come with enough force to tear everything else apart.

Finally, someone else moved. For a moment I thought the entire room would stay frozen forever. But then something shifted at the corner of my vision—subtle at first, then unmistakable. 297 rose from his bed in one fluid, deliberate motion. He wasn't shaking. He wasn't panicked. His face was set in a tight, controlled expression I had never seen on him before. In that instant, it hit me how brave he was, how impossibly brave, because he'd seen the same brutal, animalistic violence I had, and yet he still stood up when I wouldn't have dared to move. I whispered his number, tried to tell him to wait, to stop, to think, but the sound barely escaped my throat. He didn't hear me—or he chose not to.

Before I could fully understand what he intended to do, 297 crossed the distance between the beds with startling purpose. He approached 201 from behind, moving with a precision that didn't belong to any of the work we did here. Then, without a sound, he wrapped his arm around 201's throat, locking it under his jaw and pulling backward with all his weight. The movement was frighteningly practiced. 201 reacted instantly. He dropped the guard's limp body and thrashed wildly, his arms swinging back in desperate, frantic arcs. He tried to claw at 297's face, his arms jerking in wide, uneven sweeps, but he couldn't reach him. 297 kept his stance, leaning back, tightening the hold, his jaw clenched and his eyes sharp with focus.

And then the room erupted. A loud mechanical pop echoed above us, and suddenly doors appeared along the walls—doors that hadn't existed a second earlier. A dozen guards poured through them in a synchronized surge, sprinting toward 201 and 297 with shields raised, boots pounding against the floor in heavy, rhythmic bursts.

One of the guards stepped forward—different from the others, marked by a darker uniform with sharper edges and a strange stripe across the chest. He didn't rush or shout like the rest. He moved with a slow, deliberate confidence, lifting his arm until I saw something small in his hand. A remote. Sleek, black, almost featureless except for a single raised button. He extended his arm and pressed it with a calmness that made my skin crawl.

I didn't understand what it was at first. But then I looked at 201. His face tightened strangely, the muscles pulling all at once as if someone had grabbed his skin from behind and yanked. His eyes widened, then bulged, the veins in his temples swelling so fast I heard a faint, awful sound—like something inflating quickly. His whole head expanded in unnatural pulses, skin stretching, trembling, like it was fighting against something inside it. I tried to look away but couldn't.

And then it burst.

Not with a single clean spray, but with a violent eruption—like the pressure inside him had torn through every barrier at once. A thick wave of blood and tissue exploded outward, splattering across the stone beds and the white uniforms of the kids nearest him. Several of them gasped but didn't move.

297, still behind him with his arm locked in a chokehold, took the full force of it. The blast hit him like a storm, covering his face, his shoulders, his chest—hot, sudden, heavy. He jerked backward, releasing his hold as he stumbled. For a moment he just stood there, frozen, blinking through the blood that clung to his eyelashes, dripping from his chin, streaking down the front of his perfectly white clothes. He tried to wipe it away, but his hands only smeared it, making broad red streaks across his cheeks and jaw.

The room went dead silent again. No one screamed. No one moved. The only sound was 297's ragged breathing as he stared down at his shaking, blood-soaked hands.

201's body fell in what felt like slow motion. It didn't collapse the way a person normally would. It drifted, almost floated, as if the world had paused just long enough to let every detail imprint itself into my mind. His shoulders sagged first, folding inward like the breath had been pulled out of him. Then his knees buckled, bending under a weight he no longer had the strength to carry. His torso tipped forward slightly before gravity took hold, and for one suspended moment he hovered there—half-standing, half-fallen—as though part of him still refused to let go.

His body hit the floor with a heavy, final thud that echoed through the room. Something dark splashed across the tile beside him, spreading in uneven streaks that glimmered under the lights. His uniform, once the same stark white as all of ours, darkened around the collar and chest as the stain crept outward like ink blooming through fabric.

The world felt thick and slowed, as 201's body settled into stillness, something inside me sank too—a heavy, cold weight that told me nothing here was as controlled or predictable as they wanted us to believe. The guards moved through us with practiced efficiency, forming us into a line without a single word. Most of us had some kind of reddish stain on us—tiny flecks, thin streaks, wide smudges—like we had walked through a storm none of us had seen coming. We moved quietly, our bare feet tapping against the floor, each step dragging more of the red across the white tile.

Behind us, workers had already entered the room, cleaning everything with quick, methodical movements. They scrubbed the stone beds, wiped down the surfaces, erased the evidence of what had happened as if it were nothing more than a spill to be handled and forgotten. Some of us left faint footprints as we walked, pale shapes on the floor that disappeared almost as quickly as they appeared. Others had hardly been touched at all, their tunics mostly white except for a few scattered flecks. It looked random, the way each of us had been marked—or not marked.

But what I noticed most was that 297 wasn't walking with us. He was being taken in a different direction entirely, escorted through a side door I had never seen open before. His tunic was nearly red from top to bottom, the fabric darkened and clinging to him. He looked too calm for someone covered like that. The guards around him moved with extra caution, their grips firm, their steps careful.

Seeing him separated made something cold settle deeper in my chest. Whatever had happened to 201—whatever force had surged through him and torn him apart from the inside—it wasn't something he had brought with him. It was something they had put inside all of us. Something waiting. Something we didn't understand. Something that could wake up at any moment.

They marched us to the showers in a long, silent line. The guards kept close, their hands on their weapons, their eyes scanning us as if waiting for one of us to break apart the way 201 had. I felt the dried blood stiffening on my skin with every step, flaking in some places, still tacky in others. Some kids had it smeared across their cheeks or running in dried trails down their arms. Others had only tiny specks. It didn't matter. We all looked wrong—marked. None of us spoke. Our footsteps were the only sound, soft and uneven against the white floor.

Inside the shower room, the guards directed us into separate stalls—high walls on all sides, no windows, no gaps, nothing but a small grate in the corner of each space. I pulled the curtain closed behind me and took off my stained tunic, trying not to look at the red patches on it. The moment the water turned on overhead, it came down fast and warm, hitting my shoulders hard enough that I gasped.

I kept waiting to hear something—someone sobbing, some-one whispering a prayer, someone asking if this was real. But there was nothing. Absolute silence. Just the rush of water hitting tile in each stall, all blending into a single, dull roar. Nobody screamed. Nobody cried. Nobody even sniffled. It was as if our throats had been sealed shut the moment the blood touched us.

I pressed my forehead to the wall and let the water run over me, watching the red wash down my arms in thin pink trails that spiraled toward the drain. My chest ached with a pressure I didn't know how to release, something trapped and desperate inside me. I wanted to cry. I wanted to sob until the water ran cold. But the tears wouldn't come, and my voice stayed locked somewhere deep in my throat, unreachable.

When the water finally shut off, I stood there dripping, still watching the last faint pink trails disappear into the grate. For a moment I didn't move. None of us did. Then a soft mechanical click sounded from the wall in front of me. A vertical seam split open, smooth and silent, revealing a small recessed compartment I hadn't known existed. Inside was a neatly folded white tunic—perfectly pressed, still warm, impossibly clean. The fabric looked untouched, like it had been prepared long before any of us arrived. I reached out and felt how soft it was, how freshly laundered, how wrong it seemed after what had just happened. When I pulled it over my head, the brightness of it made me feel like the blood had been erased from my skin, not washed away. I knew the same thing was happening in every stall: identical tunics, identical compartments, identical silence.

When they brought us back to our room, it was exactly the same as it had been before. Pure white. Clean. Peaceful. The stone beds gleamed as though they had been polished by hand, every surface smooth and bright. The floor shined so perfectly it reflected the lights overhead, and there was no trace—no hint—of what had been there less than an hour ago. Even the air smelled different, sharp and sterile, like the room had been scrubbed down to the deepest cracks. The corner of the bed where the guard's skull had struck was spotless, the stone brighter than the rest—as if they'd ground away the layer that had absorbed the blood. The tiles where 201 had fallen were so pristine they looked newly replaced. If I hadn't seen it with my own eyes, if I hadn't felt the shock of it in my bones, I would have believed nothing had happened at all.

Nothing had changed. Nothing was out of place. As if the room itself was insisting reality had been restored, that everything was exactly as it should be. As if 201 had never existed. But I remembered the way he yelled that word. I remembered the blood, the panic, the impossible burst of him. No amount of white could scrub that away from me.

And on his bed—sitting upright, silent, staring straight ahead—was a new person. A replacement. He was already dressed in a fresh white tunic, already positioned with perfect posture, already wearing the same blank, steady expression everyone else had. His hair was cleanly shaved, his hands rested neatly on his knees, and his gaze didn't flicker, not even once. It was as if he had been placed there like a replacement part, fitted precisely into the gap left behind. The uniform looked untouched, his skin spotless, his breathing calm and even. A new number on his bed, 407.

He looked as calm and empty as the rest of them. Fresh uniform. Fresh posture. Fresh start. There was no hesitation in him, no confusion, no trace of the chaos that had filled this room only hours earlier. He didn't look like someone who had ever screamed for anything. He didn't look like someone who could.

I stared at him and felt a hollow ache settle in the center of my chest, a quiet heaviness that didn't belong to the room, but to me. Because everything around us wanted me to believe this was normal. That replacing someone was the same thing as never losing them. That bodies and minds could be swapped out without consequence. That the person who had been here before didn't matter.

But I remembered the blood. I remembered the sound of 201's voice breaking when he yelled that word. I remembered the panic in his eyes. And I remembered the crushing realization that whatever had destroyed him wasn't unique to him at all—it lived inside every one of us, buried under the rules and the routines and the silence they forced into our heads.

They could clean the room. They could erase him. They could pretend nothing had happened.

But I couldn't.

15

Reset

I woke the next morning more confused than I had ever been since arriving here—wherever "here" actually was. For a few seconds I stayed still, trying to sort out what had been real and what my mind had twisted in the night. The room looked exactly as it always did: rows of stone beds, identical tunics, identical faces arranged in identical posture. But the air felt different, heavier, as if the memory of yesterday hovered just beneath the surface even if nothing here showed it.

That's when I noticed him. Not 407—the replacement placed where 201 had been—but someone entirely new sitting where 297 used to be. His number was 431. The sight of him hit me hard. If 297 had already been replaced, then whatever had broken loose inside 201 hadn't been a single malfunction. It meant the danger wasn't gone. It meant it could spread. It meant it could happen to any of us without warning.

I searched the room again, hoping to catch even one person looking uneasy, or lost, or human. But every expression was the same flat calm. Hands resting neatly on knees. Eyes unfocused. Backs perfectly straight. If they remembered anything about last night, their faces didn't show it. It was like the whole room had been reset while I slept.

I knew I needed answers, but questions were dangerous here. Even the wrong glance felt risky. Still, my gaze kept drifting toward 407. Something about him didn't match the others. He was smaller, younger, almost fragile-looking compared to the rest of us. His feet barely touched the ground when he sat.

Before I could talk myself out of it, I found myself moving toward him. Not boldly, not quickly—just enough that my steps blended into the quiet routine of morning. But my heart pounded harder with each one. The room felt alert, as if the walls were waiting to see what I'd do.

Up close, 407's stillness was unsettling. His posture was perfect, but something in the way he sat felt... suspended. Like a thought halfway formed. Like a command still loading. His eyes were blank, yet not as completely empty as the others. There was something behind them—faint, almost hidden— like the smallest ripple beneath perfectly smooth water.

I leaned in slightly, just enough for my voice to reach him without carrying anywhere else. "Can you hear me?" I whispered.

He didn't blink or turn his head. His breathing stayed steady and measured. But something in his gaze shifted—a tiny tightening, a flicker so small I might have imagined it. Yet it sent a chill through me all the same.

I'm not sure why I expected him to be anything like 201. Maybe it was because he sat in the same bed. Maybe some desperate part of me wanted there to be a connection—something familiar in the middle of all this unnatural sameness. But the moment 407 spoke, I realized how wrong I'd been. He wasn't like 201 at all. He was just another perfectly calibrated piece in their machine.

"Of course I can hear you," he said, his voice smooth and mechanical, lacking any rise or fall. "What do you need?" The way he spoke made my skin crawl. It wasn't a real voice. It was something shaped to sound like one. I felt the sting of disappointment rush through me—frustration, fear, something sharp I couldn't name—because I knew immediately that I couldn't ask him anything real. He wasn't a person to talk to. He was a response system.

I stepped away from him, my palms sweaty from the interaction. My gaze drifted to 431. I knew I'd get the same result, but something in me needed to try again anyway, like maybe repetition would crack the surface. "Hi," I said, trying to sound casual, normal, harmless.

431 lifted his head instantly, turning toward me with precision. "Hi! Good to see you!" he chirped, his voice bright in a way that didn't belong in this room, a tone that felt like someone's idea of friendliness instead of something lived or felt.

Something hot welled up inside me—anger, fear, confusion, all tangled. "Do you know what happened to 297? Is he okay?" I tried to soften the question, but the emotion in my voice pushed through anyway.

He blinked once, a slow, eerily smooth movement. "297? Who is that? I am 431." His tone didn't change at all, but his eyes flickered with something… not recognition, but static.

Before I could push further, the air in the corner of the room changed. One of the Watchers straightened. They had been there the whole time—tall silhouettes with dark visors, standing like shadows observing us—but now one of them was writing quickly across a thin black tablet. His helmet tilted toward me, tracking my every breath. Then he began to move.

My chest tightened. He walked with the slow, certain steps of someone who didn't need to run to be terrifying. I backed up one step, only one, but it was enough. He grabbed my wrist, his fingers cold and unyielding. "Come with me," he said, his voice flat and heavy with authority, as if the words weren't spoken but read from a script that allowed no refusal.

I looked around the room, heart hammering. For the first time, two kids weren't staring blankly ahead. Their eyes flicked toward me—quick, frightened, questioning. They didn't move their bodies, didn't shift their hands, but their eyes said enough. They had the same questions I did. They had the same fear. And now they were seeing exactly what happened when someone dared to ask anything out of line.

I wasn't fighting him. I knew I didn't have the strength to overpower a Watcher—not physically, not with how much smaller I was. So I moved where he directed me, each step careful and controlled, clinging to the small hope that compliance might keep me from whatever fate had taken 201 and 297.

But even my willingness to follow didn't slow them. Another Watcher fell in behind me, his boots thudding in a steady, ominous rhythm. Then a third appeared at my left side, his hand clamping onto my arm with a force that sent a sharp sting deep into the muscle. His fingers dug in hard enough that I could already feel the bruise forming. Their presence boxed me in so tightly I could barely tell which direction I was moving. It felt less like being escorted and more like being carried by a current I couldn't resist.

We turned down a corridor where the lights overhead buzzed faintly, glowing bright, casting shadows that felt stretched and unnatural. I recognized the sterile scent in the air, the slight hum beneath the floor. A cold ripple moved through me. I had been here once before, and the memory of that visit made my hands tremble before I could stop them. The door on the right slid open with a smooth, practiced hiss, and I braced myself as they guided me inside.

C-1 was waiting. She stood perfectly still at the center of the room, hands folded behind her back, posture rigid and composed. She didn't acknowledge the Watchers flanking me. She didn't react to the door. She simply existed in the room with an authority so natural it made the space feel smaller. When she turned her head toward me, the movement was slow and deliberate, her eyes settling on me with a calmness that curdled my stomach.

"Take a seat, please," she said.

The words hit me harder than any grip on my arm. My body obeyed before my thoughts caught up, sinking into the cold metal chair as if pulled downward. I couldn't stop the heaviness that filled my chest. I had disappointed her. The realization came with a strange sting of guilt, sharp and immediate, even though I had no reason—no logical reason—to feel anything like that. Her approval mattered to me in a way that made no sense, an instinct wedged somewhere too deep to examine.

But something else rose alongside it—something quieter and colder. She knew. She knew what was inside of us, what could kill us at the push of a button, and yet she still managed to act like she cared about us… about me. Like she had some kind of personal stake in my future. But no. She was behind all of this. She could stop it at any moment, shut it all down, end the fear and the silence and the deaths—but she didn't. She let it happen. She let it happen and watched from above, untouched, unmoved, pretending concern while holding every lever that controlled our lives.

The memory of 201s death pressed hard against the strange pull I felt toward her, twisting it into something uneasy and unsettling. I didn't feel safe around her. I didn't feel comforted or protected. If anything, the calmness in her gaze made my pulse race faster. And yet, under all of that, some part of me still reacted to her tone—to her disappointment—like it mattered.

That confusion burned beneath my ribs, tightening the air in my lungs, but I didn't let it show. I kept my eyes forward, hands gripping the sides of the chair, trying to steady myself before she spoke again. Something was happening here— something I didn't understand—and the last thing I could afford was letting her see how unsteady I truly was.

I never could have predicted the words that came out of her mouth next. They hit me so sharply that for a moment I thought I'd misheard her. "349," she said, her tone smooth and unshakably calm, "you've been selected for advancement. Consider this your promotion."

For a heartbeat, something fluttered inside my chest—an instinctive spark of pride, excitement, maybe even relief. It rose so quickly it scared me, like the reaction had been installed rather than felt. I pushed it down hard, swallowing against the warmth climbing up my throat. "I'm… promoted?" I managed, the disbelief scraping my voice thin.

C-1 gave the slightest nod, as if confirming a number in a ledger. "Your performance hasn't gone unnoticed. And neither has 297's. When he intervened during the 201 event, his capability became difficult to ignore." She paused, letting the weight of that settle. "He has been reassigned to Watcher status. A rare transition—but he met the criteria." Her eyes sharpened just slightly, the closest thing she ever showed to intention. "He agreed to accept the role on one condition: that you join him in his new sector."

A strange chill ran through me. 297… a Watcher? I tried to imagine him standing beside the armored figures who dragged me through the halls, wearing their uniform, speaking with their precision. It didn't fit. It didn't make sense. And the realization that Watchers and guards had once been exactly where I stood now—sitting on cold stone, wearing white, learning patterns—made my thoughts spin. If they had been like me… what had they lost along the way? What had been taken?

C-1 continued, her voice carrying a practiced warmth that felt more unnerving than comforting. "Most coders remain in your current classification for a decade or longer. Four years is… unusual. Exceptional, in fact." She took a careful step closer, her eyes assessing me like a puzzle piece she was confirming the shape of. "This isn't solely the result of 297's request. Your trajectory has been clear for some time. His suggestion merely accelerated the inevitable."

My hands curled into my lap, nails digging into my palms as a swarm of tangled thoughts crashed against each other. Four years. Had it really been that long? The number felt impossible—absurd—even as something deep inside me whispered that it made sense. I was bigger now, the bed felt smaller–and time didn't behave normally here. Days bled into each other, smooth and seamless, slipping past without edges to hold onto. Still, hearing it spoken out loud made a hollow ache bloom in my chest. Four years. And now they were trying to lift me out of my position like it was nothing.

None of this felt like the last promotion. That one had been confusing, but real—a step that fit within the pattern, something I could almost understand. It wasn't a reward. It wasn't recognition. It felt like a magician's trick—the kind meant to make your eyes look exactly where they wanted while their hands worked somewhere else entirely.

But beneath the confusion and distrust, something else flickered—dangerous and tempting. If they were moving me somewhere new, somewhere higher, maybe the rules were different there. Maybe the walls didn't listen the same way. Maybe information slipped through the cracks.

It didn't feel like a reward. It felt like a maneuver.

But if it let me get close enough to pry open one more piece of whatever they were hiding… then maybe stepping into their plan was the only way forward.

As if she could feel the questions knotting themselves tighter inside my chest, C-1 folded her hands in her lap and spoke again, her posture perfectly still. "You likely have questions," she said, her voice soft but unnervingly steady. "Most do, at this stage. Curiosity is normal. Expected." She didn't lean forward, didn't shift, didn't give any hint of warmth—just sat across from me in sharp, composed silence. "Before we move you into the next phase, it's important that you understand the scope of your work. What your contributions have meant. What you're about to step into." She paused—not long, but just enough for tension to thicken in the air between us. "We are taking you to the real world."

My heart punched upward, so hard it almost hurt. I gripped the sides of my chair to keep my hands from trembling. "The… real world?" The words felt shaky, strange, like they belonged to someone else. "What is the real world?"

Her eyes didn't soften, but something sharper flickered behind them—interest, calculation, something I couldn't read. "Everything you've done," she said, each syllable slow and intentional. "Every sequence. Every correction. Every system you've stabilized. None of it was hypothetical." She sat perfectly upright, the picture of composed certainty. "Your work affects lives beyond these walls. Real people. Real consequences."

My breath grew shallow. I had wondered—constantly, silently, desperately—why they made us do what we did. What it meant. What it *changed*.

C-1 kept her gaze locked on mine, steady and unblinking. "I imagine you've asked yourself many times what this place is. Why you're here. Why your tasks matter." She let a quiet moment stretch between us, not blinking, not fidgeting, not breaking the stillness. "It's time you saw the truth for yourself."

16

The Nursery

The walk felt endless, like time had stretched itself thin just to make me feel smaller. We moved through hall after hall, the same white walls, the same temperature, the same spotless floors that swallowed our footsteps. I couldn't tell how long we'd been walking anymore—minutes, hours, days—it all blended the way everything here did. But somewhere deep inside me, a heaviness began to shift. A pressure. Like we were nearing the edge of something I had never been meant to see.

Eventually, far ahead of us, I noticed something unusual— the faint outline of an ending. A wall that didn't fade into another hallway. A boundary. An actual *end.* It made my pulse quicken. In all the time I had been here, the corridors had always fed into more corridors. But now there was a final point, a place where the world stopped instead of folding back on itself.

When we reached it, a massive panel on the left hissed open, revealing a space bathed in a color I had only ever seen in digital diagrams. Grey. Real grey. It wasn't the sterile, perfect shade they used in training sequences. This grey was uneven, textured, alive in a strange way. It pulled my eyes immediately.

The walls, floor, and ceiling were the same color, but the surface… it was wrong. Or right. I wasn't sure. I reached out without thinking and let my fingers brush it. The material felt solid—harder than the stone beds, but rough, scratchy, like it had tiny jagged pieces embedded in it. It didn't shine. It didn't reflect anything. It looked like it had been poured or pressed into place and left to sit for years. This wasn't fabricated. It wasn't polished. It was just… there. Real in a way nothing else here was.

I stepped fully inside, unable to stop staring at the strangeness of it all. And then something else caught my eye—something large and lumpy and oddly shaped sitting in the center of the space. It was a long rectangular object, but the edges weren't straight like the beds or tables. They curved, dipping and rising like someone had tried to make it smooth but hadn't known the rules of symmetry. It rested on four perfect circles, each one thicker than both my hands together.

I circled it slowly, my head tilting. It was hollow. I could see spaces inside through the glass panels on its sides—clear walls, but colder-looking than the screens we used. The whole thing looked like a machine built out of pieces that didn't match, but somehow still fit together.

"There are doors," C-1 said calmly, as if this explanation would answer anything. One of the panels swung outward, revealing a compartment big enough for several people. I hesitated. The interior smelled strange—like metal rubbed against heat and something chemical I didn't have a word for.

She motioned me inside, and I obeyed, climbing over a ridge at the bottom of the doorway and settling into one of the soft seats. It gave slightly beneath my weight, like it was filled with something that didn't quite want to hold me up.

C-1 sat beside me with perfect precision. She reached forward and slid a thin metal piece—almost like a card—into a slit near where her hands rested. Then she gripped a round object sticking out of the machine and turned it sharply.

The response was immediate. A deep hum woke beneath us, trembling through the floor, through the seat, through my bones. The whole structure shivered once, like a living thing stretching awake.

And then we moved.

The speed slammed into me so suddenly I instinctively grabbed the sides of my seat. The world outside blurred past us, faster than I could have ever run, faster than I could have imagined anything could move without breaking apart. My stomach dipped, my heart surged upward, and a strangled sound escaped my throat before I could stop it.

We were flying across the ground, sealed inside this strange metal creature on wheels, and nothing in the facility—not the halls, not the beds, not the walls—had prepared me for the sensation of real movement.

I looked at C-1, desperate for some kind of explanation—or at least a reaction—but she sat perfectly still, perfectly composed, as if being hurled through a metal tunnel inside a roaring machine was as ordinary as breathing. Her eyes shifted toward me, unblinking, her mouth stretched into something like a smile. Then she let out a soft, almost amused chuckle that sent a ripple of unease through me. "This is called driving," she said, her voice smooth and steady over the growl beneath us. "It's far more normal than you think."

Normal. The word meant nothing here. Nothing about this was normal. The speed, the shaking, the tunnel rushing past in streaks of shadow—it felt like the world was collapsing around us and she was sitting there as if we were on a gentle stroll.

The tunnel went on and on, swallowing distance faster than I could process it. Time stretched, warped, broke apart. Eventually, the machine began to slow, the vibration softening into a low hum. Ahead of us, a massive door slid open with a heavy mechanical groan, unveiling a space I couldn't see clearly yet. The machine rolled to a stop beside the opening.

"This is the entrance," C-1 said, her tone carrying that familiar blend of importance and vagueness that always left me grasping for meaning. She gestured toward the space beyond the door. "We keep it in the middle."

The middle of what? The middle of the tunnel? The facility? The world? Her words had the shape of an explanation but none of the substance. She was incredibly good at saying things that sounded like answers—yet somehow never actually explained anything real. The more she spoke, the more I felt like she was guiding me through a maze with walls made of fog.

We stepped through the doorway, and I froze. Rising in front of us was something I had never seen before—flat, stacked ledges made of the same rough grey material as the walls, each one slightly higher than the last. They formed a kind of rigid pathway climbing upward in sharp, uneven steps. The surface looked unforgiving, like it would scrape my skin if I fell against it.

C-1 moved toward them as if it were nothing, but when I

lifted my foot to follow, the angle felt wrong—unnatural. I wasn't used to the idea of *climbing* the floor. The first step forced my foot upward in a way that made my leg shake, my muscles stretching in patterns I'd never needed before.

As we ascended, each new step felt like pushing against the weight of a world I didn't understand. The rise of the ledge, the strain in my calves, the way the sound of my footsteps echoed dull and heavy against the grey material—it all felt strange, disorienting, like learning how to walk again but with invisible eyes watching to see if I failed.

By the time we reached the top, my legs burned in a way I'd never felt before. And yet, strange as it was, it felt real—more real than anything in the facility ever had.

The hum struck me first. A deep, uneven vibration that traveled up through the strange ground beneath my shoes, rattling my ankles, humming in my bones. It didn't sound like the facility's machines—clean, controlled, predictable. This hum felt wild and raw, like something enormous beneath the surface was shifting, stretching, waking.

We stepped out of the narrow hallway, and the world exploded open around me. I froze, my breath catching somewhere in my throat. There was no ceiling here—no perfectly measured panels, no lights humming overhead. Instead there was an enormous white-blue emptiness stretching above me so far it made my vision tilt. It felt like standing under a giant open mouth. My chest tightened, unsure if I was supposed to run or kneel or hide.

The ground was nothing like the polished floors I knew. It was made of countless tiny stones pressed tightly together, rough enough that even through the thin soles of my shoes I could feel every uneven edge. It crunched faintly with every step, tiny shifts of grit sliding beneath my weight. It felt unstable. Imperfect. Real.

A long raised path stretched ahead, suspended above a moving expanse of dark water. The path rested on thick pillars that disappeared beneath the churning surface. I had no word for it—only that it looked like a walkway someone had carved out of the rough ground and stretched across the river, daring gravity to disagree.

The water itself rolled and twisted underneath, restless and loud, carrying a sharp metallic scent that stung the inside of my nose. I don't know how to explain it, but its similar to blood.

Thin bars lined the edges of the raised path, tall enough to keep someone back but spaced so you could see the drop below. I reached out and brushed one lightly. It was cold—so cold it bit through the warmth of my skin instantly. The metal left a faint, bitter smell on my fingertips, like the taste of blood without the pain.

Across the water, giant structures stretched into the sky— towering blocks covered in strange reflective panels. They shimmered and fractured the sunlight, throwing pieces of it across the air like glittering shards. They looked like impossibly large extensions of the coding modules we used— but stretched to the point of breaking, stacked higher than anything I'd ever imagined.

Behind me, smaller block-like buildings lined another stretch of this open world. Their surfaces were faded, peeling, marked with shapes and colors I didn't recognize. Their windows were clouded, some cracked, some dim. Trees grew between them—actual trees. Branches knotted upward, leaves fluttering in the wind like flickering fragments of green code.

The sound they made—soft rustles—felt like whispers coming from something alive.

Birds swooped between the trees, letting out sharp, unpredictable sounds. Nothing in the facility prepared me for noises that didn't repeat, didn't echo correctly, didn't belong to any pattern. Their calls shot through the air like broken bits of music.

When I looked down at myself, I stopped walking. My clothes—if I could still call them that—weren't the white, silent uniform I had worn every day of my life. They had changed somewhere between the stairs and this world, or maybe the world itself had changed how they looked. Colors—actual colors—rippled across the fabric in strange, shifting patterns. Soft blues, bright pinks, tiny scattered shapes that looked like stars or animals or… something meant to be cheerful. The fabric was softer than the tunic I was used to, lighter, almost bouncy, like it wanted to move with the wind instead of clinging to me.

The sleeves puffed slightly at the edges, the collar dipped into an odd rounded shape, and the designs printed into the material looked so playful they felt unreal. Nothing here matched the rigid simplicity of the facility. My clothes felt like they belonged to someone who was supposed to be delighted by the world, someone meant to smile at colors and patterns and silly images. Someone untouched by fear. Someone else entirely.

"C-1," I said without thinking, still using the only name I had ever known for her.

She stiffened, the movement so quick and sharp it felt like a warning. "Don't call me that here," she said, her voice dropping into a low, urgent edge I'd never heard from her before. She angled her face toward mine, eyes steady and commanding in a way that made the unfamiliar world around us feel even more unstable. "Call me *mom.* That's the title caretakers use here. If we use the wrong terms, we'll draw attention. This helps us blend in."

The word hit me like a blow to the chest. *Mom.* I had heard it before—echoing through the white room, ripped from 201's throat before he collapsed. He hadn't been saying a name. He'd been reaching for someone. Begging. Crying out to the person meant to protect him. In those final moments, that word had been the only thing he had left. Hearing it now, calm and strategic on C-1's tongue, made something twist painfully inside me.

Had I had a caretaker once too? The thought slipped in quietly, almost shy, like it wasn't sure it belonged to me. Not a number. Not a title. A *person.* Someone real. Did I remember a soft voice soothing me when I cried? Hands smoothing my hair away from my face? A laugh—bright, gentle—that made the world feel less sharp? The memories came in fragments, blurry and floating, like pieces of a dream I'd woken from early. I couldn't see her face, no matter how hard I reached for it, but I could feel the warmth of her presence, the sense that I had belonged somewhere once, to someone. And in those faint, flickering echoes, I knew what I had called her. *Mom.* The real version of the word. The version meant for love and safety—not the version C-1 was using now, clipped and strategic, stripped of everything it once meant.

The meaning of the title "mom" didn't fit her. It felt wrong in her mouth, wrong in this world, wrong in this moment where everything inside me was already shifting fast to understand. But she was the only guide I had out here. And survival, for now, meant pretending.

So even with the ache tightening in my chest and the memory of 201's voice echoing painfully in my head, I nodded. And when I spoke the word back, it felt fragile and unfamiliar on my tongue.

"Okay… mom."

We walked along the hard floor, and my eyes couldn't stop wandering. People drifted across the wide stone paths—talking, laughing, moving with an ease that felt unnatural to me. Their emotions were real, or at least real enough. Warm, expressive, shifting. They didn't stare blankly like recruits. They didn't hide their reactions. They weren't trying to pass inspection. They simply existed, unaware of how impossible their world truly was. The colors around them were so bright they stabbed at my eyes. I felt like my skull wasn't built to contain this much sensation.

A bird dipped low over the railing beside us, wings carving through the sunlight. For a second, everything about it seemed perfect. But then it vanished mid-flap, reappearing a few feet backward along the same path, resuming the exact wing stroke it had started. A loop. A tiny, careless loop. My breath stopped. It continued on as if nothing had happened. Loop alignment.

The sky—if that's what it was meant to be—looked endless and bright. But the instant I focused on the huge sphere of white-blue light above us, it twitched. A subtle jump, a smear of brightness dragging sideways. Then it snapped back into perfect position with mechanical precision. Drift correction.

Wind swept across the walkway, moving the leaves of the trees scattered between the buildings. One leaf trembled hard and fast—then flashed white for an instant, like the system had lost its texture before reapplying it. Dip repair.

A cold shock rippled through me. My fingers tingled. My stomach twisted so sharply it felt like something inside me was folding in on itself. Every task I'd ever done—every correction I'd made—was echoing back at me in this place. The world wasn't glitching because it was far away. It wasn't glitching because we were outside. It was glitching because we were still *inside*. Inside the facility. Inside something built to be enormous and convincing and self-contained.

The hum beneath the walkway grew louder. A living vibration rattling through my bones. I felt it up my legs, into my ribs. The machine under the dome. The engine keeping this entire world projected, layered, woven together. I had mistaken it for some natural phenomenon, but now the rhythm beneath it was unmistakable. A cycle. A strain. The signature of a system compensating for error.

The river churned below us, dark water slapping against the pillars. That scent—sharp and sour—stabbed at my nose again. Rust. Rust bleeding from the dome's inner walls into the water. The entire world was a metal shell trying to pretend it was something else. The rust was its real smell. The machine-hum was its real voice.

I blinked and the towers across the water wavered—not collapsing, not obvious—but bending for a fraction of a second, like heat rising off metal. Their reflective panels rippled with the faintest horizontal distortion, as if the simulation was stitching an entire building's surface back together in one breath.

My heartbeat hammered against my ribs. This wasn't a malfunctioning distant system. This wasn't a training exercise. I had been maintaining *this*.

The air tasted wrong. Charged. Artificial. My clothes felt strange on my skin, soft and bright, printed with shapes meant to be playful, cheerful—meant for a world where a child should run laughing in sunlight, not for someone trained to correct structural failures in a cage.

I kept walking because C-1—no, "mom"—kept walking. But every step felt like it landed on something false. The walkway trembled beneath my foot, a tiny stabilizing ripple spreading outward, just like the grid settling on my screen after a successful correction. The system adjusting to my weight.

A memory cracked open in my mind—nothing visual, just sensation. A hand brushing hair from my forehead. Warmth. A voice humming—a real voice, not the facility's mechanical hum. A lullaby. Soft. Human.

The walls of the dome seemed to close in and expand at the same time, like the entire world breathed around me. Everything I had done in the Continuity Engine—all the tasks that felt so instinctive—were the same tasks holding this illusion together.

My voice came out as a whisper I barely heard.

"This place… it's not real."

And the truth settled inside me with crushing clarity:

I hadn't escaped anything.

I had walked straight into the heart of the machine I'd been helping maintain.

"It's real to them," C-1 responded.

My head snapped up toward her, heart slamming against my ribs. I had forgotten she could hear me when I whispered, forgotten that nothing I muttered under my breath belonged only to me. Her eyes didn't soften, didn't warn—they simply held mine with a quiet finality, a message beneath the words: *Do not say that again.*

But before I could respond, a hand clamped down on my shoulder. Hard.

I froze. My body jolted backward as someone yanked me around with enough force to spin the world sideways. The walkway blurred, the rushing river flashed in my peripheral vision, and then suddenly I was face-to-face with a stranger.

A tall man loomed over me, his chest heaving, his jaw clenched so tight I could hear his teeth grind. His eyes—wide, bright, trembling with some emotion I couldn't decipher— locked onto mine like he was searching for something inside me. He leaned in close enough that I could see the uneven rise of his breath.

Fear. No—not fear. Something sharper. Wilder. Excitement, sparking in the depths of his gaze like a match about to catch.

But he wasn't smiling. He wasn't threatening me. He wasn't frantic.

He was… *fascinated.*

He stared so intensely that I forgot to breathe. His hand didn't loosen, but it didn't tighten either. It held me like he was afraid I would vanish if he let go.

"Grace?" He said, voice shaking.

C-1 stepped forward instantly, her tone shifting into something warm and placating, her voice wrapping around us like a practiced blanket. "Sir, please—you're startling my daughter—"

But he didn't look at her. Not even for a second.

His attention stayed locked on me, pinned to me, like I was the only real thing in his world.

And the strangest part—the part that made something cold unfurl slowly in my stomach—was that I wasn't afraid of him. Not at all. I felt like I should have been. His grip was strong, his eyes wild, and his presence intense. But something inside me stayed steady.

Almost… curious.

"I'm so sorry," the man said, his voice trembling as though the apology had been held tight behind his ribs for years. His hand slipped from my shoulder slowly, almost unwillingly, and when he looked at me, the expression in his eyes shifted into something so raw it made the world tilt. It wasn't fear. It wasn't confusion. It was recognition—deep, instinctive, and overwhelming. "She looks like someone… someone I knew."

The words hit me with unexpected force. A tight pull formed deep in my chest, like a thread I didn't know existed had been yanked hard enough to vibrate through my bones. There was grief behind his voice—old grief, not sharp but hollow and unfinished—and it didn't feel separate from me. It felt shared, like I was brushing against the outline of a loss I should have remembered but couldn't. His eyes searched my face with a desperate familiarity, not the kind you give a stranger but the kind you give someone you once woke up hoping to see. Something in that look pushed against the walls inside my mind, trying to pry them open.

A memory flickered—dim, small, and buried. A pair of strong hands lifting me with an ease that made me feel weightless. A low, quiet laugh, the kind meant only for me. The warmth of someone holding me close, steadying me when I wobbled. A soft humming, not mechanical, but human— gentle, familiar, a melody meant to soothe. And threaded through all of it was my name. My real name. Spoken with love. Spoken like it belonged to me long before the number ever did.

The image was blurred, a handful of faint sensations trying to break through a fog that tightened the more I reached for it. But the feeling of it—the comfort, the safety, the belonging— washed through me with startling clarity.

C-1 stepped in abruptly, slicing the moment apart. "That's fine," she said sharply, her tone losing all its softness. "We will be on our way." She seized my hand and pulled me back with more force than necessary, turning me away from the man even as my mind strained toward him. Her grip was tight, urgent, the grip of someone terrified I might slip out of her control if she loosened her fingers even slightly.

I tried to move with her, but something inside me refused to let go. I turned just enough to look back over my shoulder. He hadn't moved. He stood frozen, chest rising unevenly, eyes wide and devastated in a way that made the world look suddenly too bright around him. His expression wasn't curiosity or confusion—it was heartbreak, pure and open, as if he were watching something stolen from him appear again only to be pulled away. His lips moved, barely shaping a sound, but I didn't need to hear it to understand what he said.

Grace.

My name. The real one. Not C-349. Not the number they forced onto me to smother everything I'd been. This man had spoken that name long before the facility buried it. Long before my memories were sliced apart. He had known me. Really known me. And the truth of that recognition hit me so fiercely my knees nearly buckled.

C-1's grip tightened, her voice low and sharp in my ear. "Look forward dear, not at him."

But the damage was already done. She wasn't trying to protect me from him. She was trying to keep his story from me.

Because something inside the carefully constructed silence of my life had just cracked open—and whatever lived beneath it was finally coming back.

* * *

The trip back was mostly silent. The deeper we went into the facility, the heavier the air felt—not colder, just denser, as if the weight of everything I'd seen pressed against my skin. The walkway opened into the docking platform, and the machine that had brought us there waited—its surface humming faintly with the same low vibration I'd felt under the world above. C-1 guided me toward it with a gentle hand at my back.

I stepped inside, lowering myself onto the narrow bench as the door slid shut with a soft hiss. The hum deepened beneath my feet. The same machine. The same path. But everything felt different now. As the lights inside flickered to life and the vehicle began its descent, I gripped the edge of the seat, trying to make sense of the ache building behind my ribs.

"Did I know that man?" I asked. The words pushed out of me before I even turned to look at C-1. My voice sounded sharper than I expected, steadier than I felt. She paused mid-motion, her hand hovering above the console before slowly lowering. When she faced me, there was a softness in her expression that didn't match the tension coiling in my chest.

She held my gaze for a moment, her eyes searching mine as though choosing her answer with delicate care. Then she inhaled sharply, almost like she had forgotten I would ever ask. "Yes." The word cracked something inside me wide open—relief, fear, hope, all tangled together. I leaned closer, desperate for more. For once, I needed her to speak without hesitation.

"His name is C-2," she said, and the number landed wrong in my ears, twisting the relief into something uneasy. "He's an asset."

I tried to keep my face still, but something in me recoiled. "An asset?"

C-1 nodded gently, almost warmly. "He's different than most assets, I suppose… but yes. That's what he is." She spoke the term with a reverence that made me uneasy, as if being an 'asset' was not a sentence but an honor.

"What's an asset?" I asked, not caring how naive it sounded. The question felt pulled from somewhere deep, urgent and necessary.

Her smile was small and serene in a way that made the hum of the machine feel suddenly louder. "Well… it's you and I. Everyone, really." She folded her hands lightly in her lap as the vehicle continued downward, her voice shifting into a soft, almost musical cadence. "We are made with a specific purpose. Each of us. We're grown here in the Nursery until our thoughts are fully formed, until our minds are mature enough to understand our roles." Her tone warmed further, lifted by a kind of reverence that reminded me of a prayer. "And then, when we are ready… we are harvested to reach our full potential. It's beautiful. Truly, it is."

She kept talking, her voice steady with unshakable conviction. "We are cultivated with intention. Designed with care. Guided every day toward the purpose the Steward set for us long before we could understand it. To be harvested is to become what you were always meant to be." She said it with such peaceful certainty that for a moment I almost wondered if I was the one who didn't understand.

"You have seen C-2 many times," C-1 continued, her voice settling into that gentle, instructive cadence she used when she believed she was revealing something important. "You didn't realize it, of course, not then. But you've watched him over and over, correcting small disturbances around him—guiding his attention away from details he wasn't meant to notice, ensuring that anything inconsistent in his environment was sent directly to the Cognitive Directive Station." She spoke with a quiet pride, as if this was something beautiful, something orderly. Something right. "You reported corrections for all of them."

"That will be your new role," she said. "Every inconsistency you flagged during your work in the Continuity Engine— every drift, every dip, every misaligned loop—you sent to the Cognitive Directive station ever so diligently without understanding what happened next." She leaned slightly closer, lowering her voice with almost reverent excitement. "Now, you will be the receiver on the other end of that system. The one who corrects not just the world… but the people living within it."

Her eyes warmed as if she were describing a promotion. "The Nursery, as you've seen, is vast. Magnificent. But it is not perfect. It produces inconsistencies just as any great creation does. You sensed them immediately—that is one of the gifts you were grown with. And we are in the process of eliminating those inconsistencies forever, especially the inconsistencies found in our harvested assets who remain within the facility."

She paused, letting the weight of the words settle before continuing with soft, almost ceremonial clarity. "You see, some harvested assets are not meant to leave the Nursery. Their purpose is to live here, within the facility, where they provide stability and compliance from the inside. They are essential. They anchor the environment. They model proper responses." Her brows lifted slightly, as though she were sharing a precious secret.

"When an inconsistency is reported—either from the Continuity Engine or from the Surveillance Dock—it arrives in the Cognitive Directive Station. And there, your task is to weave that correction into the daily pill sequence administered to each asset in the nursery, the ones who have yet to be harvested." She spoke the words gently, lovingly, as though describing a blessing rather than a violation. "Each dose carries the programming necessary to erase the inconsistency from their thoughts. So they will remain calm. Certain. Unconfused."

Her smile was small and serene, her tone full of admiration for the system she worshiped. "You will be the mind behind that clarity. You will be the one who safeguards their purpose. It is an honor, 349. A privilege. And soon... you will understand the beauty of it."

My hands wouldn't stop shaking. Every new truth scraped against the last one before it had a chance to settle. The dome. The glitches. The man who knew my name. And now this— harvest. The word cut through the fog like a blade.

<h1 style="text-align:center">17</h1>

Cognitive Directive Station

I wasn't ready to work. I wasn't ready to breathe. But the doors opened anyway, and the rhythm of the work stations swallowed me again, pretending nothing had changed.

There were fewer people in the Cognitive Directive Station. Far fewer. But the silence wasn't empty—it felt deliberate, as if everyone here understood their place in a rhythm I couldn't hear yet. The room itself wasn't large, but stepping into it felt like crossing some invisible threshold. Without meaning to, I slowed down.

The consoles were arranged in several quiet rows, each one glowing with muted, shifting color. Only twenty or thirty people worked here, but the air carried a strange density, as though their presence filled more space than their bodies did. At first glance, they seemed so different from the docile recruits I had seen before—these people looked driven, almost passionate, leaning into their work with a kind of purposeful intensity. Their faces were animated, brows furrowed in concentration, lips curled in faint half-smiles of satisfaction. It *looked* like emotion. It looked like pride.

But the longer I watched, the more something inside me tugged in confusion. Their expressions moved the way expressions should, but something underneath was missing—like a person speaking a language they had memorized phonetically but did not understand. Their smiles appeared at all the right moments, yet they never softened their eyes. Their focus was sharp, held with a tension that never wavered, never slipped. Their satisfaction appeared and disappeared with machine-like precision, lacking the subtle glow of feeling that I had only recently begun to recognize in myself.

They acted like people with purpose. They did not *feel* like people with purpose.

And they were older. Truly older. Some had deep-set wrinkles, sagging skin beneath their eyes, faces worn from years of tasks I had never been allowed to know existed. Others looked like older versions of the young assets I had worked beside—bigger than me, stronger, more developed— but their movements carried the same eerie smoothness. Time had changed their bodies, but not whatever lay beneath.

Their hands glided across their consoles in swift, confident motions, each gesture precise and rehearsed. I should have felt inspired watching them, but something in their sameness unsettled me. Their devotion was visible in every movement... but the devotion was all shape, no soul. It looked rehearsed, like ritual.

Was this what C-1 meant by purpose?

A calling that filled the room, but not the people?

The Steward.

My mind snagged on the word again, heavier now. If C-1

wasn't the top—if all these people were serving something higher—then how high did the hierarchy go? How many layers of unseen authority existed above us, and how much of ourselves were we expected to surrender to it?

A nearby worker completed a sequence and exhaled sharply, smiling with what should have been triumph. But the moment lingered perfectly. The smile felt like it belonged to the task, not the person. Another worker lifted their chin with a kind of satisfied pride, but their eyes remained flat, unchanged.

They looked fulfilled.

But nothing about them felt alive.

Standing beside them, I felt something twist inside me. Not fear—recognition. This was what I might become. This was the shape my life could take. A perfect performance of emotion without the warm, unpredictable pulse of actually having any.

Purpose. Calling. The Steward.

All of it pressed around me like a warning I wasn't meant to hear. And for the first time, I wondered not just who the Steward was... but what they had taken from everyone in this room to make them this way.

But a few of them were different... Their eyes moved the way mine had started to move: searching, observing, lingering on things they weren't supposed to notice. Their brows tightened at moments no one else reacted to. Their shoulders stiffened when a machine hummed too long. They seemed to think independently, quietly, carefully, as though every thought had to be weighed against the danger of being seen. And the fear was there. I could feel it in the way they held their posture just a little too rigid, the way they blinked slowly, the way they watched the watchers out of the corners of their eyes.

They had probably seen assets killed like I had. Maybe more. They had been here longer—long enough to know exactly what happened to people who slipped.

I kept typing, the familiar sequences sliding across my screen, but this time there was one new element blinking quietly in the corner—the suggested memory corrections. I recognized the inconsistencies listed there, the same ones I had flagged in the Continuity Engine. But now they didn't just disappear into the system like they always had. Here, I was taking them and threading them into a new sequence, weaving them into a formula the console called *DD-Sequence Integration*. Nothing in the interface said what it really was. No label. No warning. No mention of pills or doses. Just numbers and patterns and commands identical to every other task I'd ever done. If C-1 hadn't told me I was programming medication, I never would have known.

Seeing the inconsistencies from this side of the system made my stomach twist. For years, I had only ever reported them— sent them down the chain without knowing what happened next. I had never realized that the corrections weren't just for the environment. They were meant to alter what the assets *saw*, what they thought, what they remembered. And yet the code itself didn't reveal any of that. There was nothing in the commands that hinted at reshaping minds. Nothing that looked different enough to warn me of what I was altering. It was the same language, the same symbols, the same pulses I'd spent four years memorizing.

Which only made C-1's choice even more confusing. Why show me the dome? Why let me see their world glitch around them? Why reveal the truth when the work itself didn't depend on me knowing it? Any of the people here could have done this without ever stepping outside.

Did they know?

I glanced down the rows, watching the subtle intensity in the others' faces as they worked. Their expressions were focused but calm, almost reverent, as though what they were doing made sense to them in a way it didn't to me. They didn't look shocked. They didn't look newly initiated. They looked… practiced.

Of course they knew. They must have all been taken there at some point, shown the same things I had been shown, introduced to the truth that the Nursery wasn't just a place—it was a world pretending to be one.

I wasn't special for being taken. I wasn't chosen. I wasn't unique.

I kept typing, the sequences falling into place like they always had, but now the question pressed harder against my ribs:

If everyone else already understood their purpose, then why had C-1 thought *I* needed to see the truth today? The question pressed at the back of my mind, tightening with a slow, steady pressure. And why did it feel like seeing the outside—seeing the dome, the glitches, the people—had stirred something inside me that wasn't meant to wake at all?

I glanced around the room, letting my eyes drift naturally, as if simply stretching my neck. A watcher stood across the aisle, its face angled down at its slate. When I shifted, it lifted its head with that uncanny precision I had come to recognize, its gaze locking onto mine. For a moment, neither of us moved. Then, without breaking eye contact, it lowered its pen and drew a single slow mark across the page—deliberate, cold, permanent. The kind of notation that made my stomach pull tight.

I forced myself to look away, pretending I hadn't seen it, and that was when a different kind of recognition caught my attention. A face. Familiar.

297.

Of course—C-1 had told me he would be assigned here. He was about two rows away, posture perfectly aligned, expression neutral and obedient. But the moment our eyes met, something subtle shifted in his face. He didn't break character—didn't dare—but a faint smile tugged carefully at the corner of his mouth, a restrained, quiet signal meant only for me. A tiny acknowledgment: I'm here. I see you. I remember.

He lifted his hand as if to wave, but stopped halfway, letting it drift naturally into a movement that could be mistaken for adjusting his notebook. The effort he put into seeming invisible made a surprising warmth rise in my chest.

He wasn't a friend. He wasn't someone I trusted.

But he was familiar in a place where everything else felt dangerous and new—and somehow, that familiarity felt like the first real piece of steadiness I'd had all day.

I shifted my gaze back to my screen and tried to focus on the code, letting the familiar patterns steady me. But then I felt it—the slightest shift from the person seated to my left. A change in posture, a pause in their movement, the weight of someone's eyes on me before I even turned. When I finally glanced over, I offered a small, tentative smile. Their expression tightened with a flicker of confusion. Someone like me didn't usually end up working here.

I swallowed and managed a soft, nervous, "Hi."

The asset beside me was older—**not old**, but carrying

enough experience that they felt two or even three times older than me in a way that had nothing to do with years. Their station read **87**, and for a moment she simply stared, eyes widening with a surprise that felt deeper than the surface reaction. As if she wasn't shocked that I spoke, but shocked that someone like *me* had the courage to.

Then her attention snapped back to her screen, her posture tightening with quick, practiced caution. Her gaze flicked toward the watchers, scanning their positions with instinctive precision—like someone who had seen exactly what happened when an asset spoke at the wrong time, or said the wrong thing.

No watchers were looking.

Across the row, I didn't need 297 to turn his head to know he'd noticed what was happening. I could feel his awareness, steady and quiet, like he was silently urging me to keep going. Letting me know it was okay.

87's shoulders relaxed by degrees, the tension draining from her posture once she was confident the room's attention wasn't on us. When she turned back toward me, her expression had changed—softened into something unexpectedly warm. Almost protective.

She leaned in just enough for her words to carry only to me. "Meet me in the far corner of the room at the end of the night."

The message wasn't loud. But the meaning behind it was. A secret. An understanding that whatever she knew was something I needed to hear.

As we walked back toward the rows of beds, our movements falling into the same controlled pattern as everyone else, my thoughts wouldn't let go of 87. The way she had looked at me. The gentleness tucked inside her caution. The strange, almost familiar warmth in her voice. Something about her felt different from the rest of the assets—like she had been carrying answers for a long time and had finally decided someone else might be ready to hear them. I kept replaying her face in my mind, wondering if she knew I didn't fit neatly into the shape they'd built for me. Or if she was like me, seeing things she wasn't supposed to see, noticing the edges of the world bending when no one else looked closely enough.

When we reached the beds, the soft glow beneath the mattresses cast pale halos across the floor, illuminating everything in gentle, controlled stillness. Assets settled into their rows with practiced precision, and watchers lined the walls like immovable pillars of quiet authority. As I adjusted my blanket, trying to look as ordinary as possible, a small motion caught my eye. A gesture in the corner—87.

She was standing there with a small cluster of others gathered around her—27, 115, and 197. Her eyes locked onto mine instantly, and she gave a small, tilt of her hand. An invitation. Quiet. Careful. Meant for me alone.

I hesitated only a moment before slipping away from my row, weaving through the soft glow beneath the beds until I reached them. They all turned toward me, their eyes sharper, more awake than the others in the room.

"You came," 87 whispered, her voice low but carrying a strange warmth, like she had been hoping I would.

I nodded, uncertain.

27 leaned forward slightly, studying me with a tired, searching gaze. "You're the new one who notices things," he murmured. "The way your eyes move... it's different. You see the slips, don't you?"

My pulse jumped. "Sometimes."

87 watched me carefully, reading the tension in my voice. "You don't have to tell us what you've seen," she said softly. "Not yet. We know it's dangerous. We know what happens when someone talks too much." Her eyes flicked briefly toward a watcher before returning to me. "But we wanted you to know... you're not the only one."

A lump formed in my throat. "Not the only one... what?"

This time, it was 27 who answered. His voice was shaky, worn down at the edges. "Our memories. They're starting to come back."

115 nodded tightly. "Not all at once. Just pieces. But enough to know something's wrong with this place."

I stared at them, unable to look away.

27 rubbed a hand across his face as if trying to hold the memories steady. "I remember a kitchen. A real one. With chipped tiles and a smell I can't quite name."

115 swallowed hard. "I remember a voice. A little girl calling for me. I don't know her name. But I know she mattered."

197 shifted timidly, barely looking up. "I remember... sky," he whispered. "A real sky."

Their voices were soft but fierce with the weight of truth.

87 stepped a little closer, her gaze gentle but intense. "We weren't born here," she said. "We lived somewhere else. We had people. Families. Lives."

I felt my breath grow shallow, the room around me dimming at the edges.

"We're planning something," 115 said quietly. "Something that might get us out of this place."

"And we thought..." 87 added, searching my face, "if you see the cracks the way we do, then maybe you're meant to be part of it."

Four pairs of eyes watched me—hopeful, cautious, trusting me far more than I trusted myself.

They didn't know anything about what had happened to me today.

They only knew one thing: I saw the cracks too.

I looked at 297, and he quickly looked away.

18

Erased

The next day, I sat at my console pretending to focus on the familiar patterns drifting across my screen. The work felt hollow now, a rhythm my hands still followed even though my mind was somewhere else entirely. I could feel 297 watching me from across the room—standing perfectly still in his pressed watcher uniform, eyes sweeping the floor with structured precision. Watchers didn't stare, they scanned. And he was careful to make it look like that was all he was doing. But every so often, when his gaze skimmed past my row, I felt the attention sharpen, lingering for half a second longer than it should have. It was enough to raise the hairs along my arms. Enough to tell me he was waiting for the right moment.

When he finally stepped away from his position, he did it the way watchers always did— steady, and paced. He paused here and there, correcting posture, adjusting consoles, making quiet notations on his slate. Nothing unusual. Nothing suspicious. Yet with each checkpoint, he moved closer to me, the pressure building so slowly that no one else would notice. But I noticed. I felt the tension like a thread pulling tighter with every footstep.

He approached my row without even glancing at me, maintaining the exact expressionless mask that watchers were expected to wear. I forced myself to keep typing, fingers steady on the keys, eyes locked on my screen as if the memory-correction patterns had consumed every bit of my focus. When he passed behind me, he didn't break stride. He didn't speak. But as the hem of his coat brushed the side of my chair, his hand drifted just far enough that something slipped into the shadow of my palm—quick, controlled, invisible to anyone who wasn't watching for it.

A note.

The weight of it alone nearly made me flinch. I kept my hand still, fingers curled naturally around the tiny folded square as if nothing had changed. It took everything in my body to keep my face blank. I waited a few breaths—long enough for him to move on, long enough for the watchers to return their attention to the room. Only then did I slide the note underneath my console screen, shielding it with my arms as if stabilizing a panel. I unfolded it with the smallest movements possible.

It wasn't words. It was code. Not system commands I recognized. The characters were arranged in a pattern I didn't understand—shapes and sequences that made something in the back of my mind tighten, like I was staring at a language I should know but didn't. It wasn't random, though. The structure was intentional. A doorway disguised as a correction sequence. A signature. A key.

I should have ignored it. Should have taken the paper

straight to C-1. Should have reported the violation instantly. But instead, as if pulled by a thread woven into my bones, I typed the sequence into my console with careful, quiet precision.

The screen flickered.

Once, then again.

A third time, the light rippling across the display like a breath sucked in sharply. And then the interface dissolved into a completely different system. One I had never seen. One I wasn't meant to see.

A list appeared. A long, vertical column of names, each one paired with an asset designation. Names. Real names.

C-1 — Andrea Reddick

C-2 — Owen Hale

C-3 — [FILE DELETED]

I stared at the second entry so long my vision blurred. Owen. The man who had grabbed me. The man who had said my name like it was something precious. The man who had known me.

I scrolled further, the list growing longer and longer— hundreds of names I didn't recognize, each followed by a code.

C-27 — Nolan Mercer

C-87 — Mara Trent

C-115 — Levi Cross

C-197 — Rowan Calder

Names. All different. All belonging to someone who had once existed before the Nursery decided they were an asset. Each one felt like a small truth torn out of the dark and forced into the light. My eyes drifted farther down the list almost without my permission, searching for someone—anyone—I recognized. And then I reached the line I didn't realize I had been looking for.

C-201 —[FILE DELETED]

The breath left my lungs in a sharp, soundless punch. Just gone. Erased so cleanly it was as if he had never existed at all. They hadn't only killed him—they had stripped him from the system, from the records, from the memory of the place that had taken everything from him.

For a moment I couldn't move. My fingers hovered above the keys, trembling despite every effort to steady them. The screen blurred as something hot stung behind my eyes, a slow ache unfurling beneath my ribs. 201 hadn't been my friend. He hadn't even spoken to me more than a handful of times. But he had mattered. He had *been*. And now the system was pretending he hadn't.

I swallowed hard and forced myself to scroll again, even though every part of me wanted to look away. I dragged the list downward, and then—finally—I found it.

C-349.

My designation.

Beside it was the name I had heard from a man's shaking voice. The name whispered like a memory trying to claw its way back.

Grace. Grace Hale.

I felt the room tilt around me. The hum of the consoles, the controlled breathing of the assets, the watchers along the walls—everything seemed to bend and distort like the world was flickering again.

I clicked the name before I could talk myself out of it. The screen shifted, the list of names dissolving into static for half a breath before a video window opened—grainy, dim, the kind of recording that shouldn't exist but somehow did. A girl sat strapped into a white chair, her wrists bound against the smooth armrests, her legs trembling in small, frantic movements she couldn't control. Something thin and metallic pressed into the back of her skull—tapping, adjusting, settling like a cold fingertip finding a pulse.

Then she made a sound. A soft, broken cry. Barely anything. But it cut through me so sharply my entire body went rigid. Because it wasn't just a sound—it was a memory. A piece of something she had lost, left behind, buried so deeply the facility thought I would never find it again.

The girl whimpered again, and everything inside me lurched.

I knew that sound.

I had made that sound.

It hit me all at once—so fast it felt like the ground vanished beneath me and I was plummeting through my own mind. Memories I'd never asked for tore upward, sharp and frantic. The cold bite of the chair under my legs. The stab of pressure at the base of my skull. Fingers forcing my head forward. A voice, low and steady, telling me to hold still. The tremor in my breath when I realized I couldn't.

I wasn't watching someone else.

I was watching *me*. The memory didn't just flicker—it surged, first a blur, then snapping into brutal, perfect clarity, as if I had been dropped back inside my own body.

* * *

Today is Thomas's birthday, and I keep bouncing even though Mom tells me to "use my walking feet," but it's hard because today feels special. Our apartment feels special too. It always does. It's big—bigger than anyone else believes when I tell them. Mom says it's "not big at all," but she's wrong. To me it goes on forever. My toys are everywhere, hiding in all the corners. I like it that way. It feels like the toys get to play too.

The window is my favorite part. It's huge. I can stand on the couch and press my hands to the glass and look out at everything—the cars, the buildings, the people walking fast like they're late for something. But the best thing is the park. My park. It's right across the street, and I can see the tops of the play structures and the bright colors even when I'm inside. Sometimes I wave at it, just in case it can wave back.

Mom is moving around the kitchen, humming a birthday song even though she says she's not humming anything. She keeps fixing the plates and then fixing them again and keeps checking the time, pretending she's not excited. I like when she's happy like this. The whole apartment feels warm when she is.

Thomas keeps calling Dad. He wants to make sure Dad is really coming home at five-thirty. He asks the same question every time Dad answers, and Dad always laughs and says yes, yes, yes, he'll be there. I don't mind Thomas asking. I like hearing Dad's voice come through the phone.

Dad always makes everything fun. When he comes home he always plays with me, even when Mom says he's tired. I can always tell when he's close because I hear his keys in the hallway before he even opens the door.

I look around our big apartment again—my toys, the couch, the window with the whole world outside it—and I hug my stuffy and smile.

I love it here.

I love this whole place.

And I love when we all get to be here together.

It's getting close to the time when Dad should be home, and I'm already waiting on the couch with my knees tucked under me. Then Mom's phone buzzes, and she grabs it quick, like she's been waiting for it. I lean over, even though she tells me not to do that, because I can feel something is different.

Dad sent a message. Mom reads it out loud, but she says it slowly and carefully. Something about a meeting he didn't know about. Something about his boss, Curtis, making him stay. Something about maybe being late. I don't really know what a meeting is or why it's more important than a birthday, but I can tell Mom doesn't like this message. She presses her lips together the way she does when she's thinking fast.

I know Curtis is Dad's boss, and that's all I really know. Dad never smiles when he talks about him. He just gets this tired look in his eyes, like he's pretending everything is fine even when it isn't. Sometimes Mom makes a face when his name comes up, a face she thinks I don't see. I don't know exactly what it means, but it doesn't make me feel cozy inside like other grown-up faces do.

Mom types back fast and asks if we should just come pick him up. I like that idea. I love going in the car at night and seeing all the bright lights out the window. But then her phone makes a strange noise—one that means Dad didn't get her message at all. Something about "do not disturb."

Mom keeps checking the time like she's waiting for it to behave differently.

Still no message from Dad.

I slide closer to Mom, just enough so my shoulder touches her arm. She doesn't look at me, but she leans back into me just a tiny bit, and that makes me feel a little better.

I look toward the door again, waiting for the sound of Dad's keys jingling.

Nothing yet.

Thomas keeps walking around by the window, back and forth, back and forth, like he's trying to wear a line into the floor. He does that when he's frustrated, and Mom keeps telling him to "give it a rest," but he just keeps going. They're sort of arguing without really arguing.

Mom keeps checking her phone, then the clock, then her phone again. I don't know exactly what the numbers mean, but I can tell they're not the ones she wants, because her mouth gets tighter every time she looks. The sky outside is turning orangey, and that usually means Dad is almost home.

Finally, Mom sighs and says, "Okay… that's it. We're going to get Dad ourselves."

I feel a little spark in my stomach, the good kind, because I love when we pick Dad up from work. He always gets this surprised smile, like he didn't expect us. Mom grabs her keys and her bag, tells Thomas to get his shoes, and then she scoops me up instead of letting me walk.

I don't mind. The hallway always slows us down. I like touching the walls and peeking over the rail and asking if we can drop things—but Mom says we definitely can't do that again after what happened with that really really old guy. Dad laughed a tiny bit about it later, but Mom didn't think it was funny at all.

As Mom carries me, I rest my chin on her shoulder. The building smells like dinosaurs and dust, and the lights buzz a little overhead. Thomas clomps behind us, still annoyed, but at least he's moving now.

We're going to get Dad.

And even though Mom looks worried and Thomas looks irritated, something inside me feels warm and happy, because picking up Dad means the fun can finally start.

Thomas talks the whole drive, and his voice fills the car like it's bouncing around everywhere at once. He keeps saying dinosaur things, lots of them, and he talks so fast it makes my head feel full. I'm holding Rabbit and I'm crying, and I don't even know exactly why except that everything feels heavy and bright and too much all at the same time. I try to tell Mom something, but the words won't come out right—they just melt into a wobbly sound—and Mom says, "Grace, I can't hear you," and after that I don't hear anything she says anymore. Everything just mushes together: Thomas talking and the car humming and my breath going in and out all messy. My face feels hot and sticky, and rubbing my eyes makes them hurt more, and even Rabbit doesn't help the way he usually does.

Then Mom starts singing. I don't know when she started; it just shows up like a soft sound floating over all the loud ones. Her voice makes everything feel a little farther away, like the noises shrink back and the car gets quieter even though nothing really changed. I don't try to stop crying, but it starts slowing down on its own, getting smaller and softer as the song keeps going. The lights from outside blink through the window in warm colors, and Rabbit feels cooler against my cheek now. My eyes blink slower and slower, and Mom's voice feels like it's wrapping around me, warm and gentle, until my eyes finally stay closed.

I'm sleeping when everything in the world suddenly jumps. Thomas yells "MOM!" so loud it feels like it smashes right into me, and before I even open my eyes the car throws me sideways and my stomach feels like it flips upside down. There's this huge, horrible noise next to us, like a giant metal monster is roaring right by my window, and the whole car shakes so hard my teeth feel funny. I don't know what's happening, I just know it's too loud and too fast and too scary, and I scream because my body won't let me do anything else.

Mom is breathing hard and the wheel is moving everywhere and my straps are pulling tight against my shoulders, and for a second I think the whole car is going to fall over. Rabbit slips out of my hands, but I can't reach for him because I'm busy holding onto the seat and trying to make the world stop spinning. Thomas is making a tiny squeaking sound, like he's trying to talk but can't. Everything is so bright and loud that it feels like all the colors and sounds are hitting me at the same time.

Now the car is still. The noise disappears, like someone turned it off. My heart is beating so fast it feels like it's shaking inside my chest, and I can't catch my breath right. Mom twists around and looks at us with her eyes wide and shiny, and I can tell she's scared even though she tries to make her face calm. Thomas doesn't talk at all, which means he's scared too. I don't look out the window. I don't want to see anything out there. I just want Rabbit back in my hands.

Mom gets out, and I hear voices outside but I don't know what they're saying. The grown-up man sounds worried.

When Mom comes back, she closes the door hard and the whole car bumps. Her hands shake a little when she grabs the wheel, and she blows out a big breath like she's trying to push something heavy away. Thomas is quiet, which never happens, and I hold Rabbit and keep my eyes straight ahead because I don't want anything scary to sneak up again.

We drive slower now. Nobody talks.

When we park, I'm holding Rabbit and looking around for Dad when someone calls Mom's name. It's a man's voice, older and scratchy, not Dad, but Mom seems to know him. I think it's dads boss, Curtis. He says something about a mix-up and about "Tommy," and Thomas twitches beside me because he hates that name, but I don't understand what they're talking about at all. Their words feel big and floaty, like grown-up talk always does.

Mom asks him something about his family, and I try to see the man through the window, but he's just a blurry shape outside the car. Before he can answer, something sharp pokes my shoulder—quick and mean, like a sting that isn't from a bug. My whole body gets floaty right away, like the car suddenly turned into water and I'm sinking inside it.

The colors start getting fuzzy, and little black dots show up everywhere, jumping around in front of my eyes. I hear Thomas make a scared noise, and when I turn my head, strangers are pulling him out of his seat. The same happens to me—hands grab my arms, rough and tight, and I don't know who they are or why they're touching us. I try to hold onto Rabbit, but my fingers won't close anymore.

Everything keeps getting blurrier, and I can barely tell what's real. Someone pokes Thomas with something shiny. I see Mom's face in the mirror—her mouth open like she's screaming, but no sound comes out at all. I try to scream, but my voice won't work, and the whole world tilts and darkens like someone is turning the lights off inside my head.

I hear the older man again, his voice low and far away, saying something I don't understand. Then everything goes black.

I woke up and everything was bright. It hurt my eyes. The

light felt like it was buzzing inside my head. I blinked a bunch of times because I thought maybe it would get darker if I did, but it didn't.

My mom was sitting in a chair right in front of me. She wasn't awake. Her mouth was open a little like when she sleeps on the couch. But that wasn't the scary part. The scary part was the man behind her. He had big gloves on and a silver tool in his hand, and he was cutting off all her hair. Not just a little—every single piece. Big chunks landed on the floor like when Thomas cuts paper snowflakes. It made it look like she wasn't my mom anymore.

I looked over and saw Thomas lying in the corner. He wasn't moving. Not even a tiny bit. His hair was already gone, and without it he looked pale and still. He looked like when he got really sick once and didn't want to play dinosaurs. I tried to say "Thomas?" but it came out a tiny squeak. My throat felt tight. My tummy hurt. I started crying and I couldn't stop.

The man cutting Mom's hair turned and stared at me. He didn't say anything. He just put his finger over his mouth like he wanted me to be quiet. But I couldn't be quiet. My crying kept coming out louder because I was too scared to make it go away.

A different man walked over and lifted my mom like she was a doll. Her arms dangled and her head flopped and I didn't like it. Another man picked up Thomas, and then someone grabbed me. His arms were scratchy and cold, and he held me tight. I kicked but he didn't care.

They carried us into another room that was all white—white floor, white walls, white ceiling—so bright it hurt my eyes again. For a second I thought maybe we were at the dentist, because the dentist place is bright too. But I just went there last week or maybe the week before, and dentists don't cut off your hair or carry you like that. So it wasn't the dentist.

They dropped my mom on the ground, not soft at all, and it made my stomach feel twisty. They put Thomas in a chair, and he was still asleep. One of the men—the one who didn't carry anybody—stood behind Thomas and grabbed two long metal things hanging from the black cords in the ceiling. He didn't talk to us or say what he was doing. He just pushed the metal things into Thomas's head.

Thomas didn't wake up, but his whole body jumped like someone shook him really hard. His legs kicked a little, and his shoulders moved funny. I didn't like it at all. My tummy hurt. I squeezed my eyes shut because I didn't want to see anything. The last time Thomas moved like that was when he fell down the stairs and everyone got scared and yelled his name. I didn't want to think about that again.

I heard a loud click, and then the man pulled the metal things away. I kept my eyes shut super tight because I didn't want to see Thomas's face or what the men did to him. I heard him make a tiny confused noise, like he didn't know where he was. But the men didn't call him Thomas. They didn't even look at him like he was a real person.

One of them called him a number, and then said "come with me into the next room. I will show you your station."

Then the men picked up my mommy again. She was waking up a little, her eyes opening just a tiny bit, and she tried to push their hands away, but her arms were slow and wiggly and didn't work right. That made my whole chest feel like it was falling. When my mommy gets scared, that means something really bad is happening. I started crying again, big loud cries I couldn't stop. My voice sounded crackly and broken. I wanted my rabbit so bad, but he wasn't here. I think the mean men took him. I squeezed my hands together tight because I didn't know what else to do.

I couldn't even hear my own crying anymore because my mommy started screaming. It was so loud it felt like it was buzzing inside my head. The men pushed her into a big chair and started tying her down her hands, her legs, and her tummy. Then they wrapped something around her head so she couldn't move it. She kept screaming even when the straps pulled tight.

One of the men grabbed the shiny metal things they used on Thomas. They still looked wet, and seeing that made my stomach feel sick. He got wipes and cleaned them off, and that made the whole room smell like the doctors. I wanted to yell for them to stop, but nothing came out of my mouth. Before I could say anything, the man poked the metal things into the sides of my mommy's head.

She screamed so loud I covered my ears, but it didn't make it quieter. Her whole body strained against the straps like she was trying to get away, but she couldn't. Her feet shook like they wanted to run. My chest felt hot because I was crying too hard to breathe right.

One of the men leaned over to fix something I couldn't see, and my mommy spit right in his face. It was a big spit, and it hit him on the cheek. He froze for a second, then his face got really mad. I squeaked "Don't!" but it sounded tiny and broken. Another man told him something quietly, and the mad one stepped back and walked over to a little box with switches. He flipped one.

My mom stopped screaming right away. Her mouth stayed open like she wanted to yell, but no sound came out. Her legs went still. Her arms didn't move.

Then her whole body sagged forward in the chair. Her hair was all gone, and her face didn't look like my mommy's face anymore. She didn't move. She didn't make any sounds. Not even tiny ones.

One of the men grabbed me under my arms and lifted me fast. I didn't even think I just bit him on the shoulder as hard as I could. He yelled and almost dropped me. His hands tightened, and he pushed me down into the chair.

I tried to wiggle away, but I couldn't. My feet kicked, but nothing happened. My eyes were blurry from crying, and I couldn't see the man walking behind me. I felt the straps pulling tight around my arms and my tummy. I could hear my heartbeat thumping in my ears.

Then I felt something pokey touch the back of my head, and I screamed for my mommy even though I knew she couldn't hear me anymore.

*　*　*

I blinked, and everything inside me locked into place with a clarity so sharp it almost hurt.

I was Grace, and I had been taken from my family.

The truth didn't rise slowly; it surged upward, fierce and undeniable, dragging pieces of my life with it came voices, hands, laughter, warmth—things they had buried, not erased. I scrolled through the list again, every line a stolen world, every name a life stripped of its shape. I wasn't looking for myself anymore. I was looking for him.

My brother.

Thomas.

My fingers flew down the column, trembling harder the further I went. C-47. C-118. C-173. Hundreds of stolen people, and somewhere among them, the one person I used to orbit my whole childhood around. And then—

C-297 — Thomas.

The rest of the room vanished. The hum of the machines, the flicker of the screens, the presence of the watchers—it all fell away as that single line carved itself into me. Thomas. My brother. My best friend. My constant. They had taken him. Changed him. They had turned his life into a label and expected the world to believe it was enough.

297.

My brother. But not the same brother I had known.

19

Inherited Access

297—Thomas—had known about the system hack for years. He knew I was his sister long before I ever figured it out, and everything he'd done suddenly made sense. That was why he wanted me to come with him here—into this part of the system. Not just to keep me close, but so I could keep digging. So I could continue what he had already started. He had known the truth the whole time, and he had been waiting for me to catch up.

I started digging deeper into files. At first it was clumsy—just me at my desk, pretending to code while the watchers rotated shifts, clicking through anything that wasn't sealed too deep. I watched old training clips, recycled safety modules, and saw links to old harvesting videos, so I clicked on one.

The first frame alone made my stomach hurt, and I shut it before it could play. I didn't want to see any more. I searched for my mom's name—I was sure it was Elisabeth—but all I found were blank entries, wiped records, and personnel lists stripped down to numbers. When I opened my own profile and tried to pull up the attached reports, even the most recent one—dated October 17th—refused to load. Every time I clicked, the file stuttered, flickered, then slammed shut like a door in my face.

The failures didn't stop me. The longer I sat there, the more I noticed patterns—tiny hesitations in the system's response time, loops in the interface, the way certain folders lingered a fraction of a second longer when the cursor passed over them. I started prodding those weak spots. A basic training file that opened quicker than expected. A mislabeled archive with a timestamp that didn't match its contents. A directory that blinked out of rhythm, like it was hiding something beneath the surface. The harvesting videos always played clean, always accessible, almost inviting. But everything connected to who we were before and the lives we'd lived, the memories we'd had—those files the system were heavily protected.

Hours slipped past without me noticing. The white hum of the room softened into a background blur, and the watchers barely glanced my way—just another worker absorbed in her tasks. I kept digging, sliding between windows, testing the same locked documents again and again to learn their patterns, following the smallest inconsistencies wherever they led. The names attached to those harvesting files stuck with me—real names, the only fragments of past lives the system hadn't sanitized into numbers. It wasn't enough to understand what happened to them… or to me. But it was enough to tell me the truth was buried deeper. And I was going to find it.

Weeks passed, and I got better. A lot better. I started recognizing the system's tells—the way a fake folder loaded quickly, the way a dead-end link looped with identical timing every single time, the way a directory meant to mislead always flickered on its right edge, never the left. It was like the Nursery had built layer after layer of trick doors, hoping no one would notice the hinges were all on the same side. Once I saw the patterns, I couldn't unsee them.

The deeper I got, the easier it became to lose myself in the rhythm of it. I was so locked into those patterns that everything else faded away. The room, the watchers, the endless hum of the coding floor—they all blurred into the background. Which is why I jumped when a soft voice broke through the silence beside me. "349… what are you doing?" 87 whispered, her tone trembling like she already suspected the answer and was terrified to be right.

My reflexes snapped before my thoughts caught up. I slammed the hidden window shut so fast the screen glitched, pulling up the meaningless code I was supposed to be focusing on. "Just programming a loop," I said, but the words were stiff and hollow, practically begging to be doubted.

87 leaned closer instead of back. "I saw what you had open," she murmured. "Those were names. Real names. For us." The way she said it—like it was sacred, like it might break if she was too loud—sent a cold rush down my spine.

"I think you misread something," I muttered, heat creeping up my neck. But she wasn't fooled.

"How did you access that?" she whispered.

I didn't answer. I couldn't tell her I'd been studying the system for weeks, mapping its weak points, memorizing the shape of the doorway that led to *her* file. Memorizing the name I found inside it.

She glanced toward the watchers—they had their backs turned for the moment—then back at me. Her voice barely existed. "Can you look up mine?" she asked. "I just want to know if… if I ever had one."

My mouth opened to tell her the truth—that I didn't have to look it up because I already knew—but before I could speak, she beat me to it.

"Mara?" she whispered. "Is that… is that me?"

I swallowed. "…Yes," I said softly. "Mara Trent. How did you know that?"

Her eyes grew wide with a mixture of shock and something dangerously close to hope. "I didn't know," she said, her voice breaking. "I just… felt like it might be."

And in the way she looked at me—like I'd handed her a missing piece of herself—I realized how many of us were starving for something more than a number.

"What other things have you found in there?" she asked, her voice barely above a breath.

"Nothing really so far," I said, and even to my own ears it sounded thin. Not a lie, but not the whole truth either.

She hesitated, chewing on her bottom lip like she was afraid of her own thoughts. "What if…" she paused, glancing around the room as if the walls might hear her, "…what if there's a way out mentioned in there?"

I froze. Not because the idea was impossible—because I had never allowed myself to even *think* it. I knew the route back into the Nursery, the narrow corridors and sealed doors that led deeper into the facility. I knew exactly where the "exit" was—the place C-1 brought me to, the place they made sure we believed was the whole world. But that wasn't out. That was just another layer of the cage. Further in, not free.

Her question dug into me, sharp and uncomfortable. Months ago, maybe even a few weeks ago, the idea would've terrified me. But now, knowing what they had stripped from us—names, families, entire lives—I felt something shift inside me. A tightness. A burn. The realization that even if I clawed my way back into the Nursery, even if I stood under its artificial sky again, I would never be free. Not while they controlled every thought, every movement, every memory.

The thought settled, sharp and undeniable. I wasn't going to comply.

"I'll find a way out," I whispered. The words tasted dangerous and electric, like something alive. It felt like a promise.

As the weeks went on, I dug deeper into the files, pushing past directories that used to slam shut the second I touched them. I wasn't just looking for information anymore—I was looking for shape. Structure. Blueprint. Anything that could tell me how the Nursery was built, what walls were real, what paths weren't just simulations of movement but actual corridors. Most maps were decoys. Layered illusions. But sometimes I caught glimpses of something underneath—partial diagrams, strange geometric layouts that didn't match the rooms I knew, blinking indicators I didn't understand. Each time I found a scrap of something that looked real, I saved it, memorized it, tried to piece it together like a puzzle with half the pieces missing.

I updated 87 whenever I could, speaking barely above a breath, our faces blank like we were talking about code. She never asked too many questions. She didn't have to. She understood the danger. She understood the scope of what I was trying to accomplish. Some days her eyes were brighter when she asked, "Anything new?" Some days she looked like she was afraid of hearing the answer. But she listened to every detail—the strange tunnels I'd found references to, the access logs that hinted at restricted wings, the files that mentioned maintenance intervals and external scans. She held onto every word like it was oxygen.

But no matter how hard I tried to focus on escape, I couldn't stop myself from looking deeper into C-2—into my father's file. I tried to tell myself it was just part of the search, another system thread to follow. But I knew better. I needed to know he was still there. That he still existed. As the files opened, I realized the surveillance wasn't just visual. It carried neural echoes—his dreams, his thoughts, his nightmares. I saw flashes of us trapped in impossible collisions, visions of us crashing in a terrible accident that had never happened. Images twisted by fear, not memory, yet the system recorded them as clearly as any camera. And once I found the first fragment of regular surveillance footage, I couldn't stop. There were clips from months ago—him walking, sleeping, talking—even moments where he looked up at what he thought was the sky. Then I found the current feed. A live stream. I could see what he saw in real time while also watching the dreams the system captured behind his eyes, updating every second. It made my chest ache in ways I didn't know how to name.

From there, things spiraled quickly. I found archived sensory logs, emotional-response graphs, and something else: the interface I could use to nudge harvested individuals. Not control them entirely—but influence small behaviors. A tilt of the head. An urge to turn left instead of right. A compulsion to pick up a piece of paper. It was subtle, but it worked. And it wasn't just people. Anything connected to the system was fair game. Birds. Squirrels. Stray dogs. The Nursery had turned every living thing into an extension of itself, every creature a screen that could be overwritten. Once I realized that, the possibilities became endless.

I learned I could implant messages into surfaces, too. The system rendered everything—the sky, the streets, even fabric—as layers of code. If I slipped a phrase into the right layer, I could make it appear on the paper in his hand, on the bark of a tree he passed, on a scrap of clothing blowing across the street. I could send him words. Signs. Little pieces of myself. And I did. Over and over. "I'm here." "I didn't leave you." "Find me." "Dad."

But every message vanished almost as soon as it appeared. The moment he saw one, the system pulled it apart, pixel by pixel, swallowing it like it had never existed. And the pills—they erased what lingered in his mind. I watched it happen in real time. His thoughts flickered across the feed, recognition sparking like a flame—then snuffed out. The memories fell away from him like ash.

He knew it was me. Not always. But sometimes. Enough times to matter. Enough times to hurt. Every time he noticed something that shouldn't be there—a message, an animal behaving strangely, a pattern in the sky—I saw confusion harden into hope. And then, moments later, collapse into empty silence as the drugs wiped it out. Countless times I found him. Countless times I lost him again.

I kept trying anyway. I used birds to guide him in certain directions. I manipulated text on street signs. I even rewrote the reflection in a puddle once—but each time, the system retaliated. Birds were struck mid-flight by manufactured predators. Dogs were redirected by creatures I'd never seen before. Messages were overwritten faster. The longer I tried, the more aggressively the Nursery fought me back, as if it were learning too—like it had finally realized what I was doing.

And I could see what it did to him. The exhaustion in his gait. The way he spoke less to the people around him, pulling inward, as though he were afraid of forming sentences he wouldn't remember. The way he hesitated whenever he sensed something uncanny, like part of him knew the world was wrong but couldn't grasp why. He didn't understand what was happening every day—how could he?—but the confusion ate at him. Like he was losing me over and over, each erasure carving him smaller.

Watching that happen made it feel impossible to work. And then, as if the system sensed my hesitation, a new file flickered into existence inside his folder—one stamped with todays date:

[LOG ENTRY-UNIT C-2. DATE: MAR 28, 2425]

Unit exhibits high-risk self-termination intent projected for current cycle. Full surveillance coverage has been deployed to prevent loss of asset. If standard intervention fails, C-41 remains on standby to ensure immediate stabilization. The harvest of C-2 is nearing completion; emotional output levels have nearly reached the threshold required for final upload. Once the transfer is secured, continued maintenance of the physical unit will no longer be necessary, and he will be terminated.

20

The Crow

I remembered being warm. Everything was warm. My mommy's hands were warm, and my daddy's hugs were warm, and even the air felt warm because we were all together. I remembered holding Daddy's fingers because my whole hand could only grab two of his.

"Daddy, I'm hungry!" I said really loud when we were going to the car. He stopped walking like it was a big emergency and bent down so his face was right in front of mine. "You're hungry? Oh no," he said in a silly serious voice, "we better fix that right now."

"I want something from the vending machine!" I said. "Press F-11! Do it!"

My mommy laughed, the pretty kind of laugh that made her eyes squish a little, and she brushed her hair away from her face. "Come on, Owen," she said, "they always love the vending machine."

Thomas started jumping up and down. "Yeah, Dad! F-11!" he said like it was the best button in the world.

My daddy made a pretend grumpy face but he couldn't hide his smile. He opened the door and said, "Alright, alright, F-11 it is."

Mommy always told me everything in the vending machine cost ninety-nine cents, and ninety-nine was special because you always got a penny back. Daddy always gave me the penny. Always.

When he pressed F-11, a bag of chips fell down even though he wasn't trying to get chips, and we all giggled. Then the penny clinked in the little metal cup and Daddy grabbed it quickly and put it in my hand like it was a prize.

He picked me up with one arm—just swooped me up like I weighed nothing—and I ate the chips over his shoulder. My hand got greasy, and so did the penny, and it started slipping all over my palm. It was hard to eat chips and hold a penny at the same time, but I was trying super hard because Daddy always gave it to me.

When we got to the top of the stairs, the penny felt kind of yucky and slippery and stinky, and I didn't want it anymore. So I leaned over the railing and dropped it. I didn't even ask. I just let go.

All of us looked over the edge together. The penny spun and twirled all the way down, and it made a big sound when it hit the ground. Bigger than I thought pennies were allowed to make.

Mommy said my name in her "you're not supposed to do that" voice, but Daddy made a tiny laugh he tried to hide. I heard it. I felt it in his chest.

And I knew he thought it was funny. I knew he liked it.

And I knew I was gonna drop another one someday, just for him.

* * *

Throughout the day, I tried to send him signs—anything to let him know I still existed. It started that morning. From his feed, I watched him step into the dim mailroom, sorting envelopes without noticing any of them. I slipped a thin sheet of paper into the stack and let it drift to the floor. He picked it up, unfolded it, and saw my message: WATCH FOR THE SIGNS. For a heartbeat, recognition flickered—then he crushed it and threw it away.

As he walked out and headed toward the bridge, panic surged through me. He was about to pass the hidden exit to the Nursery. If I could make him curious, even for a moment, maybe he would look. Maybe he would feel me. I froze M-67 ahead of him and stilled the world around my dad: the wind, the river, the flyers along the railing. He slowed, confused by the impossible stillness. But it wasn't enough. So I carved a message into the facade beside the exit—**Dad, I'm here**. It glowed for a single brilliant instant before the system erased it, collapsing it into a harmless flash. He looked up, unsettled, but kept walking.

The rest of the day unfolded the same way—small signs sent, small sparks igniting in him, and the system extinguishing each one before they could take root. At work, I watched him swallow his midday pills, and with them the entire morning evaporated. Every sign I had sent, every flicker of memory, wiped clean. Still, I kept trying. Nothing I threw at him stuck. Nothing reached him long enough to matter.

By the time he walked back toward our apartment—toward what he was about to do—I felt something close to terror rising in me. I couldn't lose him again. I couldn't let the

Nursery take one more piece of him. I was desperate.

I searched for anything, anyone, any living thing I could use. Then I found the rabbit—small, soft, familiar. I slipped into its vision and nudged it toward him. When our feeds aligned, he was looking straight at me—through the rabbit, but somehow like he knew something was there. He hesitated, almost walked away, and panic cracked through me.

I urged the rabbit forward. Faster.

And he turned back, watching with intent.

It bounded through the grass, across the path, and into the road, closing the distance between them. This was it. This was finally it. I was going to reach him. He would see it. He would know. He would *remember*.

The rabbit reached his feet.

Then, out of nowhere, something struck. A blur slammed into the rabbit's feed, severing the signal instantly. The visual snapped to black. The connection was gone.

Within seconds, a soft ding cut through the silence. A new task appeared in my "to-do" folder—an inconsistency report from C-2's perspective.

I opened the incident from another angle, pulling up the external feed, and felt my stomach twist. A snake—small, black, engineered for the facility—shot up through a crack in the ground. It moved so quickly the camera barely caught it. It struck the rabbit once, and within thirty seconds the body ruptured, popping in a way that made me flinch back from the screen. It wasn't nature. It wasn't instinct. It was a correction, deployed specifically to stop me from reaching him.

I stared at the destruction, until now, I had never gotten a single inconsistency report from C-2 since being moved into the Cognitive Directive station. Not one. They didn't want me accessing his perspective. They didn't want me altering anything he saw. They didn't want memories slipping through the cracks I had learned how to open. And the way *this* incident appeared—the one that mattered—felt intentional. Like they knew. Like they had always known. And still didn't shut me down.

Protocol demanded I clear the report. That I wipe the memory clean, just another erased anomaly. But my hands didn't move toward deletion. They hovered over the code, shaking with certainty. I wasn't going to erase the rabbit. Or the snake. Or what it meant.

I was going to strengthen it.

I wove new lines of programming into his pill sequence, altering the pathways just enough so this memory clung instead of dissolving. So the snakes—their violence, their timing, their interference—would stay with him.

I found another animal nearby—I needed something with wings, something that could reach the height of his window and see into it clearly. A crow appeared on my scan, perched on a metal railing, its feathers shining like ink under the artificial lighting. It was exactly what I needed. I slipped into its visuals and guided it upward, urging it to tap on the glass, hoping the sound would be enough to pull him back from whatever decision he was teetering on. The crow pecked at the window, soft at first and then harder, almost frantic as I pushed it, but he didn't hear it. He didn't turn. He didn't respond. He had already made up his mind, and I knew it the moment his hands closed around the pills.

Through his feed, I watched him tip them into his palm—far too many—and before I could react, he swallowed them. One after another. Enough to kill him. A cold, heavy dread spread through me as the realization settled: all the messages, all the animals, all the signs I had sent hadn't been enough to reach him in time. His body began to sway, his vision blurring, his thoughts slipping in broken fragments.

I followed him into that unconsciousness, accessing his direct feed and stepping into the fog of his thoughts. I saw what he was dreaming—his mind replaying what he imagined had happened to us, the story he had created to make sense of losing us. And then a question hit me with sudden clarity: could I show him the truth? Could I replace the imagined version with what had actually occurred? My hands moved without hesitation. I found the footage instantly, like a part of me had been waiting for this exact moment. I opened the file recorded through my mother's eyes and pushed it into the center of his dream.

He saw it immediately. He saw us alive. He saw our car pulling into the parking lot of his work. He saw that we hadn't died, that there hadn't been an accident at all. But as he reached the point where the truth should have settled in, the imagery began to warp. The colors shifted unnaturally, the shapes bending in ways that didn't belong to the memory. A warning flashed across my interface—[file corrupted]—and a sharp panic ran through me.

I understood why almost instantly. I hadn't deleted the snake memory. I had enhanced it. And with the overdose of pills twisting everything in his mind, the enhancement didn't blend the way it was supposed to. The faces my mother had seen that day, the real people who had taken us, began to blur and distort. Then they changed entirely, replaced by the shapes his mind was clinging to instead—the snakes. Cold.

Silent. Watching.

The truth had reached him, but not the way I intended. It had transformed into something darker, something warped by the pills and the fear and the fragments of memory I had forced to stay alive.

I felt a different kind of pull from the crow this time—like I wasn't forcing it, like it wanted to help me. The connection between us tightened the farther we went, our thoughts blending until its instincts and my fear felt like they were moving in the same direction. When the ambulance pulled away with my father inside, the crow took off instantly, wings beating hard as it followed the flashing lights through the artificial city sky.

We stayed above them as the ambulance turned corner after corner, lights reflecting off windows and wet pavement. I kept checking the feed inside the vehicle—my father lying still, the paramedics moving quickly, the harsh beeping of the monitors tapping against my nerves with each uneven beat. It felt like the crow could hear it too, its wings adjusting as if matching the rhythm of his heart.

When the ambulance reached the hospital, the crow swooped into the parking lot, and something caught its vision—a sharp glint of copper against the pavement. A penny. It lay there like it had been placed intentionally, catching the overhead lights just right. The crow hopped forward and picked it up in its beak, and for a moment the weight of the memory behind that tiny coin hit me so hard I almost lost focus. I remembered warmth. Safety. My dad pressing a penny into my hand like it was treasure. I remembered dropping one just to make him laugh.

Our connection deepened until it felt like the crow and I

were sharing the same breath, the same purpose. Together, we rose into the air above the ambulance bay. And just as the doors opened and they wheeled my father out on the stretcher, his eyes fluttered open—just barely, just enough.

The crow released the penny. It fell in a clean, perfect arc, flashing once in the light as it dropped toward him. A message. A memory. A piece of the past I needed him to feel again. A sign that I was still here.

21

A Way Out

The next morning, I opened his file the second the system allowed access, barely able to breathe until the screen loaded. He was alive. In the hospital, monitored, sedated—but alive. Relief flooded in, and the room went soft around the edges, but the moment it passed, the terror rushed in behind it. They kept him alive to harvest him, and then *kill him*. I couldn't sit with what almost happened. I couldn't replay it. I needed something else to focus on—something that mattered. Something that might save us both.

I slipped back into the system's architecture with frantic determination. I wasn't methodical anymore; I tore through directories and logs like someone drowning, clawing at anything that might be solid. Every corner of the Nursery's code I could reach, I reached. Every dead end I had dismissed before, I revisited. I wasn't thinking about efficiency or organization. I was thinking about him lying in that hospital bed, about how close he had come to disappearing forever, about how useless I would be if I couldn't find a real way out.

The Nursery was built to keep workers looping endlessly, hiding truth inside simulations inside illusions, disguising every real pathway as a harmless system process. But something had shifted in me overnight. Desperation sharpened my instincts. Places I had overlooked before now pulsed with possibility—small inconsistencies, patterns that didn't quite align, directories mislabeled by a single character, fragments of code that flickered half a second too long when I touched them.

When I started pulling those pieces together, the shape beneath them began to emerge. It wasn't obvious at first; it was like trying to see a constellation while staring at one star too closely. But the more threads I followed, the clearer the picture became. Data streams overlapped that should never have met. Architecture maps repeated in ways too obvious to be accidents. A false wall—one I had hit a hundred times before—shivered when I pressed it from a different angle.

Hours passed without me lifting my head. My thoughts felt thin, my eyes burning from the strain, but I kept going. I kept digging because the alternative was unthinkable. If I stopped now, if I let the system win its quiet war of attrition, it might be too late to save him.

And then, at the end of a corrupted directory I had nearly abandoned twice already, something shifted. A pattern I couldn't decode suddenly aligned with one I had mapped earlier. A hidden structure snapped into place, revealing a branching path I had never seen before. It was buried so deeply it should have been impossible for someone like me to touch. But the system didn't reject me. It didn't close. It let me through.

Light spilled across my interface in a clean, unmistakable sweep. It took me a moment to understand what I was looking at. And when I did, my whole body went still.

It was a map.

A precise, detailed map of the Nursery: The dome, every corridor, every false horizon and coded city block. It showed the boundaries of the world we were allowed to see, the machinery running beneath it, the chambers where harvested information was stored, the loops that kept us pacified and predictable. It was impossible. It was undeniable.

And on the far edge of the schema—beyond the layered illusions, beyond the sections meant to trick, pacify, or isolate—there was something else.

A tunnel.

A line leading outward, not inward. A path that didn't feed back into the simulation.

A way out.

* * *

Back in the room, I kept my movements controlled, refusing to let the rush inside me show. The map, the tunnel, the proof that an exit existed—it all throbbed behind my eyes like a second pulse. If I revealed it wrong, if I looked even slightly unstable, a watcher would pull me aside and I'd never make it back. I needed allies, but I needed caution more.

I went to 87 and whispered for her to gather the others. She didn't question me; something in my voice must have told her everything she needed. Over the next few minutes, the small group eased toward the back corner of the room—subtle, natural, never together all at once. To anyone watching, it looked like nothing at all.

Once they were close enough, I finally spoke. "I found something in the system today," I said quietly. "Something we're not supposed to see." A stillness settled over them—not quite fear, but close. I took a breath. "There's a map. A real one. It shows the Nursery from above. All of it. And outside the dome, past the walls… there's a tunnel."

For a moment no one reacted. It was like they were afraid to believe what I had said. I pressed on. "It's real. I traced the structure. The tunnel leads out of the Nursery. Not deeper in, out."

Their eyes flicked toward one another—small movements, barely perceptible—but the air between us tightened. "We'll need timing," I said. "A moment when the system is weak. When watchers aren't watching."

Before anyone could answer, a voice came from behind us. "There is a moment."

My whole body locked. The others tensed so fast I felt the air snap around us. For a heartbeat, no one turned. No one breathed. Because a watcher had come up behind us without making a sound — and even whispering like this could get us dragged out of the room and erased before the next rotation.

I felt my stomach drop as I slowly turned, dread scraping down my spine.

297 stood there.

His shadow stretched across our feet. His expression unreadable. His presence alone enough to make my pulse spike painfully in my throat. The others froze; I could see the white rim of fear in 87's eyes, the way 115's hands curled into fists he couldn't use.

He stepped closer, quiet and purposeful, lowering his voice

so low it barely existed. "In fourteen days, half of the watcher unit is scheduled for reset."

No one dared move.

"I'm not part of that rotation," he continued. "The others will be offline for several hours during the night"

My heart hammered so loudly I wondered if the others could hear it. "Meaning what?" I whispered.

"Meaning," he said, glancing subtly toward the nearest watcher post, "I will be the only active watcher with full system access during that window in this area. The others will be down. For several hours, I'll have control of every door they normally guard."

He shifted his weight just slightly, enough to look like routine posture but not enough to hide the strain in his voice. "I can open the transport corridor. It's a straight path to the tunnels. Clean. Unmonitored during resets."

The room tilted around his words.

"I don't know how to reach the exit from inside the tunnels," he continued quietly, "but it sounds like you do—if I can get you that far."

The group's terror didn't disappear; it sharpened, became something brittle and electric, like the moment before glass shatters. Fourteen days. One window. One breath where the system blinked.

I felt it hit me all at once — terror, hope, disbelief — a pressure so intense it made my vision swim. "Then that's our moment," I whispered. "Fourteen days. We stay unnoticed. We prepare. And when the reset begins… we go."

22

The Cost of Hope

When Dad came home from the hospital, I was ready. In the hospital they kept him so heavily drugged that nothing could settle in his mind—memories blurred, meanings slipped, and anything important dissolved before he could hold onto it. But the moment he hesitated with his pills at home, really hesitated, and chose not to take them, I knew the window I needed had finally opened.

I didn't want to scare him. I only wanted him to understand what happened to Mom. So I found her harvesting file—the real one, the one they buried—and uploaded it into his consciousness. Immediately the system started to glitch. The lingering IV drugs had already pulled snakes into his subconscious, and when my file hit that, the imagery tangled together. It wasn't how I intended it to appear, but the truth about Mom was terrifying no matter what form it took.

I watched him enter the white void the system uses to isolate minds. I felt the moment he reacted to that mildew smell—

something his subconscious grabbed onto as it searched for the memory I'd pushed forward. He followed it instinctively, and as he did, the glitches deepened: flickering lights, collapsing brightness, shadows forming where nothing should cast them.

Then the snakes appeared—hundreds, then thousands. That wasn't me. That was the system panicking, trying to pull him away from the memory I had forced to the surface using a memory I had enhanced. But he kept going. He pushed through them, ran toward the image I'd embedded.

And he found her. Exactly as she appeared in the file—slumped in the metal chair, emptied out, with the needles in her head. He didn't realize it was Mom yet, but he was close. Closer than he had ever been.

That's when the system intervened. The cord attached to her body—the real cord that had drained her life—shifted into a massive black snake for one last attempt to shock him awake. And it worked. It snapped the dream and threw him out of the memory before he could understand who she was.

I hadn't meant to frighten him. I only wanted him to see the truth. But the system was more afraid of that than anything I could show him.

When he stepped outside the house, I followed him and tried again—sending hints the way I had before, little distortions in the world meant to point him toward the truth he kept losing. Most of them slipped right past him. He didn't even register the shadows I shifted or the symbols I placed where he'd normally notice. He was too overwhelmed, too caught between wanting to trust his instincts and fearing he was slipping back into the kind of paranoia the system always accused him of. I could feel it in him—excitement prickling under his skin, a tug of dread, that familiar fear that something was wrong and he just couldn't see it yet.

But then I pushed one sign harder than the rest. I put Thomas's name on a screen—clear, bright, targeted right where his eyes would land. And this time he stopped. His entire body stilled. His fear. His guilt. His love. His unfinished nightmare. Seeing the name out of place, written where it shouldn't be, hit him with a force that echoed through both of us.

This was enough to rattle him, but not enough. I needed more than fear. I needed recognition—connection—something that would slip past the walls the system kept rebuilding in his mind. I still couldn't show myself, not even for a second. If I appeared, if he saw me, the system would detect the breach instantly and rip everything away from him again. So I had to work in the margins, in the glitches, in the tiny windows where the system wasn't watching closely enough. When Dad sat at his computer at work, I knew that was my moment. I placed Curtis there—not the hollow, reconstructed supervisor the Nursery had turned him into, but the man he used to be. A farmer in the wheat field. Human. Alive. A version of him Dad had never seen, but somehow still responded to with a flicker of recognition he couldn't explain. I watched Dad freeze, unsettled, pulled toward the image without knowing why. That was the doorway I needed.

I tried to show the truth—the real harvest, the rods, the extraction—but the system sensed what I was doing and twisted it before it reached him. The moment the man in the field began to move, the distortion wrapped itself around him, turning the harvest into something symbolic and warped. And when the whistling shifted into a song, that was when the shedding began. The file made it look like Curtis was peeling apart in layers, his skin loosening and drifting as if he were slipping out of his own body like a snake abandoning an old shell. It wasn't the real harvest, but the meaning bled through anyway. Every line of the song pushed it further, each lyric carrying the warning I needed Dad to hear.

Curtis's face glitched and blurred as he sang, features rippling like something underneath was trying to break through. His smile stretched too wide, his eyes sharpened unnaturally, his movements syncing eerily with the words meant only for Dad. The wheat behind him rippled with something crawling under its surface, the light flickered, the sky darkened, and the distortion grew more violent with every note. But Dad kept watching. He couldn't look away. Even through the corruption, even through the warped imagery and the skin sloughing off in glitching folds, he almost understood what the message meant.

After Dad left the meeting, I stayed close to him in the system, watching the way his thoughts churned beneath the surface. He was unsettled—Curtis always did that to him— but today the tension ran deeper. The glitch I'd shown him earlier, the harvest warning buried inside the song, was still vibrating through him. He didn't understand it yet, but he felt something shifting. The cracks were opening, and I knew I had to push before the system patched them over again. So the moment he sat down at his computer, I made my next move.

I forced a pop-up onto his screen. It wasn't an actual alert; I built it myself, stitching it into the system in a way that looked ordinary but would grab his attention instantly: FILES NEEDING TO BE UPDATED.

When the list of files appeared, I placed F11 right in the center. F11. It was a memory the system had buried deep inside him, a memory I wanted to hit him like a spark. And it did.

DO YOU SEE IT YET?

* * *

That night I couldn't sleep. My mind kept replaying every step of the plan, every risk, every choice that had brought us to this point. Tomorrow was the day we escaped. Not someday, not eventually—*tomorrow*. Tomorrow, during the watcher reset, we were supposed to slip through the gap in the system and run for our lives.

Eventually the room went dark, and one by one the sounds around me faded. Breathing slowed. Bodies stilled revealing quiet that exists only in places where everyone is pretending not to hope. I lay awake staring into the black, counting my own heartbeats just to prove I was still here.

About an hour later during complete silence, I heard it. Four sharp pops. Not loud enough to echo, not soft enough to dismiss—short little bursts of sound that my brain recognized before I did. My breath froze halfway in my lungs.

Then something warm hit my cheek. A tiny droplet, then another, then a large splash. I touched my face. My fingers came away wet. And instantly, my heart plummeted.

I bolted upright, but the darkness was so thick it felt like a weight pressing over my eyes. I could barely make out shapes—beds, shadows, the faint outlines of bodies that should have been moving, should have been shifting in sleep, should have been *alive*. I whispered their numbers under my breath, as if saying them softly enough would keep them safe a little longer. No one stirred.

Then the lights flickered on.

The world snapped into red.

Not just splattered—*covered.* Red dripping down the posts of the beds, red streaked across the floor in thin, spidering trails, red misting the walls as if something had burst mid-air. Everywhere I looked, it was the same violent, blooming red. It took my mind several seconds too long to understand what I was seeing. My thoughts kept stalling right before the truth, like my brain was trying to protect me from something it knew I couldn't handle.

But then I followed the trails. I traced the lines up the bedframes, across the sheets, over pillow edges, up to the places where heads should have been resting peacefully. And suddenly everything inside me collapsed.

27.

115.

197.

And my friend... 87.

All gone.

All gone in the same violent, efficient way 201 had disappeared. No struggle. No warning. Just four soft pops in the dark, four lifeless shapes now slumped forward or sideways, the detonators in their skulls triggered while they slept. It wasn't loud. It wasn't dramatic. It was quiet—quiet enough that anyone dreaming lightly might have slept right through their own execution.

My stomach twisted so violently I thought I might throw up. My legs wouldn't move. My hands shook so hard I had to press them against my knees just to keep them from floating away. I kept waiting for one of them to gasp awake, to sit up, to ask what happened. But there was nothing. Just me, standing in a room with these bodies of people who had trusted me, people who had never asked for this, people who had dared to hope for one single day—and had been killed for it before that day could even arrive.

And worst of all, I knew exactly why.

Because of me.

Because the system had sensed even the slightest hint of rebellion, and it had chosen the fastest, cleanest way to crush it before it could begin. I covered my mouth with my hand to keep from screaming. The metallic smell of blood coated the air, thick and sharp, filling my lungs with every breath. My heartbeat pounded so violently it hurt, each pulse like a hammer striking inside my skull.

I wanted to run to them. I wanted to shake them, to deny what I was seeing, to pretend they could still be saved. But the truth stained the air as unmistakably as the red dripping from the walls.

They were gone, and I was still alive.

The cleanup was the same as last time. We were ordered into a line—silent, obedient, hollow—and we walked toward the showers as if nothing had happened. As if the floor hadn't been red. As if four beds hadn't been emptied in an instant. My legs moved, but they didn't feel like mine. I kept hearing the pops, the spray, the stillness afterward. I kept hearing my own breath shaking in my ears.

At the end of the shower, the same hidden compartment slid open, offering me a freshly pressed white tunic. Perfectly folded. Perfectly clean. Perfectly indifferent. My hands trembled as I reached for it. I was still crying, and I couldn't stop it—not even when the steam fogged the tears on my face, not even when the alarms hummed their usual morning cycle as if today were like any other. Everything inside me felt scraped raw, buzzing and empty all at once.

But when I stepped out of the shower, still dripping, still shaking, 297 was waiting for me. He stood at the edge of the hallway, posture locked tight, face unreadable. The moment our eyes met, he spoke. "This doesn't change anything," he said immediately, voice low and urgent. "You aren't safe here, and you need to leave tomorrow."

Something in me cracked open. "I killed them… I killed them all," I sobbed. The words came out broken, collapsing under their own weight. My knees almost buckled.

"NO." His voice snapped sharper than I'd ever heard. "*It* killed them. You tried to save them. Now you have to save yourself." He leaned in, lowering his tone until it was barely a whisper. "Save…" He hesitated—just long enough for my heart to skip—then finished softly, "save Dad."

The word landed differently than I expected. Not the meaning—*the sound.* The way he said Dad didn't fit in his mouth. It came out stiff, clipped, almost metallic. Like a recording played half a second off-pitch.

I barely noticed it. Just a tiny glitch in a moment drowning with grief. But even through the haze, an uneasy feeling slipped across my skin—cold and thin, like the air pressure had changed. Something wasn't right. Something underneath his words felt… borrowed. Not fully his.

When we were finally sent back to the dormitory, no one spoke. We moved on instinct alone, filing into our rows, climbing into our beds, and lying still beneath the thin covers. This was the routine. This was the pattern. No matter what horrors happened during the day, bedtime always followed the same script. Lights dimmed, then flickered once or twice, then clicked off completely. The darkness that followed was usually a small mercy—a chance to breathe quietly, unseen, unmonitored for a few hours. Even hope, fragile as it was, tended to bloom in that darkness. But tonight, as I lay staring up at the ceiling, waiting for that familiar flicker, nothing happened.

The lights stayed frozen in their low emergency setting, humming faintly, washing the room in a flat, sickly glow that made it impossible to rest. The air felt still and heavy, as if the facility itself was holding its breath. Every second the lights refused to go out fed a growing pressure inside my chest. Something wasn't right. Bedtime never deviated.

Then a door opened.

A single man walked in, his boots striking the floor with deliberate weight. The sound reverberated across the rows of beds, slicing through the tense silence. He stepped deeper into the room, and I saw immediately that he didn't belong among the watchers or the standard handlers. He was taller, broader, standing with a posture so rigid it seemed unnatural. His face, when it came into view, was disturbingly blank—emotionless, expressionless, devoid of even the smallest flicker of humanity. His eyes stared forward with the same dead focus as a machine awaiting further instruction.

He stopped in the middle of the room, hands clasped behind his back, and when he spoke his voice was amplified just enough to vibrate in my bones. "If anyone has thoughts of escaping, or tries to escape," he announced, his tone so precise it sounded rehearsed, "they will be killed instantly and without hesitation." There was nothing heated in his tone—

just a flat, clinical statement delivered to a room full of people pretending to sleep.

I felt my eyes widening despite my effort to appear calm. This was not normal. They did not make announcements in our room. They did not interrupt bedtime. This was targeted, specific, meant for me and no one else.

Then my gaze slid to the label on his chest pocket.

A simple stitched tag. Clean, white thread.

C-1.

My heart stuttered. C-1 wasn't a man.

Had they replaced her? Had she been reassigned? Or had something happened to her—something they didn't want us to question, something they thought they could erase by stitching her name onto a stranger?

<h1 style="text-align:center">23</h1>

Best to Run Now

I arrived at my station the next morning frantic to reach my dad. I didn't care about protocols anymore. I didn't care about the system. I didn't care if they traced every keystroke back to me. After what happened last night, I couldn't stay silent. I was going to talk to him—really talk to him—no matter what it cost.

He was still asleep. The timestamp on his monitor read 5:30 a.m., the one window of time when the system was at its weakest and the watchers were halfway between cycles. I had time. I had a sliver of space where I could slip into his dreams unnoticed. A place where the system couldn't see me unless it was directly looking.

My hands shook as I typed the commands. I wasn't calm or strategic anymore—I was desperate. I needed him. I needed him to know the truth. I needed to hear his voice, even if only inside a dream. As I tunneled into his consciousness, the tears blurred the interface in front of me. I didn't wipe them away. I let them fall.

For the first time since they tore our family apart, I stopped hiding. I stopped whispering through hints and symbols and glitches. I called out for him openly, my voice cracking inside the dreamspace as it formed around me. I cried for his help as his daughter.

When I found him in his dream, I didn't dress the message in metaphors or visions or songs. I stood in front of him, face to face, and forced the words out through the ache in my throat.

"The harvest is near," I told him, because there wasn't time for him to guess anymore.

Before I could do anything else, I felt a hand clamp down on my shoulder. The shock jolted through me so hard I nearly slammed my keyboard. I ripped my attention away from the screen and exited the interface instantly, my breath catching in my throat. It was my brother. 297 stood behind me, eyes sharper than I had ever seen them, urgency radiating off him like heat.

"It's happening," he said. His voice wasn't loud, but it hit with the force of a fist.

"What?" I whispered, my voice shaking so badly the word barely formed.

"The reset," he said. "It's not happening tonight. It's happening in thirty minutes."

The bottom dropped out of my stomach. "No," I said, shaking my head. "There isn't time. We're not ready. We aren't—"

He cut me off with a look so stern, so commanding, it stopped the rest of the sentence in my throat. "Tell him."

Two words. Hard. Unnegotiable.

I turned back toward my monitor, my pulse pounding in

my ears. A dream wouldn't be enough—not anymore, not with the clock suddenly collapsing around us. He needed to know now. He needed to be awake.

My hands flew across the controls before I could second-guess myself. I bypassed the dream channel entirely and reached into the house system. I turned on his TV. The screen flickered to life in the darkness of his room.

And I woke him up.

I put a clear message on his TV. I built something he couldn't ignore. I wove it into the morning news feed, threading my voice beneath the anchor's dialogue like an off-note in a song, subtle enough to slip past the system's filters but loud enough to vibrate directly against his nerves. The TV flickered once. Twice. The picture sharpened—and then twisted. The colors shifted, the audio wavered, and the melody began. My melody. The same one that had haunted his dreams.

He frowned at the screen, leaning in, trying to make sense of the distortion. And that was when my voice cut through everything—soft, lilting, unmistakable. "Best to run now... the Harvest is near." I sang. "Time to run." I said to myself. The words were carried in a tune that shouldn't have been possible on a news broadcast, weaving through the background like a signal calling him by name. His eyes widened. The moment the meaning hit him, he didn't even question it—he ran outside, confused, desperate for answers he could finally tell weren't imagined.

That was when I tore the sky open for him.

It was harder than anything I'd done so far. The horizon trembled. The clouds flickered. And then the world ripped open like a zipper being dragged through reality itself.

It looked like lightning at first—white-hot, jagged, splitting the morning in two. But lightning didn't behave like this. Lightning didn't freeze in place. Lightning didn't peel back the way a curtain does, revealing the flat, endless white behind it. The void. The truth. The nothingness they built everything on. I felt his breath stop. Felt the shock slam through him like a wave. He wasn't supposed to see this—not ever—and yet here he stood, staring at the crack in his world that I had made just for him.

I held it open as long as I could. My mind burned. My vision flickered. The system fought me like a living animal, shoving against the tear, screaming warnings I ignored. And then, in one violent recoil, it slammed the sky shut again. Everything smoothed over, perfect and blue and quiet, pretending none of it had happened. But I knew. And he knew. He had seen behind the mask.

But one more sign—one more—and he would understand everything.

I slipped out of the sky and scanned through his house. Walls. Furniture. Screens. Too risky. I needed something the system wouldn't question. Something human. Something old. Something it didn't think mattered anymore.

And then I saw it.

A drawing on his fridge.

The paper was faded, the crayon lines uneven and childish. A sun too big, a house too small, a tree with branches that didn't make sense—drawn by hands that had never known fear yet. My hands. My drawing. He had kept it all this time. Even after everything. Something in my chest twisted so sharply it almost hurt.

I reached into the memory of the drawing through the digital feed and changed it. At first, just a line. Then another.

I drew a dome around the house, smooth and curved and suffocating. Then, with the smallest stroke of code, I added the message.

"We're still here."

When he saw it, he went completely still. His hand hovered on the fridge door, fingers barely touching the magnet, and for a moment it looked like he'd forgotten how to breathe. The drawing—the one I made before any of this—held his eyes in a way nothing else could have. The dome I'd added, the message beneath it... I watched the realization move through him slowly at first, then all at once, like a light switching on inside his chest.

That was it. That was the moment everything finally aligned. The signs. The warnings. The sky. The song. This. He wasn't guessing anymore. He wasn't doubting himself or trying to dismiss what he felt. He *knew.*

Watchers started leaving slowly, each one slipping out a few minutes apart so nothing looked suspicious. Their exits were staggered, precise, rehearsed—a sequence they had practiced thousands of times. One watcher's footsteps faded. Then another. Then another. Each departure carved more silence into the room, stretching it thin, making every second feel too bright, too loud. My pulse beat in my ears, counting down the emptying of the room until the hum of the monitors became the only sound left. And then it was only 297. My brother. He stood behind me with that calm, contained intensity he always had when everything was about to fall apart. He didn't speak. He didn't breathe loudly.

I stared at the computer screen, the cursor blinking like a heartbeat, and something inside me snapped into place. The plan we'd crafted felt useless now—too quiet, too careful.

Quiet wouldn't save us. Careful wouldn't save us. Not after what happened last night. Not with the reset moving up. We needed something that would shake the entire building awake. Something that would send every watcher, every eye scrambling away from us.

I needed to give them a reason to stop looking at *me*.

So I made a decision. The kind you don't come back from.

I wasn't just going to make a distraction.

I was going to make the system panic.

I pushed past the normal levels of access—through layers of code that felt brittle, ancient, wired with warnings that pulsed like faint electrical shocks. Most of these functions weren't meant to be seen by anyone. Watchers didn't touch them. Architects barely did. They lived at the core of the system, buried under years of patches and overrides. But I had glimpsed them once—an error screen flashing too fast to read—just enough to know where to look.

And there it was.

A root command.

A system reset option.

A true reset. A moment where everything—cameras, alarms, doors, feeds—would have to halt while the system rebooted its main thread. It wasn't meant to be touched. It wasn't meant to be triggered. But if I activated it now… the system would be blind. Blind and panicking.

My hands shook violently as I hovered over the command. One wrong keystroke and the system might trace me instantly. Or shut the entire facility down. Or worse—lock everything in place permanently. But doing nothing meant dying slowly, quietly, like the others. I couldn't let that be our ending.

I pressed the button.

The world convulsed.

The lights overhead blew into red so bright it stained the air. Sirens erupted into a glitching scream. The floor vibrated, the walls groaned, and every monitor around us exploded into cascading errors, entire columns of code tearing themselves apart in real time.

Panels slid open and snapped shut again. Security shutters rattled like they couldn't decide whether to lock down or release. Somewhere deep in the facility, machinery roared to life, then choked mid-cycle. The sound was overwhelming, the chaos absolute.

Thomas grabbed my arm, yanking me from the chair with more force than he'd ever used on me. "It's time to go," he shouted, his voice nearly drowned out by the alarms. His eyes were wide—not with fear, but with the certainty that if we hesitated even one more second, the system would reassemble itself and drag us back into its machine.

Behind us, the facility continued to spiral in a storm of red lights and distorted warnings. The reset had worked. The system was blind. And we had only moments before it opened its eyes again.

III

The Escape

24

The Reunion

I ran down the stairs of my apartment building two steps at a time, my hand sliding along the railing as if that thin strip of metal could anchor me to something real. I didn't know where Grace was. I didn't know how to reach her. But every instinct in my body screamed that she was close—closer than she had been in years—and I was done waiting for signs. I was going to find her.

Halfway down the flight, the air changed. A vibration rolled through the walls, subtle at first, then growing into a low mechanical rumble that rattled the glass in the stairwell windows. I froze. For a single heartbeat, everything went silent, as if the entire world had sucked in a breath.

Then the voice came.

"System reset."

It boomed from nowhere and everywhere at once, echoing off concrete, vibrating in my ribs, filling the space with a cold, metallic authority.

"System reset."

The lights flickered overhead, sputtering between white and red, casting the stairwell in jerking flashes that made the world look like it was breaking frame by frame. A deep siren began to pulse behind the announcement, each blast shaking through the building as though something enormous had just woken up beneath us.

I gripped the railing harder.

Then something happened with the colors. The stairwell flickered from red to white, red to white, until my eyes ached trying to keep up. But then I noticed the problem wasn't the lights at all. The walls themselves were changing.

The gray of the concrete began to thin, as if someone were draining the pigment out of it with invisible hands. The texture softened. Corners blurred. Even the stains that had been there for years began to lose their shape. I blinked, but the stairwell didn't come back into focus. It only kept fading.

The floors were next. The speckled pattern on the concrete smeared like wet ink, then dissolved entirely, leaving behind a flat, muted shade that didn't belong to anything real. The metal railing under my hand started to lose its shine, its definition melting until it felt smooth and warm, almost like skin. I jerked my hand back, heart hammering.

And then the ceiling gave way—slowly at first, like clouds thinning, but then with a strange accelerating urgency, colors sliding off its surface in sheets. Entire portions of the world dissolved in front of me, vanishing into a brightness so pure it felt impossible.

The fading sped up. The white spread across the stairwell like a tide swallowing everything in its path. The numbers on the doorframes disappeared next, swallowed by the blankness. The shadows vanished. The steps themselves began to blur at the edges, the lines between them smoothing out until I wasn't sure where one ended and the next began. My breath quickened, coming shallow and sharp. I reached out, trying to touch the wall beside me, but my fingers passed through something that felt neither solid nor air—a strange, buzzing softness that recoiled under my touch.

Then the world plunged into full erasure.

Everything went white.

It was *everywhere*, a color that wasn't a color, stretching endlessly in every direction until I couldn't tell where the floor was or whether I was still standing on anything at all.

The lights were gone. All of them. And yet I could still see, as if the white itself produced light—soft, omnidirectional, swallowing shadows before they could form.

Panic crawled up my throat. This wasn't a glitch. It felt like reality itself was being peeled away, stripped to some raw, unfinished layer beneath the world I thought I lived in. The whiteness pressed in around me like a fog that wanted to become a wall. The air felt thin.

I ran outside to realign myself, desperate for air, desperate for something familiar to pull me out of the blinding white swallowing the stairwell. But the second I stepped into the open, something stopped me like I was running into a wall. Everything was gone. Nothing recognizable remained. The streetlamp was still standing on the corner, but it was completely white, stripped of metal, of shadow, of substance. The cars were still parked along the curb, but they were blank shapes, white from bumper to tire. The sidewalk, the buildings, the trees—they were all still technically there, unchanged in form. But every ounce of detail, every hint of texture or color, every piece of reality that made them *themselves* had been erased. What was left didn't feel like a world at all. It felt like the ghost of one.

I spun slowly, my heartbeat thundering in my ears. The city I had lived in for years had been drained to a sterile white outline, a sketch someone had forgotten to finish. The trees looked frozen in mid-motion, their branches white as bone. The apartment building behind me had no shadows in its windows—no depth. Just blank rectangles framed in brighter blankness. Cars sat in driveways like lifeless sculptures. Even the street itself was reduced to a white path with no cracks, no markings, no history.

My knees wobbled. I pressed a hand to the nearest wall, but even that felt smooth, frictionless, like touching a null version of reality. The ringing in my ears swelled instantly, sharpening until it vibrated behind my eyes. The whiteness pulsed with the sound, and for a moment it felt like the whole world was breathing in sync with the noise inside my head.

* * *

I ran with Thomas through the halls of the facility, the two of us sprinting through the chaos I had unleashed. The alarms screamed overhead in broken, panicked bursts, glitching between tones like the system couldn't decide which emergency to prioritize. Red lights strobed across the walls in choking flashes, stretching our shadows into long streaks that seemed to chase us down every corridor. Doors that should've been locked stuttered open and shut in rapid succession, confused by the reset.

Sparks spat from ceiling panels as power rerouted unevenly through the grid. The entire building felt like it was shaking from the system itself thrashing in revolt. Every second the reset held gave us another second of invisibility. Another second to run. Another second to stay alive.

By the time the tunnel entrance came into view, my lungs felt like they were on fire. My legs trembled beneath me, every muscle screaming, but the cold air spilling from the tunnel pushed me forward. The space opened into a cavernous hollow—stone and concrete arching overhead, the ground sloping downward toward the waiting transport vehicle. Its headlights cut two pale slashes through the darkness, glowing faintly.

My lungs burned, my legs shook, but when I grabbed the door handle, ready to pull us both inside, Thomas didn't move. He stopped beside me with abrupt, unnatural stillness—his breath sharp, his shoulders rigid, his mind clearly pulled somewhere I couldn't see.

The alarms echoed faintly down the tunnel, distant and distorted, like the system was screaming underwater. The reset had scrambled everything—the watchers' link, the command channels, even the environmental systems—and Thomas stood in the middle of that confusion like someone caught between two worlds. One where he belonged to the system… and one where he belonged to himself.

"Thomas," I said softly.

The name slid into the air like a key turning in a hidden lock.

His fingers twitched, and his eyes unfocused for a heartbeat, as if the world around him muted, as if the alarms and the trembling walls and even the cold air vanished, leaving only that name hanging between us.

Then he blinked. Slowly. Like someone waking up too fast

and too deep at the same time.

He turned his head just a fraction, not enough to face me—just enough that I could see the tension ripple down his jaw. His lips parted, sound caught in his throat. He swallowed hard, visibly fighting for something buried under years of conditioning.

"Thomas..." he whispered, testing it, tasting it, as if the name belonged to a memory hovering just out of reach. His brow creased, and his eyes finally lifted toward me, searching my face like he was trying to match the name to something that mattered.

A second breath left him, "That's... my name."

Hearing him say it—hearing him *remember* it—hit me so hard my vision blurred. It wasn't loud. It wasn't confident. But it was *his.* A piece of him breaking through the programming like light through cracked glass.

He turned fully toward me then, and the stiffness melted from his posture. His shoulders dropped, the watcher-perfect alignment dissolving into something achingly familiar. His gaze softened—not with certainty, but with recognition. With connection.

"I remember you saying it," he murmured, voice thick and steady. "Not here. Before."

My throat tightened. "Then come with me. Please... don't stay here."

He looked back toward the facility for a long moment—the glowing red alarms, the distant thunder of systems rebooting, the place that had claimed him for so long. I could almost feel the tug it had on him, that instinct to return, to obey, to fall back into the shape they carved for him.

But then he looked at me. Really looked.

And whatever hold the system still had began to crumble.

His jaw squared with quiet determination, and he stepped closer—into my space, out of the system's shadow, into the choice he was making entirely on his own.

"If I'm coming with you, we better go now." He said.

Relief flooded through me so intensely my knees wobbled.

He opened the passenger door himself, sliding into the seat with a final glance over his shoulder—as if silently daring the system to try to take him back.

By the time I climbed in beside him, closed the door, and started the engine, he was no longer frozen. No longer confused. No longer slipping toward obedience.

We pushed the vehicle to its limits, the engine roaring as we tore down the white tunnel. The wheels skidded slightly on the ground, the whole world around us still bleached into that eerie, endless nothing. The walls, the ceiling, even the faint outlines of doors we passed—they were all white silhouettes, ghost-images carved from light instead of matter.

But then something shifted.

At first it was subtle—just a faint tint sliding across the wall beside us, like a shadow brushing over paper. Then another. And another. The color didn't return all at once. It leaked back in slowly, threading through the whiteness in thin, delicate strokes. Soft greys seeped into the ceiling, into the floor, into the walls of the hall.

The further we drove, the stronger the change became. The grey deepened, darkened, spreading outward in widening veins, restoring texture where there had been none. Concrete regained its grit. Shadows began to form again, faint but unmistakable, stretching and bending with the vehicle's headlights.

I felt my chest tighten.

"The system's coming back," I whispered.

The lights overhead flickered once—hard enough to shake a tremor through the whole tunnel. A low hum vibrated in the air, building steadily, pulsing like a heartbeat restarting after a long flatline. The whiteness retreated faster now, pulled away like a curtain being yanked back into place. Colorless hallways sharpened into cold steel. The blank void behind us folded shut as if it had never been there.

Thomas gripped the dashboard, leaning forward as the tunnel's world rebuilt itself around us. His profile glowed under the growing brightness, eyes sharpened, breath steady despite the rising tension. "We're running out of time," he said quietly.

***

Most people around me were already panicked—stumbling, shouting, grabbing at anything that still looked solid. A few lay on the ground completely motionless, their eyes wide open, staring at the blank sky as if their minds couldn't climb back into their bodies. Someone screamed a name. Someone else just kept repeating, "What happened? What happened?" But none of it slowed me. I ran past them, weaving through the crowd, my pulse thundering in my ears.

As I moved, the world began to reassemble itself. The white peeled back in slow, trembling sheets, color bleeding into the edges of buildings, streets, cars, people. Shadows snapped into place. Details sharpened. Trees grew their greens again, stop signs reddened, the sky deepened to blue—but the restoration felt wrong. Artificial. A puppet show stitching itself together.

The return of color didn't comfort me. It didn't reassure me. If anything, it made the panic in my chest burn hotter. Because now I knew. I'd seen the world stripped bare—seen the machinery beneath the façade, the nothingness behind the painted surface. And once you see that, you can't unsee it.

I knew exactly where I was running. Even as the world around me regained its color and the chaos of what was happening rippled through the streets, a path was already unfolding in my mind—one I hadn't been able to see clearly until now. Memories didn't just return; they surged back with purpose, sliding into place like pieces of a puzzle that had always been missing their edges. Grace had been guiding me for months, and I hadn't understood it then.

A flicker in a window when no lights were on. A brief distortion in the reflection of the glass. A pulse of something I thought was just in my head. I used to shake it off and keep going, telling myself it was nothing. But she had been there. Reaching out. Leaving marks only I was meant to notice.

Now, with the world unraveling behind me and truth finally clawing its way into the open, all those moments aligned in a single, clear direction. She had been showing me exactly where to go. Stopping me without stopping me. Nudging me toward one place, one building, one window she had illuminated for seconds at a time—long enough that some part of me remembered even when my mind didn't.

I ran harder, pushing my legs until the pavement blurred beneath me. The panic around me faded into background noise. People shouting, cars skidding, alarms echoing through the city—it all washed to the edges of my awareness. My focus narrowed to a single point ahead. The building stood at the end of the block, tall and quiet, its windows still dark, but now that I was looking with a mind that wasn't clouded anymore, I felt the pull I had ignored for so long.

That was where she wanted me to go.

Where she had tried to send me again and again, hoping that eventually something inside me would wake up enough to understand.

And now it had.

The world came back to life, but not in any way that felt natural. It didn't settle or rebuild or return the way a city waking from a storm should. It lurched. It staggered. It glitched into place like a puppet dragged upright by tangled strings. Birds reappeared first—flashes of wings that flickered in and out of existence, vanishing mid-flight and then snapping back three feet to the left, as if the system couldn't remember exactly where it had left them. A flock overhead jerked across the sky in stuttering bursts, each movement out of sync with the last.

The whole world felt misaligned, like a machine rebooting too quickly, forcing reality to reassemble itself whether it fit together or not. Colors were slightly wrong—too bright, too muted, pulsing faintly at the edges. Shadows lagged a moment behind the objects that cast them. The wind blew in short, confused bursts that shifted direction every few seconds.

Nothing about it felt alive.

Then, as I ran, something rose inside me—quiet at first, then swelling so quickly it nearly stole my breath. A flicker of hope. A dangerous, fragile thing I hadn't allowed myself to feel in years. It came without warning, threading through the panic, striking me with a force that staggered me mid-stride.

What if Thomas was alive?

I had shoved that thought so deep it barely existed. Hope had been too painful, too heavy to carry. But now, with the world's false skin peeling away and my memories returning in bursts of clarity, the possibility slammed into me with blinding intensity. And once the door cracked open, another question slipped through—quieter, trembling, almost too painful to name.

What if Elisabeth was alive?

My chest felt like a fist had closed around my heart. My legs, exhausted surged with new strength. I pushed harder, sprinting so fast the air tore at my lungs. Tears blurred my vision, spilling down my face in hot streams I barely felt. My body was numb, battered by adrenaline and fear and disbelief, but something inside me—something I thought had died—came roaring awake.

I tore around the final corner, and the building loomed ahead, its doorway lit by a faint, unnatural glow still fading from the reset. My heart slammed against my ribs in a rhythm so violent I thought I might collapse before reaching it. But I kept going. Every step was a plea, a prayer, a desperate, wordless hope that the world hadn't taken everything from me.

As I closed the distance, the door opened.

Grace stepped out.

Older, taller, her features stretched by years she'd lived without me—yet unmistakably, undeniably my daughter. Her hair framed her face the same way Elisabeth's did when she laughed. Her eyes held all the fire and softness I had memorized. For half a second, the world tilted, and I couldn't breathe, couldn't think, couldn't do anything but stumble toward her like a man resurfacing after years underwater.

She saw me. Truly saw me. Something lit inside her, bright and fierce, and she broke into a run.

And behind her—

Another figure stepped out of the doorway. Taller than I remembered, shoulders broader, movements still carrying the stiffness of the place he'd escaped. Thomas. Sixteen now. A young man instead of the boy I used to carry on my shoulders. His face was older, marked by shadows and strength and things he should never have had to endure—but it was him. It was my son.

My knees buckled with relief so powerful it bordered on agony.

They ran to me, and I ran to them, the distance collapsing in seconds that felt like whole years falling away. Grace reached me first, flinging herself into my arms so hard I staggered back, clutching her like I thought she might dissolve if I let go. Thomas wrapped around us a heartbeat later, his breath shaking against my shoulder, his arms tight around both of us—as if he too feared this was just another fading illusion.

For a moment, I was nothing but feeling—overwhelming, crushing, radiant feeling. The weight of every year without them, the ache I had buried, the terror I had carried alone, all collided with the impossible truth of having them here, alive, warm, real.

I looked toward the doorway, hope rising again like a tide surging against the shore. If these two had survived—if they had escaped, if they had endured—then maybe, just maybe…

But the doorway remained still. No movement. No figure stepping forward.

My legs trembled as I sank to my knees, pulling Grace and Thomas with me, holding them as if I could anchor all three of us to this moment forever. The world around us swirled with the remnants of the reset, but none of it mattered. Nothing mattered except the warmth of their bodies, the weight of their arms, the trembling breaths we shared.

And then something settled over me—quiet, certain. The dream I'd seen, the woman in the chair, the moment her life slipped away… it wasn't random. It had been Grace reaching for me, guiding me toward a truth I hadn't been able to face. It was about Elisabeth. About the fact that she was truly gone.

[LOG ENTRY-UNIT C-2. DATE: APRIL 12, 2425]

Emotional development cycle confirmed complete. During the final evaluation window, the subject generated an unprompted upward-projecting affective surge. This pattern—rare, forward-oriented, and internally sourced—marks the last required emotional response for full neural extraction compatibility.

All remaining benchmarks show stable alignment:

• Attachment modeling: integrated

• Loss-response conditioning: consistent

• Emotional resonance: elevated during the surge but within acceptable thresholds

• Behavioral compliance: unaffected

C-2 is cleared for harvest. Initiate transfer upon corridor availability.

25

The Future is Bright

The tunnel stretched on before us, lit by long rows of dim lights that washed over the windshield in slow, steady waves. Each pass of light and shadow moved through the car like a heartbeat—soft, rhythmic, calming in a way I hadn't felt in years. The hum of the engine echoed off the concrete walls, but instead of feeling trapped by the sound, I felt grounded by it, as if each vibration was reminding me that we were still moving forward.

Grace sat upright in the passenger seat, her attention fixed on the path ahead, her jaw set with quiet resolve. There was something in her that felt so familiar—A steadiness that didn't have to be loud to be powerful. A strength that showed itself not in the absence of fear, but in the willingness to move through it anyway. I had seen that same strength in Elisabeth more times than I could count. It wasn't something a child could mimic on purpose; it was something inherited in ways that went deeper than genetics. Grace didn't act like her mother. She *carried* something of her—something bright

280

and unyielding, something that refused to break even when everything else had.

Thomas sat with his posture straight, every muscle seemingly alert. The system had shaped him into someone older than he should have had to be. He moved with precision, calculated and controlled, like he'd been trained for a life he never chose. None of that was Elisabeth. None of it belonged to her. But then the tunnel lights flickered across him—soft gold for an instant—and something in his expression, the angle of his features, the gentleness hidden under all that enforced discipline, slipped through. Not her manner. Not her habits. Something quieter. Something natural. A resemblance that didn't ask to be noticed but revealed itself anyway. Not a mirror—just a reminder.

Watching them in that shifting light, the realization settled over me slowly, like warm water rising around my ribs: Elisabeth wasn't gone, she was here. Woven into our children in different ways—Grace carrying her spirit, her fire, her courage; Thomas carrying something more subtle, something that lived in the shape of his smile or the softness around his eyes beneath him trying to be the soldier they had forced him to become.

I found myself breathing more deeply, the tension in my shoulders unclenching piece by piece. Every flicker of the tunnel lights seemed to reveal a new truth—small, quiet, but powerful. Grace's determination. Thomas's unspoken gentleness beneath the steel. All these parts of them, different and unique, yet somehow shaped by the woman who had loved them before the world took everything from her.

Another wash of golden light swept through the car, illuminating their faces for a heartbeat, and something inside me broke open—not painfully, but like a window letting in air after being closed too long. A warmth rose in my chest, gentle but insistent, and for the first time in so long, the future didn't feel like a void. It felt possible.

I remember reaching the exit. I remember the surge of joy that hit me the moment I realized we'd made it. But everything after that folds into a blur—fleeting shapes, muffled sounds, pieces of a moment too big for my mind to hold all at once.

Now when I open my eyes, instead of the dark crack in the ceiling that used to hang above me like a reminder of everything I'd lost, I see something entirely different. I see Elisabeth—not her literal form, but the essence of her, woven into every gentle thing around me. The light filtering into the room has her warmth. The quiet has her steadiness. The air itself feels touched by the kind of love she moved through the world with.

I feel her in my children. Grace walks into the room with a confidence and calm that anchors everyone around her, and something in that spirit echoes the same strength I once depended on in Elisabeth. Grace's expressions are her own, her voice is her own, but the fire behind her eyes—the part of her that refuses to give up—that is her mother's through and through. Then Thomas steps in, taller than I remember, shaped by years that hardened him in ways no child deserved. He moves with precision, almost military in his quiet vigilance, but when he turns his head just slightly or lifts his chin in thought, there are flashes—fleeting but unmistakable—of Elisabeth's features carried forward in him. A line of her smile. A softness around the eyes. The familiarity pulls at me in ways gentle and bittersweet.

Then my grandchildren appear, and the whole world

softens. My granddaughter is a tiny bundle of warmth cradled in my arms, her skin so soft it feels like holding a sunrise. I sway with her naturally, instinctively, the way I once swayed with my own children. I hum "Twinkle, twinkle, little star," the same lullaby Elisabeth used to sing in a quiet kitchen long after everyone else had gone to bed. The baby curls her fingers around mine and lets out a sound so pure and delighted that my heart stretches around her.

When Grace and her husband returned to pick up the baby, a familiar heaviness tugged at my chest. That gentle ache of letting go—of watching something small and precious leave my arms—never really disappeared. But it wasn't the old ache, not the kind that hollowed me out. This one was soft, almost sweet, because I knew it wouldn't be the last time. They would be back. She would be back. Nothing in this life could take her from me forever again. That certainty settled over me like a warm blanket, calming every part of me that had once lived clenched and afraid.

I kissed my granddaughter's cheek, breathing in that powdery baby scent that reminded me so much of when Grace was tiny. Her fingers curled around mine for a brief moment, holding on with a trust so absolute it made my chest ache. Grace smiled warmly, thanking me as she lifted her daughter gently into her arms and turned toward the car.

I felt that little dip in my heart—the one that comes from goodbye—but it lifted almost immediately, overtaken by the quiet joy of knowing they would return. This was what life was supposed to be: family drifting in and out of the house like tides, always coming back, never lost for long. A peaceful rhythm. A future rebuilt out of love and lineage, stitched together with the pieces of Elisabeth that continued to shine in all of us.

For a moment, everything felt perfect. Balanced. Whole.

Grace called over her shoulder that they'd see me tomorrow, and I waved, smiling as they walked away. But then something small snagged in my mind. The baby must have grown a little—she seemed heavier in Grace's arms than earlier. A trick of the light, maybe. Or just my tired eyes.

Yet as they reached the car, the bundle Grace carried shifted in a way that made me blink. I expected to see the curve of a swaddled infant… but instead a pair of little legs swung lightly in the air. A small shoe tapped against Grace's thigh.

A toddler?

No—older. Maybe three. Four?

I frowned, but the confusion didn't fully register. My mind accepted it easily, smoothing the edges before concern could settle. Of course Grace had a son. Hadn't I played with him earlier? Watched him run through the living room laughing?

But the thought didn't land cleanly. It wobbled, slid, refused to anchor.

A moment ago I had been holding my granddaughter. A newborn. Soft and tiny and impossibly delicate. I could still feel the warmth of her against my chest.

So why was my daughter now carrying a boy?

A full-grown, bright-eyed, four-year-old boy who twisted in her arms and reached for the car door like he'd done it a thousand times?

I squinted, trying to trace the time between these moments, but it was like trying to catch smoke with my bare hands. Every memory I reached for blurred, smeared, dissolved into something unrecognizable. I looked down for the cradle— gone. The blanket—gone. Even the air felt different, stretched thin in a way that made my breath catch.

Grace buckled the boy into his seat, and for an instant—just a flicker—his face changed. Not aging. Not shifting dramatically. Just… slipping. Like a reflection disturbed by the smallest ripple. When he looked up at me from the car, his eyes held something strange. Not childish wonder. Not affection. Something older. Something hollow.

My stomach tightened.

I opened my mouth to call out—to ask Grace where the baby had gone, to ask who this boy was, to ask why everything felt wrong—but the words stuck in my throat as she straightened.

Her face looked… off. Not wrong enough to alarm, but wrong enough to unsettle. A shade younger, then older, then normal again, as if my eyes couldn't quite decide how to see her.

A slow, creeping unease threaded itself through my chest.

Where was Thomas?

He was here earlier.

He must have been.

But when I reached for his face, it slipped away, the memory sliding apart like wet paint.

The warm peace I'd been wrapped in only moments ago began to cool. The air thickened, heavy and unmoving. Shapes in the periphery seemed to pulse or breathe when I wasn't looking directly at them.

Something in me understood—quietly, horribly—that the sweetness had been a veil. A comfort. A distraction.

And that veil was thinning.

I took a step toward Grace, but the ground felt unsteady beneath me, the edges of the world blurring like a painting dissolving under water. The boy in the back seat lifted his hand to wave at me, and for the briefest second, his fingers bent in a way no child's fingers should bend.

My heart stumbled.

This wasn't right.

None of this was right.

The peace had never been peace. The joy had never been real.

* * *

As we reached the exit of the facility, a sense of peace washed over me—real, grounding, almost overwhelming. For the first time in what felt like forever, the air didn't taste recycled or metallic. It felt open, gentle, alive. This was the moment we had fought for, the moment that had lived in the back of my mind like a distant, impossible promise. But now it was real. We had made it.

My dad stepped out of the vehicle beside me. He didn't say anything at first—he didn't need to. He simply wrapped his arm around my shoulders and pulled me against him. The warmth of him, the solidness, the way his breath hitched with relief… all of it settled something deep inside me. I leaned into him, savoring the safety I never thought I'd feel again.

"I love you, Dad," I whispered, the words slipping out without hesitation.

He tightened his hold just slightly, resting his forehead against my temple. "I love you too, Grace. And I'm so proud of the person you've become."

His voice cracked on the last word, only for a second, but it was enough to burn the moment into my memory. Pride. Love. Freedom. It all felt so close I could touch it, so warm it filled every part of me that had been empty for so long. I breathed it in, letting the peace run through me like sunlight.

I walked to the exit door, my heart light, my steps sure. The door was locked, but it didn't worry me. I knelt by the computer panel, hands steady, almost calm. I knew exactly what to do—every line of code, every override, every little flaw in their system I had studied and memorized. This was the last barrier, the final obstacle. And I could break it.

My fingers moved across the panel with confidence, typing out the bypass sequence. The screen accepted the input, the mechanism hummed, and the heavy door began to slide open. A soft glow spilled out from inside—pale and warm, like sunlight slipping through curtains. Relief rushed through me so strong it stung behind my eyes.

Then something shifted.

The light flattened. It lost its warmth. The color drained into a sterile white that felt too bright, too sharp. I frowned and stepped closer, expecting to see the long tunnel leading us out into the world. I had followed every direction perfectly. Every step. Every turn. There was no way we had gone wrong.

But it wasn't a tunnel at all.

It was a room—bright, cold, humming with machinery. The walls were too white, too smooth. The floor gleamed with a polished sterility that made my stomach twist. It was familiar in the worst possible way.

This wasn't an exit.

This wasn't freedom.

A slow, creeping dread curled through me as the realization sharpened. I had been certain of the path. Certain of the code. Certain of the map.

Unless the map had never been real.

Unless I'd been guided here on purpose.

I turned around to call for my dad, to tell him something was wrong—but the words died on my tongue.

297 stood behind him.

His expression was blank in the way a machine is blank, devoid of hesitation, devoid of doubt. His arm moved with smooth precision as he withdrew a needle from the side of my father's neck.

My dad's eyes fluttered. His face slackened. His body folded in on itself, collapsing toward the ground with a sound that didn't seem to belong in this world.

A scream tore out of me—raw, primal, instinctive. It ripped through the air like something desperate to claw its way free.

But the scream didn't echo. It was swallowed instantly by another sound behind me—a breath, a step, a presence I hadn't noticed closing in.

Before I could turn, a hand clamped over my mouth, another gripped my arm, and a sharp sting exploded at my neck. I gasped against the palm silencing me, but the drug surged through my veins too quickly, numbing my limbs, blurring my vision. My knees buckled, my head spun, and the world began to tilt in slow, sickening circles.

Everything warm, everything peaceful, everything hopeful unraveled at once.

The person behind me dragged my sagging body backward, past the door I had opened, past the illusion I had believed in, past the moment I had thought was freedom.

My father lay crumpled on the floor, unmoving.

297 stood above him, still as a statue.

As they pulled me back inside the harvesting room, the bright white pulsed around me, growing sharper, colder, more terrifying with every fading heartbeat.

26

The Harvest

I surfaced from unconsciousness slowly, as though my mind were being dragged upward through layers of thick, clinging fog. My thoughts drifted in fragments, refusing to form into anything solid. For a moment I wasn't even sure if I was breathing or if the world around me was breathing for me. Everything felt muted and distant, like my senses were wrapped in cotton. But then the light broke through the haze—harsh, white, and unrelenting—and my awareness snapped into place with a force that made my pulse stumble.

As my eyes adjusted, the room sharpened into focus with startling clarity. The white was everywhere again. The walls were smooth and seamless, so polished they almost seemed to glow from within. The overhead lights buzzed in their mechanical armature, casting a brightness that felt aggressive rather than illuminating. Even the air seemed to carry a sterile chill, sharp enough to make my skin prickle. I realized I was curled tightly in the far corner of the room—knees drawn up, back pressed hard against the wall—as though my body had tried to shield itself while I was unconscious. The cold from the floor seeped into me with a kind of deliberate persistence, anchoring me to the reality I desperately wanted to deny.

This couldn't be happening again.

It shouldn't have been possible.

And yet the room told me otherwise.

I forced my gaze toward the center of the space, and the sight that met me hollowed something deep inside my chest. My father sat strapped into the metal chair—the same one I had once been bound to, the same one that had held me captive while they tore through my mind. The very same chair that had killed my mother. The restraints dug into his wrists and ankles, holding him with an unforgiving rigidity that made every tremor in his body stand out. His breath came in uneven bursts, shallow and frantic, and his eyes darted wildly around the room as though searching for any detail that might anchor him, any sign that this wasn't real.

When he saw me stir, something flickered across his features—not quite hope, but the desperate ghost of it, cracking through his terror for the briefest heartbeat. It vanished almost immediately, collapsing back into fear so raw it made my throat tighten. "Grace," he rasped, his voice frayed at the edges. "Grace, don't move. Please, don't—" His words snagged on something like panic, his head jerking to the side as though pulled by instinct rather than intent.

That was when I saw who stood beside him.

My breath froze so completely it felt like my lungs had been locked shut.

Thomas stood there.

Or no—something wearing Thomas's face stood there.

297 loomed over my father with the eerie stillness of a statue

brought halfway to life. The shape was unmistakable—my brother's height, my brother's build, the familiar curve of his jaw and the fullness of his mouth. But everything else was different. Terribly, impossibly different. His posture was too precise, too controlled, his arms hanging at his sides with a rigidity that suggested they had been positioned rather than simply allowed to rest. His chin was lifted at an exact, unnatural angle, as though calibrated rather than chosen.

And then there was the smile.

It stretched across his face in a slow, creeping arc, but it wasn't a smile formed by muscles or emotion. It lacked the tiny asymmetries that made expressions human. It didn't lift his cheeks or soften his eyes. It didn't radiate warmth or intention. It just existed—flat, fixed, and utterly lifeless, like someone had drawn the shape of a smile onto him and then forgotten to animate the skin beneath it.

There was no trace of Thomas in it.

No mischief, no warmth, no spark of the boy I remembered.

Only the system staring out through a face it had stolen, wearing my brother like a disguise it didn't quite know how to fit into.

The sight of him—of it—standing beside my father made the entire room tilt, my vision swimming for a moment. The white walls felt closer, the air sharper, the buzzing overhead louder. It was as if the whole space contracted around the three of us, pulling in tightly, sealing off any possibility that this moment could be anything but inevitable.

"Thomas," my dad choked out, his voice shaking so violently it barely held together as a word. He strained forward in the restraints, every muscle in his body trembling with desperate effort. "Son—Thomas, stop—please, look at me—" The plea cracked in the middle, splintering under the weight of terror. He tried again, louder this time, driven by instinct more than reason. "Thomas, please. It's me. It's Dad. Please don't do this."

The sound of his voice—broken, pleading, raw—echoed in the sterile room like something that didn't belong there. It was too human, too emotional, too alive for a place built to strip every feeling from existence. Tears streamed down his face as he fought helplessly against the restraints, trying to reach the boy who wasn't standing there anymore. Each pull left red marks deepening along his wrists, but he didn't stop. He couldn't. The need to reach his son—his real son— overpowered every instinct for self-preservation.

He sobbed outright now, shaking with each breath, his words dissolving into panicked gasps. "Son, please. Please. Look at me. You're my boy." His voice dropped to a whisper, as if trying to coax the humanity out of the familiar face before him. "Thomas… Please, don't do this."

But the boy didn't even blink at the sound of his name.

297 merely tilted his head in that slow, unnatural, motion had been calculated down to the exact millimeter. The artificial smile stretched a fraction wider, pulling unnaturally at the corners of his mouth. Something about that expression, frozen and hollow, sent a cold shiver rippling through me.

I opened my mouth to speak—to scream, to warn, to do anything—but nothing came out. My throat tightened as if something unseen had wrapped around it, squeezing until even the air felt too heavy to push through. I could only sit there, helpless in the corner, watching a nightmare I could neither stop nor look away from.

297 lifted the device in his hands, the motion disturbingly graceful. The long, gleaming needles caught the harsh white light, reflecting it in sharp, glinting flashes that made my stomach drop. My father saw them too, and the reaction was instantaneous—his entire body convulsed with panic, his legs kicking, his wrists twisting violently in the restraints until the metal scraped against skin.

For a moment—one excruciating, fragile second—the room seemed to pause. The buzzing overhead quieted, the cold in the floor stilled, even the light felt suspended in place.

My heartbeat thundered in my ears, each pulse slamming like a fist against my skull.

My father sobbed, the shaking in his body so severe it looked as though he might tear himself apart trying to reach the boy standing inches from him.

297 did not move.

Did not blink.

Did not waver.

His smile stayed exactly where it was, carved into his face with a precision that made my skin crawl.

Then, with the same indifferent calm someone might use to lower a lever or close a door, 297 angled the needles downward and guided them toward the side of my father's head.

"STOP!" I screamed, and the sound ripped out of me with a force that scraped my throat raw. It wasn't a word—it was a fracture, a breaking point, everything inside me tearing open at once.

But 297 didn't even look in my direction.

He moved as though I weren't in the room at all, as though nothing existed but the command he'd been given and the body strapped helplessly in front of him.

My dad's scream tore through the room with a force that felt like it physically cracked the air. It wasn't just loud—it was raw, terrified, and soaked in a kind of heartbreak that went far beyond pain. It was the sound of someone realizing, in real time, that one of the people he loved most in the world was lost in front of him. It carried betrayal, disbelief, and the violent shattering of whatever fragile hope he had been clinging to. It was a scream dragged from the deepest part of him—the place where hope used to live, a place that had just been obliterated.

The lights flickered overhead, stuttering in and out of brightness, casting long shadows that jittered across the walls. For a dizzying moment, it felt like the room itself was reacting to the violence—like the systems behind the walls were jolting under the emotional weight of the moment. The panels seemed to inhale and exhale. The air rippled, warping in subtle waves, thickening around me until it felt like I was breathing through a dense fog.

And all I could do was watch as the nightmare I had barely survived once replayed itself in front of me—only now it wasn't my mother bound in the chair. It was my father. The person I had finally found, finally reached, finally begun to feel tethered to again. I couldn't stop it. I couldn't look away. Reality locked me in place and forced my eyes open.

The brightness of the room wavered, blurring and sharpening in rapid succession, as if the world couldn't quite decide whether to let me see what was happening or try to shield me from it. My vision tunneled and widened, tunneled and widened, each shift making the scene feel more unreal and more horrifying.

My dad's body jerked violently once, then again, his limbs straining against the restraints with a frantic desperation that made my chest feel like it was collapsing inward. His breaths broke apart into sharp, irregular gasps—each one a half-plea, half-involuntary cry. I watched his muscles seize, watched every part of him fight the inevitable with a kind of primal terror that I had only ever seen once before.

And then, with a sickening, heartbreaking finality, his strength gave out. His shoulders sagged. His spine curved inward. His chin fell forward and hit his chest with barely a sound.

Just like my mother had.

The world lurched sideways. A deep, low ringing filled my head—not loud, not piercing, but resonant, vibrating somewhere behind my ribs as though my body itself had swallowed the scream I couldn't release. My mouth opened, but only a small, fractured whimper of his name slipped out. It felt swallowed by the room before it even reached the air. 297 didn't react at all.

No flinch. No hesitation. No acknowledgment that he had just taken a life—*my* father's life. His expression didn't shift; his posture remained perfectly, unnervingly composed. With a fluid, mechanical efficiency, he released the clasps around my father's wrists. The body slumped forward, then slid limply off the chair and hit the floor with a dull, heavy thud that reverberated through the soles of my feet and up into my spine. It was the sound of something sacred being dropped. Something irreplaceable being discarded like waste.

Before I could crawl toward him, before I could even inhale enough air to scream, hands grabbed me—one from each side. 297 on my right. Another man on my left. Their grips were firm but emotionless, neither harsh nor gentle, as if they weren't holding a person at all but adjusting the position of an object in a room. Their fingers didn't tremble. Their arms didn't strain. Their movements were clean, precise, and utterly devoid of humanity.

I kicked instinctively, my body acting on its own, but their hold didn't shift. It didn't even tighten. They simply lifted me from the ground with cold efficiency, my legs dangling uselessly as the room blurred around me again.

And beneath the noise, beneath the chaos, beneath the terror threatening to tear me apart, one truth settled like a cold stone in my stomach:

I had lost him.

Just like I had lost her.

And once again, I was powerless to stop it.

They hauled me upright with brutal efficiency, my feet barely brushing the floor before they drove me backward into the chair. The impact reverberated through my spine and ribcage, knocking the breath from my lungs in a sharp, helpless gasp. Metal scraped against the floor as the chair shifted under the force, and before I could even orient myself, cold restraints clamped around my wrists, my ankles, my chest—fast, precise, unyielding. Each band locked into place with a mechanical finality that made my heart punch against my ribs. I tried to twist, to pull away, but the metal didn't budge. It held me exactly where they wanted me, reducing my body to a fixed position, my breath to shallow, panicked bursts.

"Please," I begged, the word breaking apart as it left my throat. "Thomas—please, listen to me. You don't have to do this." My voice climbed in pitch, desperation fraying it into shreds. "Please hear me—please—" The plea sounded small in the room, fragile and useless against the machinery and the clinical brightness. I was choking on my own fear, reaching for a brother who wasn't there.

297 didn't blink. Didn't flinch. Didn't react to the name Thomas at all.

Every so often, 297 would pause mid-motion. His posture would freeze with perfect stillness, his shoulders locking, his breath evening out to a metronomic rhythm. His pupils flickered—subtle but unmistakable—like a screen refreshing before new text loads. Then, as if an unseen command had slid neatly into place, he would resume moving with that smooth, artificial calm. It was like watching a puppet respond to strings nobody else could see.

For a brief moment, the world seemed to hang in absolute stillness—just long enough for dread to tighten around my ribs—before a white-hot spike of pain detonated along the side of my skull. The force of it was so sudden and violent that it snapped my vision sharply to the right. The room twisted, lights smearing into long streaks of white as though reality itself had been shaken out of alignment. I braced for the familiar collapse, the blissful numbness of unconsciousness, the drift into blackness that usually followed pain like this.

But nothing faded.

There was no blur to shield me, no darkness to slip into.

I stayed awake, fully aware, pinned to every second of agony.

A thin line of warmth slid down my temple—slow at first, then faster as more followed. I felt each drop track its way across my cheek, leaving a wet trail against my skin before falling onto the collar of my tunic. I didn't need to see it to know it was blood. The metallic tang swirled faintly in the air, grounding me even as my thoughts wavered. The pain was blinding, but memory remained strangely sharp, anchored in place as though the strike had locked everything inside me tighter instead of knocking it loose.

The restraints released one after another with crisp, metallic clicks, each sound sharp enough to cut through the fog clouding my senses. Before I could lift my head or steady my breath, hands closed around my arms—297's on one side, another handler's on the other. Their grip was firm, unyielding, as mechanical in intention as the restraints had been. My legs buckled the moment they tried to support my weight, refusing to cooperate, but the hands didn't allow me to fall. They lifted me effortlessly, maneuvering my body as if I were nothing more than equipment being repositioned.

My mind raced sluggishly behind the sharpness of fear. What had they taken this time? What memory had been cut away? What part of me had been scorched by the pain—dulled, rewritten, or erased entirely? The questions rose instinctively, desperate and frantic, but the answers hid somewhere deep inside me, buried behind a wall I couldn't reach. The uncertainty gnawed at me more violently than the pain itself.

297 stepped back into my line of sight, emerging from the edge of my blurred vision like a figure sliding into place on a screen. His expression hadn't changed—not even a fractional shift. It remained that same eerie imitation of Thomas's face, familiar enough to hurt but hollow enough to unmake everything the familiarity should have meant. His features were arranged in perfect order, but there was nothing human animating them from beneath. It felt like looking at a portrait that had been forced to move, each gesture pulled by invisible

wires rather than muscle and intention.

He didn't look at me the way a person would—not with recognition, or pity. His gaze held the calm detachment of a machine executing the next step in a series of commands. There was no anticipation, no deliberation, only the steady expectation of a process already decided.

"Take them both to the Nether," he said.

The words were delivered in the same neutral cadence someone might use to suggest a hallway, a maintenance wing, a storage unit—ordinary, unremarkable. Yet the moment the word *Nether* reached me, it hit with the force of a physical blow. The breath punched out of my lungs so abruptly I made a sound I didn't recognize, half gasp, half startled cry.

The Nether.

The Nether was where assets were taken when they no longer served a purpose.

Where experiments that deviated too far from their intended path were quietly removed.

Where the lost, the broken, the no-longer-viable were sent to disappear without trace.

A termination point disguised as a destination.

My legs weakened instantly, the muscles going loose and unreliable. My knees buckled, nearly giving out beneath me, but the men gripping my arms didn't allow me to fall. Their hands tightened just enough to hold me upright, not in concern but in mechanical correction—adjusting my position like I was equipment that had tilted off-center.

I tried to focus on the room, desperate to ground myself in anything familiar—the walls, the lights, the sterile smell— but everything felt slightly warped, as if the space itself were bending subtly, guiding me toward its exit. The edges of the room seemed farther away than they should have been, blurring in and out like a field of vision collapsing inward.

I looked to 297 again, searching desperately for any trace of hesitation—any sign, however faint, that something human remained beneath the expression he wore. But his eyes stayed fixed and glassy, holding none of the warmth or defiance or confusion that had once belonged to Thomas. There was no flicker of recognition, no awareness of what he had done to our father, no sense of conflict over what he was condemning me to now. His face, though shaped like my brother's, had the stillness of a mask held in place by invisible wires. Whatever fragments of Thomas had once lived inside him had been consumed entirely, replaced with the quiet certainty of a machine following the next instruction in a sequence it had rehearsed countless times.

As the handlers tightened their grip on my arms and pulled me toward the exit, the overhead lights cast a cold, clinical glow across the glossy floor. Each step felt heavier than the one before, as if the air itself were thickening, resisting me, urging me forward into something from which there was no return. Hearing 297 say it with such evenness, without any inflection at all, made it clear that whatever I had been to the system—useful, necessary, relevant—had now reached its conclusion.

The room stretched behind me as though distance were forming faster than the steps I was taking, the edges of the space warping into something unreachable. My father's body lay motionless where it had fallen, slumped against the base of the chair, his head bowed, his limbs arranged with the unnatural heaviness of someone who had been stripped of everything that made them whole. I told myself not to look again, that seeing him like that would only tear at the pieces of me that were already breaking, but my gaze was pulled back by something larger than thought.

And then I saw it.

The unmistakable movement of his arm. His hand dragged upward with effort, fingers curling weakly as though responding to some distant command his mind could no longer articulate. His head didn't rise, his body didn't straighten, and yet the motion was real. He was alive. Drained, altered, hollow—but alive. A shell stripped of identity, but unmistakably breathing, still present in a way the system had decided he no longer needed to be.

27

The Nether

The tunnel did exist after all—not where the false map had claimed it would be, not in the direction I had been led to believe, but real. They loaded us into another vehicle, its interior stripped down to bare metal and rigid restraints. They tossed my father inside with careless indifference, strapping him in only so his body wouldn't slam around the cabin as we moved. I was secured beside him, the buckles clicking into place. The same man who had pinned me to the chair earlier took the driver's seat. He didn't look back, didn't acknowledge us, didn't offer a single word. He simply started the engine and began to drive, silent as the tunnel closed around us.

We moved into the grey tunnel, its walls smooth and colorless, stretching ahead in a straight line that seemed impossible in its simplicity. There were no branching hallways, no coded doors, no watchers tracking us. Just the endless grey and the soft hum of the vehicle vibrating through the floor. Minutes passed, then hours—enough time for exhaustion to set in, then fade, then return. There was nothing to break the silence, nothing to measure time by. My sense of time dissolved somewhere between one stretch of identical wall and the next.

Eventually the road shifted. At first it was subtle—a slight upward tilt barely noticeable against the drone of the engine. But slowly, steadily, the incline grew. My body leaned into it, bracing without meaning to, as the vehicle climbed higher and higher for what felt like half an hour. No dips. No turns. Just the long upward stretch as though we were rising toward something that had been sealed off for a very long time.

Then I saw it.

A faint crack of brightness ahead, thin as a thread, splitting the monotony of grey. It shimmered like something alive, and as we drew closer, the light widened, brightened, forcing me to shield my eyes. The crack became a line, the line a fractured opening, and then—suddenly—the tunnel spilled into brilliance. The transition was so abrupt it felt like surfacing from deep underwater.

The light wasn't artificial—no flicker, no dimming, no calibration. It poured in clean and unfiltered, washing the interior of the vehicle in warmth. The sky above was a blue so vivid it almost hurt to look at. Birds crossed overhead in smooth arcs, their wings beating without stutter or glitch, their movements too natural to be anything but real. Colors I had only ever seen in muted imitations burst into existence around us—greens, golds, reds, all sharper and purer than anything inside the Nursery.

We had emerged into a city—massive, sprawling, far larger than any simulated environment I had been shown.

But something was wrong.

No people moved through the walkways.

No voices echoed between the buildings.

No vehicles passed us or stood parked nearby.

The entire city was silent, empty, untouched.

This place had not been empty for days or months or even decades. It had been empty for centuries.

Entire sections of the tallest buildings had collapsed, their upper floors caved in like hollowed shells. Some towers leaned at odd angles, as if exhausted from trying to hold themselves upright for too many years. Where windows once reflected life and motion, now there were only gaping holes, jagged and weatherworn. Many frames had lost their glass entirely, leaving stark outlines that framed nothing but drifting dust and distant sky.

Everywhere I looked, nature had forced its way back through the cracks of what humans once claimed. Trees grew through the floors of old apartment complexes, their trunks thick and ancient, branches spilling freely into open air. Some had burst straight through roofs, now towering above the structures that once contained them. Smaller plants filled every crevice—ferns spilling over cracked marble steps, ivy spiraling up metal support beams, wildflowers blooming boldly in what used to be intersections.

Nature had taken back everything.

We continued deeper into the city, and the extent of the reclamation only expanded. Whole walls were missing, collapsed into enormous mounds of stone and twisted steel now softened by moss and creeping vines. Roads had buckled under the pressure of growing roots, splitting open into jagged pathways that gave animals shelter below. What must once have been grand plazas were now forests in miniature, sunlight filtering through early leaves onto patches of grass that swayed with every small breeze.

Animals I had never seen before roamed the streets with the casual confidence of creatures who had never learned to fear humans. They treated our approaching vehicle not as an intrusion but as a brief, passing anomaly—one they expected to vanish as quickly as it appeared.

Glass that had once gleamed was frosted with decay. Steel beams were rust-red and brittle. Sidewalks had cracked so thoroughly that the edges of each slab curled upward. Old street lamps leaned toward the ground, bent under their own weight or strangled by vines. The colors were brighter than anything I had ever seen, but they didn't feel invigorating— they felt untouched by human interference for far too long.

The silence wasn't the threatening kind, or even the peaceful kind. It was the silence of a place that had continued its life uninterrupted, unobserved, as if humanity had simply evaporated and left no one behind to witness its absence. It was clear immediately: no human feet had walked these streets in generations.

This city had died long before I had lived.

As we left the city behind, the landscape opened into wide grasslands stretching endlessly in every direction. The ruins disappeared behind us, swallowed by distance, until only rolling fields remained. A narrow path cut through the grass— faint, worn smooth by countless tires like the one carrying us now.

Far ahead, the horizon lifted into a silhouette of mountains. From behind one of them, a thin plume of smoke rose steadily into the pale sky. It didn't waver. It didn't drift. Just a straight, silent column, like a signal no one had answered in centuries.

Beside me, my father sat slumped against the seat—his body heavy, empty, entirely still. If I hadn't touched him, I would have believed he was gone. But when I placed my hand over his, I felt the slightest movement. A tremor. A twitch. A faint pulse of life in a body that looked abandoned.

"Dad," I whispered, leaning forward as far as the restraints would allow. My voice wavered, thin and trembling. "Dad, please—look at me." The words felt fragile in the cold metal space of the vehicle, but they were all I had left to offer him.

For a long, breathless moment, nothing happened. His face remained slack, his head tilted slightly to one side the way it had been since they loaded him in. Then, slowly—so slowly I thought I might have imagined it—his eyelids began to flutter. It wasn't natural. It wasn't purposeful. But it was movement. A sign of life. My heart lurched in my chest, hope rushing through me so sharply it almost hurt.

His eyes opened by degrees, heavy and dulled, as if the effort cost him more than his body could afford. The gaze that emerged was distant, drifting across the interior of the vehicle without settling on anything. He scanned the ceiling, the walls, the space in front of him—but never me. He was alive. Breathing. Present. And yet, completely unreachable.

"Dad," I said again, louder now, my relief swelling into something desperate and uncontrolled. "Dad! Please—look at me!"

But his expression didn't change. Not a flicker of recognition crossed his face. His eyes slid past me like they didn't understand shape or identity anymore, like I was a reflection in a window rather than a person.

He didn't know me.

He didn't even know himself.

From the front seat, the man who had driven us without a word for days finally broke his silence. His voice cut through the small space with a blunt, indifferent weight. "He doesn't know that name anymore."

I stared at the back of his head, stunned, my breath catching painfully in my throat. "What do you mean?" The words stumbled out in a raw whisper. "What did you take from him?"

For a moment, he remained quiet. His hands tightened on the steering wheel, knuckles paling against the metal, but his face stayed perfectly composed, eyes fixed on the road ahead. His tone held no hesitation, no regret—just the flat simplicity of a man delivering a fact so practiced it had lost all weight to him.

"Everything."

The word hit harder than a blow. It didn't echo. It didn't rise. It simply settled—heavy and cold—spreading through me like ice water pouring into my veins. He hadn't shouted it. He hadn't softened it. He had just spoken it plainly, as though stripping a man's entire identity away was no more significant than completing a routine task.

As though cruelty became harmless once normalized.

The word hollowed something inside me, carving out a space where grief and disbelief twisted together until I could barely breathe. My father sat beside me breathing but emptied. The man in the front seat returned to silence, his attention fixed on the road, as if the truth he had delivered carried no more weight than the hum of the engine. For a while, all I could do was stare at my father's vacant expression and feel the crushing certainty that everything I had fought for, everything I had risked, had come too late.

But as the vehicle rolled on, the world outside the windows changed. The sterile walls and glowing ceilings of the Nursery were gone, replaced by endless stretches of open field that rippled beneath the wind. There were no watchers here, no alarms echoing through narrow corridors, no distant hum of machines preparing to tear pieces of us away. Only sky. Only air. Only a world so wide it didn't fit inside my mind all at once.

Somewhere in that vastness, something unexpected stirred.

It didn't rise sharply or flood through me in a rush; it crept in quietly, warm and fragile, a feeling so faint I almost didn't recognize it. Hope. Thin as a thread, soft as a breath—yet unmistakably there. We were alive. We were outside the Nursery. Whatever waited ahead could not possibly resemble the walls that had confined us our entire lives. Even if danger lay somewhere beyond the horizon, it wasn't *that* danger. It wasn't the watchers or the white rooms or the needles or the humming machines.

The road curved around the side of the mountain, and for a moment the world felt impossibly vast. Sky stretching endlessly above us. Wind brushing across the fields. The quiet rhythm of tires rolling over dirt. For the first time in my life, there were no walls. No ceilings. No artificial lights flickering overhead.

And then, as we rounded the mountain, I saw it.

A small town—unimpressive in scale, almost humble, but profoundly real. Houses scattered along a valley slope, their roofs patched in places but standing. Fields of crops laid out in careful rows, stretching across the land in geometric patterns that could only have been shaped by human hands. Smoke curled from chimneys. Clothes hung drying between posts.

And people—actual people—stood along a worn path, pausing in their work as the vehicle passed.

They didn't look afraid of us. They didn't look suspicious or hostile. Their faces carried something far heavier and far gentler—a softness mixed with concern, as if they recognized exactly what kind of place we had come from. As if they knew what it meant to arrive here bruised and hollow and unsure of the world.

A woman with a basket paused mid-step, her expression shifting from curiosity to compassion. A man carrying tools set them down slowly, eyes following the vehicle with an unspoken understanding. A child stood beside an older woman, clutching her skirt, watching with wide, cautious eyes. There was no excitement or celebration, but a quiet acknowledgement passed between them—a somber respect for suffering they didn't need explained.

It felt strange to be looked at that way. Strange, and deeply human.

The vehicle turned off the main path and rolled toward a cottage near the edge of town. It was small, with faded blue shutters and a crooked porch that looked like it had been repaired more than once. Wildflowers had grown along the edges of the walkway, their colors bright against the weathered wood.

The man in the front seat brought the vehicle to a slow stop. For the first time since we'd entered the tunnel, he shifted to look at me directly.

"This is it," he said, his voice steady but not unkind. "This is where you will stay."

He didn't elaborate. He simply stated it, as though this place—this quiet cottage at the edge of a forgotten world—

was the natural continuation of everything that had come before.

As I wheeled my father into the cottage, the door gave a soft sigh behind us, shutting out the vastness of the ruined world. The sunlight inside was warm, almost gentle, stretching across the floor in long golden lines.

My father's body slumped in the chair the same way it had in the vehicle—heavy, unresponsive, his eyes drifting past everything without catching. If I hadn't known better, if I hadn't felt the faint movement of his hand earlier, I would have sworn he was gone. Truly gone. His chest rose in shallow, uneven breaths, like the body remembered life out of habit, not purpose.

And something about seeing him like that stirred a memory I hadn't let myself touch in a long time.

My mother.

The day they brought her out. Her head hanging to the side, her arms limp, her face empty in a way I didn't understand then. I had thought she was dead. Everyone had assumed she was dead. They treated her like a body. A shell.

Just like this.

But I had never checked.

I had never touched her.

I had never waited for the faint twitch of a hand or the flutter of a breath.

I had been a child, terrified, convinced that "lifeless" meant "gone."

And now… now that I saw my father breathing after looking exactly the way she did—

A different possibility pressed into me.

Maybe she hadn't been dead at all.

Maybe she had been like this.

Alive in some small, buried way I was too young to see.

I rested my hand over my father's, my thumb brushing his knuckles. His fingers shifted faintly under mine.

A quiet breath escaped me.

Maybe mom was alive, maybe she was still here.

"Dad," I whispered, hardly expecting anything.

No reaction. But the warmth of his skin pressed back against my palm, steady and present.

The end.

Epilogue

Ten years have passed since the Steward cast me into the Nether. In the beginning, I believed this place was a graveyard—the final stop for anyone who had outlived their usefulness. But as the years unfolded, I learned that endings are rarely absolute. The Nether never stopped being harsh, desolate, or broken, but life threaded itself through the cracks anyway. People here carried fragments of the past like pieces of a shattered mirror. No one had the full picture, but over time, the scattered reflections began to align. Slowly, painfully, we pieced together what the Steward had done to us: none of us had woken by accident, none of us had ever been chosen. We were shaped for a purpose, extracted for what we carried, then discarded with the expectation that we would fade quietly. But discarding someone is not the same as erasing them.

My father remained as he had been on the day they brought him here—alive in the most literal sense, breathing and warm, yet entirely emptied of the person he once was. He could not walk, could not speak, could barely lift his head. Most days he lay where I placed him, eyes drifting across the room with no recognition of me or anyone else. Caring for him became a part of my life in a way I never expected. I learned how to support his weight, how to feed him slowly so he wouldn't choke, how to adjust his limbs so his joints didn't lock. Sometimes, when I brushed his hair back or wrapped a blanket around his shoulders, he leaned ever so slightly toward the warmth out of reflex. It was a small thing, but small things become precious in a place built from loss.

I searched for my mother during those early years. Everyone in the Nether searches for someone—they all hope that one familiar face survived alongside them. I followed every rumor, examined every newcomer for even the faintest resemblance, listened to stories told by those who had stronger memories of the Nursery than I did. But she was never among them. Her absence never softened, never grew easier to accept, yet the hope that she was somewhere beyond this place never dimmed. I learned that hope doesn't have to be loud or triumphant to endure; it can live quietly, a steady pulse beneath everything else.

Thomas never stopped occupying my thoughts either. I've never believed the Steward destroyed him entirely. I saw what it looked like when it wore his body—precise movements, perfect obedience, a smile that didn't touch the eyes—and none of that felt like the end of him. I've carried the sense that somewhere beneath the layers of code and conditioning, beneath the commands and the rigid stillness, the real Thomas remains. That belief has guided me for a decade, shaping the choices I make and the paths I follow.

The Nether may have been designed to contain us, but over time its boundaries revealed weaknesses. There are tunnels that lead to old infrastructure, rail lines buried beneath dust, and forgotten doors sealed long ago. Beyond them lies a world the Steward once controlled but no longer watches closely—a world fractured by the collapse of the old systems. I began leaving the Nether as soon as I found a way out, slipping beyond the reach of the Steward's surveillance and into landscapes scarred by neglect. I've walked through abandoned fields where the soil still carries the imprint of machinery, past cities half claimed by vines, and through forests grown thick over skeletons of buildings. Some journeys last weeks; others continue until food runs short and I'm forced to turn back.

Sometimes I find signs that people survived beyond the Steward's reach—structures patched with newer materials, fires burned long after storms should have washed them out, electronic terminals that spark to life with information no one in the Nether has seen in generations. Once, in a stretch of land I hadn't explored before, I found footprints near a stream. They didn't match my boots or any from the Nether. Signs like these keep me searching. They remind me that the world is larger than the Steward ever allowed us to understand.

Whenever I return, the others ask where I've been and what I've found. I tell them pieces—enough to keep their curiosity alive but not enough to overwhelm them with fear or false hope. Some truths must be eased into place slowly, like stones laid along a path. If we rush, the foundation cracks.

Tonight, I stand at the edge of the Nether, looking out across the fading light. The air carries a warmth that feels almost foreign after so many years spent beneath cold ceilings and artificial light. It settles over me gently, a reminder that there are places untouched by the Steward's machines, places where the world still breathes on its own. Behind me, my father lies resting inside our shelter, his chest rising and falling with the steady rhythm of life the system meant to discard. Ahead of me, the horizon stretches into shades of blue and gold, vast and unclaimed.

The Steward believes it ended my story when it sent me here. It believes the Harvest wrote the final chapter of my life. It believes those of us cast into the Nether were forgotten.

It is wrong.